Copyright © 2017 by Lovestruck Romance.

All Rights Reserved.

No part of this publication may be reproduced, distributed or transmitted in any form or by any means including photocopying, recording, or other electronic or mechanical methods except in the case of brief quotations embodied in critical reviews and certain other noncommercial uses permitted by copyright law. The unauthorized reproduction or distribution of this copyrighted work is illegal.

This book is a work of fiction. Names, characters, businesses, places, events, and incidents are either the products of the author's imagination or used in a fictitious manner. Any resemblance to actual persons living or dead is purely coincidental.

This book is intended for adult readers only.
Any sexual activity portrayed in these pages occurs between consenting adults over the age of 18 who are not related by blood.

KODIAK ISLAND SHIFTERS

CANDACE AYERS

KYM DILLON

LOVESTRUCK ROMANCE

CONTENTS

COLTON	1
WYATT	93
TUCKER	197
About the Author	285

COLTON

KODIAK ISLAND SHIFTERS BOOK 1

Colton Sterling is a brilliant business strategist, adrenaline junkie, self-made billionaire, and Kodiak grizzly bear shifter. Colton has no plans to settle down. Not, that is, until he sees the beautiful Hannah Cooper. His mate.

Hannah is a smart, curvy, bold doctor, who is way out of her league in the Alaskan wilderness.
Lucky for her she'll be outta here tomorrow.

Colton has just 24 hours to make Hannah fall in love with him before she returns to the lower 48.
Can he rise to the challenge?

1

"Take a seat Doctor Cooper." Hannah's lawyer proffered a chair opposite his paper-strewn desk. He adjusted his spectacles before continuing, "It's all fairly straight forward—all monetary assets are to be transferred from your uncle's estate at your earliest convenience."

Hannah smiled tightly, not really knowing what to say. It had been an overwhelming week. It began with her uncle's funeral, a man she hadn't spoken to in years and only vaguely recollected. It was now ending, on a warm Friday afternoon, in her lawyer's office, discussing the deposit of a large inheritance into her bank account.

"I have to say," the lawyer continued, "it's a rare pleasure allocating such large funds to someone so risk-adverse. You have a very healthy credit record, Doctor Cooper."

"Well. I don't come from a wealthy background, Mr. Moore. I think that helps."

"Indeed." He nodded, "There is, however, another matter I wanted to discuss with you today." He cleared his throat before continuing, "Your marriage to a Mr..." He peered down at the document in his hand, "Bradley..."

"Brad Crawford," Hannah interrupted him. "Yes. We're not actually married. I mean, we're married, technically, but... well, haven't been together for many years now. We just never got around to a divorce."

"I suggest that you do. You understand, of course, that he could cause," he hesitated, looking for the right word, "*issues* as your legal husband if you were to receive the inheritance and then opt for a divorce. My suggestion to you would be to obtain signed divorce papers before the transfer proceeds."

Hannah nodded, "I don't think that will be a problem... once I track him down."

"You don't know Mr. Crawford's location?"

"No. I haven't seen him in ten years." Hannah shrugged, she really hadn't thought about him for an entire decade. They broke up a month before she left for medical school, and neither of them had been in contact with one another since.

"Well, I suggest you locate him. My understanding is that these funds will enable you to start your own medical practice?"

Hannah nodded, "Yes... and pay off my student loans."

"Admirable. I hope it proves a fruitful endeavor. I will have the divorce papers drawn up for you by next week. Once you have the co-signature, we can reconvene and transfer the funds.

"Okay. Well, great." Hannah rose from her chair, and shook her lawyers hand. "Thank you for your help, Mr. Moore."

"It's a pleasure, Dr. Cooper."

RIDING the elevator down from Delaney, Smith and Wexler LLP, Hannah felt dizzy. She had hoped that one day she'd have the financial means to open her own practice specializing in family medicine, but never in her wildest dreams did she imagine that day would come so soon. Thank you, Uncle Henry. May you rest in peace.

All she had to do now was get a divorce. She slipped on her RayBans as she stepped out of the office building and into the bright Chicago sunshine, heading towards a Starbucks across the street. Hannah wasn't on call, so this was only the second cup of the day. If she was going to start trying to locate Brad Crawford, she reasoned, she'd need all the help she could get.

As the barista smiled at her mechanically from behind the counter, Hannah contemplated her options. She knew that neither of her parents had heard from Brad in years, and she wasn't really in touch with anyone from High School. That was one of the drawbacks of medical school; you could forget about maintaining old friendships during the four years of intensive study, as lab partners and classmates became the only faces you ever saw. The four years of residency that followed had been no easier, but at least Hannah had shared an apartment with two other young doctors who understood the need to get shit-faced drunk the first day you lost a patient, that black-out conditions were mandatory during the day if you were on night shifts, and that the fridge needed to be stocked with Diet Coke twenty-four seven.

Hannah figured her best bet for tracking Brad would be to start with his sister. A few months ago, Hannah was sure she'd seen a new baby announcement on Facebook with Brad's sister tagged in the group. Lila, that was her name. Lila Crawford. As far as Hannah could recall, she still lived back in Montana, so maybe Brad was near that area too. It would be nice to visit. Maybe she could pop by and see her parents.

With renewed vigor and a tall steaming black Columbian coffee, Hannah set off back home to her apartment.

"LILA?" Hannah asked when she heard a confused 'hello' at the other end of the line.

"Speaking. Who's this?" Lila's voice sounded sleep heavy.

"It's Hannah Cooper. We went to High School together." Hannah prompted.

"Oh, yeah. Brad's wife."

"Yeah," Hannah paused. She hadn't exactly expected a warm reception, but Lila's tone was particularly cold. "I was actually looking for Brad. Do you know where he lives now?"

"Not really. I haven't heard from him in over a year. No surprise there."

Hannah made a sympathetic noise, "Any idea where I might find out?"

"Why are you looking for him anyways? You two haven't seen each other in years."

"I just wanted to catch up with him, see how he's doing..." Hannah trailed off. "I also need him to sign some divorce papers. We never really got around to it, before, you know?"

"You getting hitched again?" Lila asked.

"No, no, just getting my paperwork in order."

There was a long silence on the other end of the phone. Eventually Lila sighed.

"Well, last I heard, he was in Alaska."

"*Alaska*?"

"Yeah. He was doing odd jobs here and there. No idea where he's at now though."

"Okay, thanks Lila. Do you know what area?"

"Port Ursa."

Hannah had never heard of it. So much for her trip to Montana.

"Great. Thanks, Lila, you've been really helpful."

"Anytime."

The phone went dead before Hannah had a chance to say goodbye. Hannah stared bemusedly at it. Lila had always been a bit of an oddball, and as far back as Hannah could remember, she'd never gotten along with her own brother.

The Crawford siblings hadn't exactly had the Leave it to Beaver upbringing, though. Brad may have been the all-star favorite on the school basketball team, but he had also been a wild card–constantly in trouble, forever in detention, and he often missed long periods of the school semester. It was that wildness that had attracted her to Brad in the first place. Hannah smiled to herself, remembering her days as a straight-laced high school student. She had been forever studying, positively obsessed with getting straight 'A's. Brad had caught her attention during senior year, and they had started dating casually.

When High School came to an end, they and a group of their friends decided to celebrate their freedom with a cross-country road trip. Predicated by a night of free drinking at a casino, and Hannah's first actual falling-down drunk, Brad and Hannah had found themselves in an Elvis Chapel in Vegas, pledging their future to one another.

Hannah went into her bedroom, and dug out a shoebox from beneath her bed. It was full of old photos and mementos. She searched through the piles, till she came to the cheaply framed picture of her wedding day. Brad had insisted on dressing up in a Rhinestone body suit. It still made Hannah laugh. He looked ridiculous, but she didn't look any better. Having drunkenly decided to go "full Vegas," she'd found the tightest, shortest mini dress she could find and the highest stilettos. In the picture they were surrounded by their friends—people Hannah hadn't seen in years. She looked at the picture fondly. Brad had been troubled, no doubt about that, but he had been fun. The foolish marriage aside, she would never regret that vacation. Her last hurrah, a taste of much needed freedom before she buckled down to carving out her career.

She was intrigued to see what had become of Brad. She was actually surprised that this much time had passed without him contacting her to get the marriage annulled. Hannah's dating landscape had been pretty barren, solely due to her working hours and somewhat narrow-minded focus on her job, but she would have thought Brad would have found a nice girl to settle down with by now.

"Do we have any ice-cream?" her roommate, Laura, stood in the doorway looking utterly miserable.

"No, honey, we don't. Are you okay?"

"No," she pouted, "Long shift working with Grayson. It was horrible. He yelled for hours, and I was so tired I didn't even know what he was yelling about."

"Yuck. I'm sorry, that sounds rough." Grayson was the Chief of

Staff at the general hospital where Hannah and Laura were finishing off their residency. He was an acidic demon, and getting on the wrong side of him would lead to shifts ending in tears. For Laura, it always necessitated buckets of ice cream.

"Come on," Hannah ushered her into the living room, and wrapped her up in a blanket on the sofa. "I'll go out and get some."

"Really?" Laura's eyes lit up, "Thank you, thank you. I'll do your laundry duty next week."

Hannah laughed, "No you won't–you never have time to follow through on that promise, but I appreciate the sentiment."

Laura smiled sheepishly.

"By the way," Hannah continued, "have you heard of Port Ursa?"

"In Alaska?"

"Yes! Do you know it?"

"Not really. My dad went fishing there once. I think it's a bit of a nightmare to get to–like, one of the islands you can only get to by boat or bush plane or something."

"Of course it is," Hannah sighed, "Salted caramel?"

"Can you get that and a cookie dough one?"

"Don't push your luck." Hannah picked up her keys and purse. "Be back in five."

Laura gave her a helpless wave from her position on the sofa.

Hannah marched down the stairs, mildly annoyed that the one rare week she got off would be spent traipsing around in Alaska, no doubt freezing her ass off, trying to locate her legal husband.

2

"I think we should expand," Colton Sterling leaned back in his chair, idly scratching his lean torso as he waited for his brothers' response.

"It's risky, Colton," Wyatt spoke in measured tones, "It makes me nervous that we couldn't cover it with the income from the current fishery."

"But we can easily cover it with Sterling Outfitters," remarked Colton, "We're running a multi-billion-dollar chain. What else do you want to do with the profits?"

Colton's brother sighed.

"Come on, Wyatt. You know he's right." Tucker Sterling broke the silence, "He was right the last time, he's right this time, and he's going to be right next time."

The three brothers sat around the table. They had been playing a game of poker, but talk had turned to business as it so often did. The whisky had stopped being poured as they tried to reach a solution, the game on pause while each man carefully considered the options.

Years ago, when their father died, the three brothers had been left running the family's small camping goods and outdoor supplies store right in the heart of "nowhereville" Alaska. Colton alone had seen the bigger picture; Alaska was growing its tourist influx every year. Visitors poured in seasonally for adventure and nature watching in the brutal, pristine Alaskan wilderness. All the small towns had an outdoor goods supply shop, but the quality varied, as did the stock. Colton's brainstorm had been to take over each of these mom and pop stores, one by one, whilst keeping on board the experts who had been running each shop, as employees. It meant more income for them, as well as access to superior quality products. Thus, Sterling Supplies became Sterling Outfitters, Inc. and within a few years, new stores popped up in various locations in a chain that encompassed Alaska, Canada, and most of the lower 48 states. Sterling Outfitters was now a household name. No one could deny that Colton had a mind for business that bordered on genius.

Now, Colton was keen to replicate the model in the fishing industry.

"You know it's not just the money, Colton," Wyatt reminded him, "The Jackson pack aren't pleased with our stronghold here. Purchasing the fishery that previously belong to their pack isn't going to help politics."

"Shit, Wyatt, Jackson drank that place into the ground. If it's not us, that place will just go to waste. There's no one here that has the inclination to take on a place with so much bad debt attached."

The brothers were at a stalemate. Both Wyatt and Colton looked to Tucker, waiting for his input.

"Look, let's talk to Joe about it, see what he says. I agree with Colton, this is a good opportunity and it shouldn't go to waste, but we also need to think about what the consequences are going to mean for relations between our clan and the wolves. I don't want more shit from Jackson and the rest of them cocksuckers." Tucker reached for the bottle of whisky. His action decreeing that the subject was now closed.

Joe Sterling was the uncle of the three men. When their father, Joe's brother, died, Joe took over as Alpha of the bear clan. Tensions between the wolf pack and bear clan had been growing steadily more precarious. Their father, Jeremiah Sterling, had died in his car, driving back home from work. The investigation into his death wasn't much at the time. Port Ursa had been such a small town that the police and legal infrastructure hadn't amounted to much, and the car had been deemed faulty. The death was recorded as an accident. The Sterling clan had their suspicions, though, grounded in the fact that two of Jackson's pack members had reportedly been seen hanging around the lot where Jeremiah's car was parked that day.

Tucker poured each of his brothers a drink, and then raised his glass.

"To the Sterling clan. Long may we prosper."

"Long may we prosper," echoed Colton and Wyatt, before each downing the golden liquid.

"How's that woman you're seeing from San Fran?" Tucker asked.

Colton had spent the last two months opening a store on the San Francisco coastline, whilst simultaneously catching the attention of a local lawyer.

"She's great. We've had a good time," Colton shrugged.

"Let me guess – you won't be seeing her again?" Tucker laughed, rolling his eyes at his younger brother.

"Woman in every port, huh, bro?" Wyatt commented, his smile wry.

"Come on, neither of you can talk. Wyatt, when was the last time you even went on a date? And Tucker, you *know* you're as bad as I am. I can't believe you're both giving me shit for this."

"Believe it, brother. We know we're all doomed to perpetual bachelorhood, so we might as well laugh about it," Tucker replied.

"Yeah, well, I'm too busy making money for you two, to think about settling down." Colton stood up and shrugged his coat on before either of them could think of a comeback.

COLTON STOOD AT THE DOCK, it was about ten in the evening but still not dark. The perpetual half-light of the spring evenings had begun, and would continue till September. He could still see the light of the horizon, just a sliver, where dawn was breaking over some far off point on the North Pacific Ocean.

The Alaskan spring had brought some warmth with it, but the evenings still remained viciously cold, and Colton pulled his jacket tighter against himself as he gazed out onto the swaying bulks of the commercial fishing ships rocking in the bay.

Colton had a good feeling about the fishing investment. He'd eventually want to expand their catchment all the way to Japan, but for now he would be content with the Alaskan coast. As much as his brothers' hesitation frustrated him, rationally he knew they had good reason.

The Jackson pack wasn't just at odds with the Sterling clan, they were also fighting within their own ranks. Drake Hansen, a wolf that had been brought up in Alaska as part of one of the oldest Yupik packs, had returned from the military to find his pack had been taken over by Simon Jackson's faction. At the time he'd had no choice but to fall into rank, but since the death of Jeremiah Sterling and the civil unrest this had caused between clan and pack, Drake had seen an opportunity to divide the pack and reconsolidate Yupik power.

The days of Port Ursa being a small, local and peaceful town were drawing to a close. As Colton had predicted, the town had grown rapidly in size–almost too quickly for local infrastructure to keep up. The police department was still based a two-and-a-half-hour drive from Port Ursa, which included a ferry trip, and that was on a good day. During winter, it was better to take a bush plane.

Colton sniffed the air, clearing his senses. He could detect an out of season snow rush coming. Earlier this week, he had considered inviting the lawyer to Alaska for the weekend. He had too much work on to travel, but if the weather was going to be bad it was wise to wait. A couple of nights with the woman would have done him the world of good, but he didn't want her getting stranded for an entire week. A week would be entirely too much together time. Better to remain solo this weekend and get on with persuading the rest of the Sterling family that fishing was the next frontier.

3

Hannah hadn't realized the logistical nightmare of getting to Port Ursa. She'd taken a seven-hour flight to Anchorage, then a one-hour connecting flight to Kodiak. Once there, she'd had to rent an SUV before taking a ferry across to Port Ursa.

She'd been able to appreciate the breath-taking beauty of the landscape, the surreal light that turned the sky a sci-fi aquamarine color, the impossibility of such a large, vast stretch of ice and ocean. The moment she'd landed in Anchorage, her phone reception had become laughably obsolete. Hannah knew she would need to lower her city standards considerably and rough it for a while. This part of the world held no prisoners, even less benevolent toward the unprepared and the foolhardy. Hannah had packed the warmest clothes she could find languishing at the back of her wardrobe, and dug out her winter parka. As soon as she got the SUV, she went and purchased an extra gallon of gas to store in the trunk. She wasn't taking any chances.

She arrived at Port Ursa around four in the evening. The roads were still icy, not yet thawed from the winter. Hannah drove carefully to pick up the keys for the cabin she had rented for the duration of her stay, which she'd hoped would be for one night only.

The town was charming and rustic, mostly wooden buildings dotted here and there selling tourist junk, restaurants and cafes, and expedition centers. Most of the commercial construction took place at the edge of the lively seaport.

Her directions, which fortunately Hannah had the foresight to print out, rather than relying on her phone's GPS, led her to a small corrugated steel shack. A sign reading 'Burke Cabins' hung over the top. Hannah peered in through the window and found a surprisingly cozy room where an old man sat at a table playing Solitaire and smoking a cigar.

She went around and knocked on the door. She could hear him shuffling to his feet, and a few moments later he swung it open.

"Afternoon. Dr. Cooper is it?"

"That's me, hello."

"Come on in. Coffee, whisky?"

Hannah wiped her feet on the welcome mat before making her way in, noticing that the old man was wearing a pair of bedroom slippers.

"I'm good, thanks."

"Suit yourself," the old man flicked on the kettle, "I need one on the hour, every hour."

Hannah's medical degree kicked in and she dearly wanted to comment on the hazards of stomach ulcers, but held her tongue. She didn't get the impression it would be very well received.

"I got your keys ready, the place is in good shape. Try not to get too lonely out here. Tourist season hasn't started yet, so you'll be the only one in the cabins. I got three up the way," he gestured up past the main road, "but you're getting the best."

"Thank you," Hannah replied, "I really appreciate it."

"Huh, don't thank me yet. You're a city girl, I can tell. If you want heat in that place, you need to burn a log fire. If you don't, you'll freeze your backside off." The man gave a short bark of laughter at his own joke, and Hannah smiled weakly.

"Ah, don't mind me. There's plenty of wood in there for you, you need more, just come down and holler."

The man shuffled over to a wooden cabinet on the wall and retrieved a set of keys.

"These are them. There's a manual in the cabin, tell you anything you need to know." He placed the keys in Hannah's palm. "What you here for anyway? One of those marine biologists? You lot are always coming and poking around."

"No, I'm... I'm a *medical* doctor. I'm just looking for a friend. Brad Crawford?"

"Ah. Yeah, I know the guy. What you want with the likes of him?"

"We went to high school together." The old man's tone didn't really surprise Hannah. It reminded her of the way teachers at school would refer to Brad. He was obviously still making a name for himself by being a little bit wilder and more reckless than the next guy.

"Huh. Surprised he went to school at all. Well, you'll find him at the garage." He shuffled around looking for something in his desk drawers. "Here–map of the area. Brad's on the other side of the island, but it's only about a twenty-minute drive. He'll be closed by now though–likes to get off early that one." The man grunted, clearly unimpressed by Brad's work ethic.

"Great, thank you," Hannah took the map and shoved it in her purse.

The old man saw her out, nodding in approval at her SUV, and gave her the directions to the cabin.

Hannah drove her vehicle slowly, following the rough track to the cabin. On arrival, she lugged her small suitcase out of the back seat and ventured inside.

It certainly had plenty of rustic charm, she told herself, whilst shivering violently, as she closed the door behind her. Before doing anything, she needed to light the fire. Hastily she pushed the logs onto the grate and crumpled up some old newspaper. Flicking the match, she was relieved to see it rapidly come to life, but it would be a while before she'd be able to remove her coat.

Next, she checked the sleeping arrangements. The bed was in the same room, which was a relief. It wasn't damp, either, but with only a duvet for night time warmth, Hannah thought it would be wise to invest in a sleeping bag, even if it was just for the night.

She checked her map and found a camping supplies store in the center of the town. Hopefully it would still be open, and plus, she was starving and far too tired to cook. It would be dinner for one tonight at the nearest, least touristy looking restaurant.

THE STOREFRONT LIGHTS were still glowing when she reached Sterling Outfitters. It was by far the largest and grandest looking store on the street, and Hannah vaguely recalled seeing a few from the same chain in Chicago. She stepped in and was welcomed by a blast of heat and a genuine smile from the rugged looking man behind the counter.

"Can I help you?" he asked as Hannah approached.

"Please. I'm looking for a sleeping bag."

The door chime rang as a family entered behind Hannah. Two children ran in, followed by their mother.

"Be with you in a sec," the assistant called to them, and gestured Hannah over to the neatly stacked sleeping bags. "We've got pretty much every type. Are you looking for a one man or two man?"

"One man would probably be best, as long as it's *seriously* warm."

The assistant laughed, "You staying at one of Burke's cabins?"

"How did you guess?"

"My aunt stayed there one winter during my wedding–house was full. She didn't stop complaining about the cold. The local motel closes over winter till start of June, so sadly there's nowhere else to stay."

"It's okay, charming really, as long as I can keep warm tonight. It's only for a night."

The man nodded and pulled down one of the bags, "This is filled with duck down, as well as some Japanese-made synthetic materials. Can't really go wrong."

"Perfect," Hannah smiled gratefully. She was about to say something else, but froze to listen to the sounds of sharp gurgling gasps coming from behind her, followed by silence.

"Jamie, Jamie!" The little boy's mother rushed over to him, waving her arms about helplessly.

The boy's eyes were wide open and desperate. His face blossomed bright red and then rapidly started to lose color. Hannah dropped the sleeping bag and was beside him in less than a second.

4

From his chair in the back office, Colton heard a commotion coming from up front. It almost sounded like the place was being held up—a loud, blood-curdling cry was emanating from a woman, and he rushed to the door anticipating wolf trouble.

He burst into the main store, his primitive bear senses kicking in as his eyes rapidly surveyed the scene. He relaxed at the absence of wolves, and mere presence of one hysterical woman crying over a child. There was also a second woman, who at the moment was standing behind the child executing an efficient Heimlich maneuver. Giving one final thrust, a bright blue object flew through the air and smacked against the glass display case. The child started crying.

"You need to get him to his pediatrician. He may have damaged his airways," the woman calmly addressed the mother of the child, whilst soothing the crying boy.

"Thank you! Oh, I can't thank you enough!" The mother took the boy back in her arms.

"Lego," the woman commented, picking up the bright blue object, "Happens all the time."

"We can't get to the doctor. We can't cross on the ferry in this weather and the flight path's closed, do you think he'll be alright until next week?" The tinge of hysteria was edging back up in the woman's voice.

"Let me have a look," the red-haired woman turned and addressed the boy, "Will you open wide for me?"

Amidst his sobs, the boy did as he was told.

"He looks okay. Get him to a doctor as soon as you can, though. Is there really no one around here, not even a general practitioner?"

The mother shook her head.

Colton stepped forward to offer his assistance, then halted mid-stride. The mother had moved, clearing his line of vision and now he could clearly see the little boy's savior.

For Colton, it was as if time stood still. Her hair flowed loosely down her shoulders, thick, deep red with natural golden highlights. Her skin was alabaster white, contrasting strikingly with full pink lips. She was curvy. Beautiful, voluptuous curves that made Colton's mouth water. Her eyes were a piercing arctic blue, and right now they were looking expectantly at Colton, as if waiting for him to speak.

"I have a plane you can use to take your boy to the mainland if you need it." Colton addressed the mother. He vaguely recognized her; she was fairly new to Port Ursa.

"Thank you, that would be wonderful. It's really so kind of you…"

"Colton."

He glanced over at the redhead. She had broken eye contact with him and was now rising to her feet. He wanted to speak to her before she left.

"Jake, will you get the flight charted?" he spoke to the shop clerk, who rapidly ushered the boy and his mother into the back room.

The redhead made her way over to the camping equipment, picking up a sleeping bag that had been dropped. Colton watched her bend down to retrieve it, admiring her thick, curvy ass encased in hip-hugging jeans.

There was something about her, besides her amazing figure, that had his bear wanting to rip out of his skin. Moments ago he had thought it was just the false threat of wolf attack, but now he wasn't so sure. His bear was screaming to be let loose, his blood bubbling under the surface of his skin. The pounding in his chest grew more insistent, thundering within his ribcage. His muscles became tauter, tensing as they physically prepared for the change his body instinctively knew was coming his way. It took effort for Colton to hold back the transformation—to halt nature's will as it strived for his metamorphosis.

"Do you work here?" the woman looked up at him.

"Yeah, hi." Colton moved behind the cash register, "It was amazing what you did back there. Are you a medic of some kind?"

"I'm a doctor, I work in Chicago." She passed him the sleeping bag, "I'm just visiting."

"Staying at Burke's place?"

"I am–hence the sleeping bag."

Colton nodded. Her smile was distracting, not helping his inability to recall how the cash register worked. They had upgraded the machinery since the days when he'd had to work behind a register, the multiple buttons and scanning codes were alien to Colton.

"You know what? Have it for free. A thank you for saving one of my customers."

"No, really, I couldn't. I was just doing what anyone would do, and a kid choking on Lego is nothing, trust me."

"I insist. How long are you staying for?"

"Just tonight. I'm looking up an old friend."

Colton wanted to ask who, but restrained himself.

"Not staying to explore?"

"I wish I could. It's beautiful here." Moving to leave, the woman smiled blandly at Colton, "Thank you for this. Much appreciated, really."

"It's no problem. I'm Colton Sterling, by the way."

He was racking his brain to come up with some excuse to keep the conversation going. In truth, this wasn't usually a problem for him. Women were usually happily flocking around him, hanging on to his every word.

"Hannah Cooper. Nice to meet you."

It was getting awkward now. The woman, Hannah, clearly wanted to get going. Colton came out from behind the counter to see her out. Holding the door open for her, he got a hit of her scent as she walked past. It almost knocked him to his knees.

He watched her get into the SUV and drive off into town. Colton groaned. He may not have experienced it before, but his instincts categorically knew that the doctor making a one-night appearance in Port Ursa was his. His mate. She also appeared to be completely unaffected by him. Not only was it a blow to his ego, but it was also damn inconvenient. Colton had less than twenty-four hours to make Hannah fall in love with him.

HANNAH SMILED to herself as she drove around town, looking for a suitable restaurant. It had been a while since she'd laid eyes on such a magnificent specimen of man. That guy had been *hot*. He'd been about a foot taller than Hannah, a quality she always appreciated, with a huge, broad frame. Even under his thermal hoodie, she'd been able to see a taut, well-defined body, but it was his face that Hannah knew wouldn't leave her memory for a long time. He wore his dark brown hair a little long so it hung slightly over his forehead, had a defined jawline covered in stubble, and bright green eyes that were shaded by thick lashes. His face was undoubtedly handsome by any standard, but it was his wicked smile that definitely made her girly parts take notice. As she backed into a restaurant parking lot, she caught a glimpse of herself in the rearview mirror and realized she was smirking. *Get a grip, lady.*

It was nice, she reflected, to know that she was still susceptible to the charms of the opposite sex. It often felt like she'd completely shut herself off from the potential of having any romantic interest in the last four years. Work had come first, and the thought of having her much-needed sleep interrupted by male companionship hadn't been at all appealing. She just hadn't had time to entertain the idea of a relationship—not with the kind of time and effort that they required. Laura swore by one-night stands, and they had been appealing during Hannah's college years, but the longer she'd gone without any intimate contact, the more the idea of sex with a stranger had started to seem like more of a hassle than it was worth.

Until today. She almost wished she were staying longer. If Colton Sterling was single, which she doubted anyhow, he'd be more than welcome to park his boots under her bed tonight.

5

Colton hadn't slept. The trees surrounding Hannah's cabin were pitch black against the rich blue purple pre-dawn light, which was starting to glow a soft pink as the sun rose over the harbor. Colton paced slowly through the trees in his bear form, the most comfortable physical state for him to be in with Hannah's nearness.

He had come here at about two am this morning, feeling restless and discontent. He had turned his attentions to work throughout most of the evening, going over the paperwork his lawyers had drafted for the acquisition of the fishery. It was watertight. He'd show it to Wyatt later today, continuing his campaign to get the brothers to accept the proposal.

Colton sniffed the air. On the icy breeze that blew off the ocean, a scent of wolf carried over. It was still some ways off, possibly a small pack hunting over on the far side of the forest, away from the harbor, where the sea cliffs yielded a high population of Kittiwakes and other birds, as well as small forest animals.

He would ignore it for now, not wanting to stray too far from the cabin. He couldn't be sure from this distance if they were naturals or shifters, either. Colton increased his back-and-forth pacing, feeling slightly on edge. He was glad that he'd come now. Port Ursa could be a wild and unwelcoming place for the uninitiated.

For a few hours all was quiet, and the scent didn't come much closer. He edged toward the cabin. He needed to be in position if any predators started getting curious. His own scent should be enough to deter them. He stayed close to the trees, not wanting to risk being seen in the clearing, and waited.

Colton heard noises coming from within the cabin, a soft padding about as Hannah woke up and re-lit the fire. He smiled to himself as he heard a loud expletive. His mate clearly wasn't a big fan of the cold.

Moments later, she appeared in the doorway, dressed in running gear and jogging up and down in place to keep warm. As he watched her, transfixed by her lycra-clad figure, her scent lifted in the breeze. It was instantaneously followed by another, the distinct reek of wolf closing in. They had come over from the north rapidly, Colton estimated they were still about three miles away, but they were running, chasing down her scent.

As it came closer, Colton could detect a strong undercurrent of human. They were shifters, not naturals. Colton riled. They had no business hunting down the scent of a human. That broke the already fragile accords completely, and he vowed that once this was over, Jackson's pack would pay dearly.

Meanwhile, he had a dilemma. Hannah was completely oblivious to the dangers the Alaskan wilderness held for her. He watched as she slipped in a pair of ear buds and configured her iPhone. All locals knew never to venture out in the wilderness without taking the proper precautions–which meant a handgun at the very least, and certainly nothing that would disrupt the ability to hear. But, Hannah wasn't a local, and Colton thought that this time that might actually work to his advantage.

She ran slowly at first, but picked up speed as she got into her stride. Colton followed in bear form, alert and watchful for a potential attack. He had hoped that his smell alone would deter predators, but the wolves were gaining on them, and by now they would have certainly smelled him. To Colton that meant that this was an undeniable declaration of all-out war on the clan.

He tried to keep a safe distance, not wanting to be seen by her. But as the wolves narrowed their distance, Colton shadowed Hannah closer, undetected due to the heavy bass emanating from Hannah's phone.

The first attack came from the side. Colton could hear paws slamming against the frosty ground, the heavy panting that emerged from a thirsty, open jaw. The wolf didn't aim for Hannah; it was headed straight for Colton. *Idiot wolf*, he thought as it leapt through a break in the trees, flying through the air towards him.

Without making a sound, Colton rose up on his hind legs, catching the full impact of the wolf's body smacking into him. He fell forward, with his jaw clamped deep into the flesh of the wolf's neck, Colton's mouth filling with blood. He held the struggling body down on the ground with his paws, yanking at the wolf's neck as it whimpered loudly, still snapping as it tried to get a jaw grip on Colton's forelegs. He swiped at the wolf, claws out, until it finally lay still.

He should have waited for the transformation back into human form to take place, to get the identity of the attacker, but there was no time. He could smell the approach of another, and sped up his pace to catch up with Hannah. Clearly, they had planned the attack, using one of their men as the distraction. They had, however, underestimated Colton's willingness to make a cold-blooded kill. Had it been any other woman running through the forest, Colton may have intended to injure only. The wolves hadn't anticipated that the woman they were hunting was his mate. Colton would have no qualms about annihilating an entire pack to keep her safe.

The second wolf ran alongside Colton, about five feet away, matching him pace for pace as they thundered through the forest after Hannah. Colton had the slight advantage of being on the dirt path, the wolf had to negate the underbrush and wild growth of the forest. It only slowed the predator down by nanoseconds, but it was an advantage to Colton.

He could smell the rancid breath of the beast, his own blood boiling with sheer rage as he heard the wolf's saliva swirling about in its mouth, drooling as he gained on his prey.

Colton had a choice. He could veer off path, heading off the wolf from the side, or he could wait for the wolf to make its move, and then attack head on. He decided the latter was too dangerous; if the wolf chose to leap, Hannah would be wounded, no matter how quickly he managed to drag the hell beast off of her.

He heard the wolf lose some ground as he hit a small, dried up ravine. The creature stumbled, swiftly lifting itself, but Colton had already veered toward it. He leapt at the wolf's side. It spun around instantly, growling ferociously at its attacker. This wolf was smarter. He didn't leap at Colton. He retracted back on to his hind legs, driving himself closer to the ground, aiming to land a blow at Colton's underbelly.

Colton bore down lower, shielding his torso. They growled at one another, slowly circling in the forest, each beast waiting for the other to make the first move. As ever, always staying true to its instincts and exposing its greatest weakness facing predators, the wolf quickly lost patience and moved in for the kill.

He leapt head on, razor-sharp claws extended and jaw bared open. Colton bade his time; when the wolf's fangs were an inch from his face, he clobbered the creature with his paw, knocking it off its trajectory whilst getting a good swipe into the wolf's front haunches. It smacked into a tree, spine first, and whimpered.

Colton gained on it, ready to finish the job. The wolf was too quick. It leapt up, scattering a light dusting of dirty snow and mud into Colton's face, and disappeared off into the undergrowth.

The wounded wolf left a blood trail that Colton could have followed, but again, he couldn't risk it. He needed to follow Hannah, to ensure that she got back to her cabin safely.

Following her again, Colton was able to keep a greater distance. He couldn't smell any danger, and let himself relax, his mind whirling as to what this incident would mean for pack/clan relations. As soon as Hannah was indoors, he would need to warn his brothers and Joe. The old man who manned the Burke's cabin desk was strictly aligned with the bear clan, as were most of the Port Ursa residents. Colton would let him know what was happening, with strict instructions to contact Colton if he saw anything suspicious.

Finally, they looped around back to the Cabin. Hannah looked pleased and tired as she slowed down her run into a gentle jog, blissfully unaware of how much danger she'd been in only moments before.

She paused at the front door, wiping perspiration from her brow. Her scent was viscerally intense due to the run, and smelled of the sweetest perfume to Colton's nostrils. Colton had to force himself to back away from her. The pain was physical as he fought his bear who was demanding he claim her immediately.

6

The garage was on the seedier side of the small town. Hannah followed the road until the traditional wood cabins became sparser, and were replaced by corrugated metal constructions and white-board homes that were falling into disrepair.

Hannah glugged down a coffee which tasted like rocket fuel, courtesy of the old man at the cabin reception. Turning a corner, she saw the garage up ahead and slowed the SUV to a halt a couple of yards away.

Car tires were piled up in the lot, along with an assortment of rusty car parts. She could see a shadowy figure moving around inside, but couldn't ascertain whether it was Brad or not. It had been too long since she'd last seen him to recognize his gait or his posture.

Hannah was partly dreading this, wishing that she and Brad had kept in touch a little so that their first meeting in over ten years wasn't on the subject of divorce papers. She didn't believe for a moment that he'd mind. He was probably just as eager as she was to get them signed, and like her, just hadn't got around to it or had a pressing need to get the marriage annulled.

Still, it was going to be an awkward conversation, and as much as

Hannah was curious about how Brad was doing after all these years, she felt slightly apprehensive as she exited the car.

As she approached, she could make out that the figure was definitely Brad. The charming high school all-star had grown taller and leaner. An oil-stained t-shirt clung to his sinewy muscles, giving his appearance a slightly hungry, malnourished look. His hair was shaved into a buzz-cut, removing the floppy locks of his younger days. She made a mental note to tell Laura to spend her next summer here. Port Ursa may be cold and wild, but its male population more than compensated.

"Can I help you?" He hardly looked in her direction, his attention focused on the contents of a popped car hood.

"Hi Brad, it's me, Hannah. Hannah Cooper."

He jerked his head up so fast he almost whacked it on the hood. "Well, shit," he turned to look at her, "Last person I expected to walk in here."

"Nice to see you, Brad."

"Likewise," Brad wiped his hands on the bottom of his t-shirt, causing it to ride up, exposing a rock-solid six-pack and a monstrous bruise covering the left side of his torso. "You look great, Hannah. Doing well?"

"Yeah, you know. Just finished my residency, so, tired more than anything else."

"You a doctor now, then?"

"Yes. Finally. And you, how are things going?"

"Good. Got a pretty sweet set-up here. Own this dump."

"That's great, Brad."

"Yeah. It gets pretty busy during tourist season, fixing up skidoos and flashy cars that can't hack the roads here," he ushered her toward the back room of the garage, "Want coffee or something stronger?"

"Coffee would be good."

Brad turned and busied himself with a kettle.

"So, I take it you're not here just for a visit. Unless you've discovered a passion for bird watching or salmon fishing since I last saw you."

"No, not here for sightseeing," she hesitated, trying to work out how best to approach the subject, "I was actually wondering if you could help me with something?"

"Sure, shoot."

"Well, we're still married, as you know, and I thought it's time we officially ended it. Don't you think? My lawyer will handle everything, I just need you to sign the papers, that's all."

Hannah winced at the silence that followed. Brad had his back to her, spooning instant coffee into mugs, so she couldn't gauge his reaction.

"You getting married or something?" Brad asked, eventually.

"No, it's not that. It just seemed like a good time. You know, sorting out my future, that kind of thing." Something stopped Hannah from mentioning the inheritance. It wasn't that she didn't trust Brad, exactly, but she no longer knew him either.

"Right."

The kettle boiled, screeching loudly and Hannah almost jumped out of her skin. She was regretting the request for coffee. She was clearly already on edge.

"I've got the paper work right here," she extracted the papers from her bag.

"No messing around, huh?"

Hannah detected a tension simmering under the surface of his jovial tone.

"I just didn't want to take up any more of your time than necessary. I'm sorry Brad."

He shrugged, holding out the steaming cup toward her.

"Thanks," she murmured.

"Do you remember that road trip? It was wild. Did you hear that Matt died?"

"What?"

"Yeah. Animal attack. Camping in the Rockies. A couple of years ago, really shitty stuff."

Hannah was stunned. The last recollection she had of Matt was him yelling out to the echoing vastness of Death Valley, head thrown back, bottle of Jack Daniels in his hand. Now he was gone? She wondered what he'd been like as an adult.

"Did you see him much after high school?"

"A bit," he shrugged, "We roomed together for a while, after you left."

Hannah nodded.

"You see anyone from school?" Brad asked.

"Not really. I've lost touch with most people, shame really."

"Well, you're here now."

Brad smiled at her. Hannah returned it, not really knowing what to say next. He'd strayed from the subject of the divorce deliberately, but Hannah wasn't sure why. Was it painful for him, even after all this time? She doubted it. When they'd parted it had been on good terms, and Brad had seemed as happy to see her go as she was to leave. Neither of them had been anywhere near ready for the commitment of a marriage.

"What about dinner?" He continued.

"I really only planned on being here for one night," Hannah hesitated, "I need to get back."

"Do you have plans for tonight?" He persisted.

"Well, no. I guess we could. It would be nice to catch up."

"And I'll definitely have a look at those papers," he grinned. "I'll get them signed, and you'll be free of me forever."

That sealed the deal for Hannah. If it meant getting the divorce papers signed, then a nice dinner catching up with her soon to be ex-husband was no big deal at all.

"Great!"

They finalized the details, Hannah insisting that she drive to the destination rather than have Brad pick her up. She wanted to keep this whole thing strictly professional. He hugged her tightly as she left, and Hannah inhaled his scent. It was so strange and familiar all at the same time. She broke the hug first, taking a step backward and smiling at Brad brightly.

"See you later."

"Yeah. See you, Hannah."

There was an odd look in Brad's eyes, but she couldn't decipher what it meant. Regret? She couldn't really say. Whatever it was, it unnerved her and Hannah was happy to step out into the natural light of the garage parking lot and hurry back to her car.

7

"Shit." Tucker ran his hands through his hair, "We've got a problem."

They'd gathered in Joe's apartment. Their offices were secure, staffed entirely by clan associates or bear shifters, but Colton hadn't wanted anyone overhearing their discussion.

"Did you get an identity on the second shifter?" Joe asked.

"No. I had to stay with the woman."

Joe nodded, "You did the right thing."

"Who is she?" Wyatt asked, "Why would they target her? Do you know her?"

"No. Not really. She's a doctor, in town looking up a friend. I didn't ask who." Colton wasn't ready to divulge to the group that he was pretty sure Hannah was his mate. It was something he wanted to keep quiet for a while, until he understood why she was being hunted, and until he better understood his own feelings.

"We need to find out who she's visiting, or if that's even the truth."

"It's the truth, Wyatt. Trust me."

"Colton, you don't know that," Wyatt argued, "Not for sure. We should keep an eye on her, see what's going on."

"Fine, I'll keep an eye on her, but I want Jackson's pack watched as well," Colton was on the defensive. He knew Wyatt was just being cautious, but when it came to the safety of Hannah, he didn't want to take any chances, nor did he want anyone else tracking her. That would be his responsibility.

"I'll speak to Derek, see if he's willing to divulge pack information," Joe reassured Colton.

"Be careful. If it gets out that he's aligning himself with us..."

"Yeah, I know, there'll be hell to pay. But, the alliances are going to emerge soon. This cold war can't last forever. I know Jackson. He'll get impatient and break soon enough. I want us to be prepared when he does."

Colton looked over at Joe. He sounded determined and strong, but observing his features more closely, Colton saw that the man looked tired. They all knew that Wyatt would soon be taking over as alpha, it would be his sworn duty, but Wyatt had always been a bit reticent to take up the leadership role. He wouldn't be able to evade it for much longer, thought Colton. Joe was becoming more insistent he step down as the years passed.

"Tucker, get a team together and start tracking Jackson's pack. Keep it spread out and below the radar, nice and easy. Colt, you keep close to the woman. Find out what her story is. Wyatt, you're contact point. All info goes through him. Got it?"

The brothers all nodded in the affirmative and started to disperse.

Tucker shadowed Colton as they left the building. As soon as they were outside, he came and walked next to him, out of earshot of Wyatt.

"You're lying, brother," murmured Tucker, "About the girl. You know more than you're letting on. What's the deal with that?"

"You're imagining it."

"Oh, come on, don't give me that crap. What's going on?"

"Jesus." Colton spun round to face him, "I don't know her. At all. She came into the shop yesterday. First time I met her..." he let out a slow, defeated sigh, "But, I think she's my mate."

"What?"

"My mate. My one true partner. The real deal, whatever you want to call it," Colton was getting agitated. He wanted to get on the road, find Hannah and make sure she was safe.

"How do you know?"

"I just know, okay. I can feel it."

Tucker raised his eyebrows as if he wasn't quite convinced by his brother's words.

"Believe what you want. I don't care, but I need to find her, so I'll see you later." They had reached the parking lot and Colton opened the door to his car, getting in without so much as a backward glance at his brother.

"Don't do anything stupid!" Tucker shouted at the departing vehicle, and then cursed quietly under his breath.

∼

Colton pulled up at the reception desk. Leaning out of his window, he gave the door a sharp knock. It opened instantly.

"She here?"

"Nope. Not back yet," replied the old man.

"I'm driving up."

Colton got back behind the wheel and continued his way up the dirt track, his tires crunching in the frost. He pulled up outside her cabin, smiling at the fading smoke still drifting from the chimney. Hannah must have overloaded the fire something fierce to have it keep going this long.

Colton desperately wanted to shift, to see if anyone had been sniffing around while she'd been gone. In human form he could usually pick up the faint scents of wolf, but his sense of smell wasn't nearly as strong as when he was in bear form. Shifting was too risky though. Hannah could return at any moment. Seeing a bear roaming outside her cabin and a stranger's vacant truck would most likely terrify her.

He checked his phone. No news yet. Putting it back in his pocket, Colton heard the sound of Hannah's SUV approaching. He prayed that he was going to be able to keep her interested enough to spend the day with her, in the interests of protecting her from harm, and his own selfish needs of wanting her, in the not so distant future, in his bed.

8

Hannah was surprised to see a truck parked up by the cabin. As she cut her engine, she was even more surprised when the door of the truck opened and the hot guy from the outfitters store emerged. He wore a North Face jacket over a plain white t-shirt and low slung jeans.

"Hey."

"Hey yourself," Hannah replied.

An awkward silence followed, Hannah waiting for the guy to explain what he was doing outside her cabin, a few miles up from the main road.

"Colton–from Sterling Outfitters."

"I remember who you are."

He shifted on his feet, and jammed his hands into his pockets.

"Just checking to see if everything's okay up this way. How'd the sleeping bag hold up for you?"

"You do that for all your customers?" Hannah hoped she looked skeptical rather than flattered. She ignored the slight fluttering in her chest.

"Nope." Colton smirked at her.

"Well, the sleeping bag was great, thanks."

"I'm glad to hear it," he hesitated, "actually, I was kind of concerned about wild animals up this way. They get pretty active this time of year. Bears come out of hibernation and there's slimmer pickings for wolves."

"Seriously? They hunt this close to the town? I'd never have thought that. Thanks for the tip." Hannah was slightly taken aback. Before she'd gone to sleep last night, she'd thought she could hear howling but assumed it was dogs or a few wild coyotes.

"They do, yeah, and you're really not that close to the town," Colton corrected her. It was true. On her run yesterday, she'd got more of a feel for the layout of the place. The 'town' was more of a thin line of houses and restaurants that followed the bay, backed by miles upon miles of forest. Hannah's cabin may have only been a short ride from the main road, but behind it lay pure wilderness. She shivered.

"Scaring you really wasn't my intention. Sorry."

"No, I'm glad you told me. It's better to know than be unpleasantly surprised. I went on a run this morning, deep in the forest without thinking. What an *idiot*."

Colton seemed to find this amusing.

"What?"

"Nothing. Just typical behavior for a city dweller."

"I grew up in Montana. I'm just a bit rusty is all." She raised an eyebrow at him. She couldn't quite figure out if he was flirting with her or just being friendly. She hoped for the former, but considering this was an excursion to get her husband to sign divorce papers, it was probably better if he was just being friendly.

"How long have you lived in Chicago?"

"Good memory," Hannah smiled, "About eight years. It's where I went to college, and then medical school. I went straight after high school and never left."

"So, a little rusty on your wilderness etiquette, then?"

Hannah laughed, "Yes, okay, it's been a long while. I'd say I'm more skilled at dealing with heart attacks and car accidents than wildlife attacks."

"Well, I hope it stays that way."

"I'll be careful. I promise."

Colton nodded, "What are you doing for the rest of the day?"

"Not much, just trying to keep warm, I guess."

"Do you want to take a ride?" When Hannah didn't respond, he continued, "I can give you a tour of the place, I guarantee that I won't convey enough of its history to bore you rigid, and I'll do my best to keep you warm."

"Sure, I'd like that." Hannah tried to keep her tone causal, but she couldn't help the small flip her stomach did at the idea of spending the day in the company of easily the sexiest man she'd seen in a very long time.

"C'mon," Colton walked toward his truck, and held the passenger door for her.

THE INITIAL PART of the drive took place in silence. Now that she was in such close proximity, close enough to smell his subtle aftershave and admire the strong forearms and capable-looking hands as they maneuvered the steering wheel with ease, Hannah found herself tongue-tied.

It wasn't as if she didn't have questions to ask. She did, plenty. She knew nothing about the man except that he was most likely the manager of a camping and outdoor goods store and obviously lived in Port Ursa. As a doctor, she was used to asking strangers all kinds of intimate, personal questions. Those on the receiving end rarely felt comfortable divulging information, but Hannah was more than capable of being straightforward and professional, barely blinking an eye, no matter how bizarre some of the answers might be.

In the car with Colton, it felt different. She didn't have any professional interest in him, and as hard as she was trying to remind herself this was just a casual outing at the benevolence of a local, her body was reacting as if it was a first date. She did a mental checklist of the symptoms—slightly accelerated heartbeat, repeatedly pushing her hair behind her ear, and then consciously trying to *stop* doing that, and a dry mouth. She really needed to get a grip.

"So, how long have you lived in Alaska?"

It was the best she could do, the silence had started to become awkwardly long.

"All my life. I was born here. My dad used to own the camping shop."

"Is he retired?"

"Dead."

"I'm so sorry," Hannah groaned inwardly. *Nice going.*

"Thanks. He was a good man. My brothers and I run it now, and a couple of other businesses here."

"Wait...you *own* the store?"

"Yes."

Sterling. Colton Sterling, he had told her his name while she was shopping in a store called Sterling Outfitters and she hadn't put two and two together. He must think she's an idiot. He and his brothers must own the entire chain. There was nothing remotely flashy or ostentatious about him, but the clothes he wore exuded wealth–subtle, but definitely evident from the well-fitting cut of everything he wore.

"You must like living here then. I've seen the Sterling Outfitters in Chicago, too."

"All across Canada and the lower 48 states," he beamed. I do. Don't get me wrong, the winters can be hard, but I like the wilderness of the place, and the privacy. I travel a lot, though, so that makes it easier. Maybe if I was stuck here, I'd have a different perspective."

"I can see that. The wilderness and privacy, I mean," she hoped she wasn't offending him. Hannah hadn't quite made up her mind about Port Ursa yet. Just because of the situation, she had briefly imagined what it would be like to be married to Brad, not just in name only, and living here in the seedier part of the small town under the potential threat of being attacked by a wolf or bear every time she went for a run. Still, the quiet of the place was nice. She'd enjoyed getting to sleep with the sounds of nature surrounding her, rather than car horns blowing and drunken revelry that made up the chaotic symphony of noise she usually slept to.

"You don't yet, but you will," Colton smirked, still looking straight ahead. His smile was deliciously wicked. It made him look sort of devilish.

"What's that supposed to mean?"

"Patience. Just trust me and you'll find out soon enough."

As soon as he finished the words, he took a sharp turn up a small road and parked in a large parking lot. It backed onto a small office, a sign reading *Kodiak Rentals* hanging above the door. The lot held a variety of outdoor sports equipment, from snowmobiles to dirt bikes and even a few jetty boats.

"Please tell me you're just running an errand?" Hannah moaned.

"Nope, 'fraid not."

"You're not getting me on a dirt bike. I'm a doctor. I see more injuries from motorcycle accidents than I have hot dinners."

"Okay, I'm not getting you on a dirt bike." He walked ahead, leading the way to the office. Hannah rolled her eyes at his retreating back and then followed. *Great*, she thought, *a guided tour by an adrenaline junky.*

He held the door of the office open for her, and she walked gratefully into the warmth. There was a very pretty young girl sitting behind the desk, who couldn't be more than sixteen years old.

"Your dad out, Lori?"

"Yeah," she paused and looked over at Hannah before continuing, "On business."

"Good."

"Can I get you anything, Colton?" She shot him a coquettish eyebrow raise, and Hannah smiled to herself. If she were a sixteen-year-old girl, she'd already be head-over-heels in crushville with Colton Sterling.

"Yeah, a skidoo. Anything that's not booked up today."

"Sure. Take number six," she pulled out a drawer and handed him a key, "The back's clear so you can drive right out. Not much snow for a mile or two, though. Take a wheel kit."

"Thanks. See you later, Lori."

Hannah tried to smile at the girl as they departed from the office, but the girl just returned her look with a suspicious stare. Clearly she didn't take kindly to Colton hanging out with strange women she didn't recognize.

Outside, Colton located their snowmobile and went about affixing wheels to its base. He casually chucked his jacket aside, leaving him in just the plain white t-shit. Hannah was stunned that he didn't seem to be absolutely freezing, but then quickly became transfixed as she saw the muscles on his back ripple in motion as he worked. He was more built than she had originally assumed. Every part of his torso appeared to be solid muscle, as compact as granite. Hannah couldn't begin to imagine how a retail owner managed to achieve that level of physical perfection. Not that it mattered - she certainly wasn't complaining.

9

The drive up the dry mountain path was bumpy. Though Colton stayed in perfect control of the machine, the small jumps were unavoidable in such a light vehicle – even with two passengers. Hannah held on tightly, convincing herself it was just out of necessity. It had nothing whatsoever to do with the feeling of Colton's rock hard six-pack emanating intense heat under the pressure of her fingers.

Soon the forest ground of rock and soil gave way to a light sprinkling of snow that got denser the further they travelled away from the port. The trees reduced in number, and before long there were wide flat plains of thick snow.

"Are you ready?" Colton asked, his profile turning so he was an inch away from her face.

"No–not if you're going to massively speed up!"

He just laughed in return and revved the engine. Hannah clasped tighter, and he held one of his hands over hers, warm and reassuring.

"Just hold on. It's going to be fun, I promise."

"Famous last words."

The snowmobile shot off across the snow, smooth and fast. The icy wind whipped at Hannah's face, lifting her loose hair up and off her shoulders. She drew in closer to Colton, trying to shield herself from the worst of the cold, and slightly terrified of looking down at the skidoo's rapid progress.

Colton effortlessly weaved around the few pine trees that crossed their path, leaning into the turns so that Hannah had no choice but to mirror his movements, carving figures of eight into the snow.

Hannah reluctantly acknowledged that she was in safe hands. After they had been driving for a while, she stopped being so anxious and let the exhilaration of the experience take over. For someone that had spent the majority of the last six years closeted in a medical facility, rarely seeing daylight between intensive shifts, being outdoors in such epically magnificent surroundings was refreshing, to say the least.

Colton must have felt her body relax. In the next moment, he sped up sending huge, arching waves of powdery snow in the wake of their track. As the wind changed direction, the powder showered them both, glinting like diamond dust in the sunshine. Hannah held on tighter, her hands reaching closer together across his waist.

She had noticed a little before, but the heat that emanated from his body was intense. It was like he was suffering from a high fever–except there was no perspiration that would lead her to confirm that diagnosis. The normal internal acclimatization process ensured that people adjusted to their surroundings. The population of Alaska wouldn't feel the cold the way she did, but this was ridiculous. It was like he was his own personal furnace.

"There's a place I want to take you–up at the top. We'll stop there for a bit."

Colton now drove straight, charting his direction to the precipice of the mountain. Pines whipped past them, and Colton repeatedly accelerated, getting the vehicle up the final, steep incline.

They reached the top at full steam, traversing the final hump by flying inches off the ground, and came to an abrupt halt. It was just in time. The edge of the precipice suddenly dropped off a few feet from their stop. Ahead of Hannah and Colton lay an empty expanse of ice-blue sky.

With trembling legs, tired from the exertion of tensing into the body of the snowmobile, Hannah stepped onto icy snow. The view left her breathless, and without looking back at Colton she edged closer to the drop.

"Careful," he called, softly.

She looked down. The various bays of Kodiak Island stretched out miles below her, and she could see nothing but the tops of pine trees. Then, most spectacular of all, the huge vastness of the rippling ocean.

"That's the Gulf of Alaska, leading to the North Pacific Sea." Colton had come to stand next to her. She was so mesmerized by the view, she hadn't been aware of his approach.

"On your left is Canada, and about seven hundred miles on your right, Russia."

"That's crazy. I know we're close, but when you say it like that..."

"I know. It makes the world seem so small."

It really did. Hannah took it all in, breathing in the cold, fresh air that tasted almost sweet this far away from pollution and the general, myriad smells of urbanization.

"This is really amazing. Thanks, Colton."

"It's my pleasure."

"You're quite the tour guide. I'm impressed."

Hannah looked at him sideways, watching a small smile soften his features.

"Well, you're my first customer. Maybe I'll start charging after this."

"I'm flattered, but do you really need the business revenue?"

She'd made the lame joke to hide the swell of pleasure that erupted in the pit of her stomach. She had actually thought that this was where he routinely brought women to impress them. Not that she minded. It was dammed impressive, but she'd believed him when he said it was the first time he'd done this. Knowing that this wasn't part of a well-rehearsed repertoire made her feel slightly giddy and light. She stepped back from the edge.

"Getting dizzy?" he asked.

"I'm okay."

"Stand a bit further back, just in case. It can get a bit weird after a while. Your perspective gets confused. You can start to feel like the ocean's right in front of you and could just step out onto it."

Hannah shivered.

"I can imagine that."

"Don't. This is meant to be an awe-inspiring wonders of Alaska trip, I don't want to frighten you."

Hannah laughed out loud.

"It's okay, consider me inspired."

"Good."

Colton's phone buzzed in his pocket. He took it out and checked the screen.

"Sorry. I need to take this."

Hannah nodded, more than a little amazed that he managed to get a signal up here. Colton walked a few paces off.

She really didn't want to listen in to the conversation, but the silence was absolute, and Colton's voice carried easily across the breeze.

"Yeah, fine...near Old Harbor, top of the mountain...Shit. They're tracking. Heard from Joe yet? Okay. Get in touch with him. I need to know what's going on." Hannah watched as he hung up abruptly, and walked back toward her.

"Everything okay?" She asked.

"Yeah. Fine. Just a delivery I'm tracking," he slipped the phone back into his pocket. "You ready to get back?"

"Sure."

"Happy to go a bit faster?"

"Within reason," Hannah eyed him wearily.

"Okay. Just punch me in the stomach if I go too fast."

Hannah smiled to herself at the last remark. *Would you even be able to feel it if I did?*

Hannah clasped him more tightly this time. They did go faster, but she didn't mind. She felt pretty content as the scenery flew by. The wind's icy blasts were nothing to her whilst she was comforted by her own personal heater. From her perspective behind Colton, she could really only see a sliver of his profile, the strong line of his jaw, which seemed more tightly clenched than on the way up. She assumed that something from the phone call had irritated him, or made him anxious. When she looked down at the steering wheel, his hands were gripped tightly, his turns sharper and more efficient than his previously languid driving.

Hannah guessed he was in a hurry to drop her off. It was a shame, she'd really enjoyed their afternoon together, and this was likely to be the last she'd see of Colton Sterling. Not that she'd ever forget this afternoon. The memory of his dangerously good looks and rock-hard physique would be something that would keep her warm on many, many nights to come.

10

The wolves were on their trail. The pack had tracked them from the shop, and kept their distance as they made their way up the mountain. They hadn't known that the clan had been tracking them in turn. A few of the clan were now setting their sights on detaining one of the wolves, and getting some much-needed information, which would be fine, as long as they didn't get to him and Hannah first.

Colton sped up. He didn't want to frighten her, but he needed to get her to safety as soon as possible. There was now a perimeter around her cabin made up of the clan members that Colton trusted most, Tucker included. She would be safe there. At least for the time being.

He hadn't wanted to ask who she was visiting in town. Hannah hadn't brought it up herself, so he felt that it would be impertinent for him to ask, but time was running out. It was likely that whoever she was seeing was the missing piece to this puzzle. Otherwise, he just couldn't comprehend why suddenly a pack of wolves would be so intently hunting her down, especially when Colton was clearly taking an interest in her. That should have been warning enough to stay away.

Colton accelerated fiercely, determined that the pack would once again be reminded why they needed to respect the Sterling clan.

When they reached Hannah's cabin, driving in from the forest rather than the main road, Colton cut the engine. Hannah's hands slid down from his waist, and he felt the loss of their coldness pressing into him. This afternoon had been agony for him, being so close to Hannah, spending the day immersed in her delicious scent, without being able to do a thing about it. Torn, as well, because he was meant to be protecting her. His physical reactions, if let rule, would jeopardize that. If anything happened to Hannah, he would never forgive himself, so it was preferable that he ignored his instincts and stuck to his job.

"Thanks for the ride, Colton." They had just pulled up in front of her cabin. Hannah looked a bit shell shocked, and Colton once again regretted the speed at which he'd had to go. It was nice to have her clinging on so tightly, but it had also made the journey a lot shorter than he would have liked.

"Like I said, it was a pleasure."

"Same here."

She made a move as if to open the passenger door, and Colton stopped her.

"I was actually wondering if there was something else I could show you–if you have the time?"

Hannah looked taken aback.

"Um, sure. As long as I'm not taking you away from anything?"

"No. You're not."

Colton reached behind his seat and brought out a canvas covered bag. He revealed two small pistols and a pack of about ten cartridge sets. Hannah was silent.

"I know this is a bit strange, but consider this wilderness training one-oh-one. This," he picked up one of the pistols, "is a Ruger Redhawk forty-four magnum. Most dependable model in its class.

Short of giving you a shotgun, this is the best protection I can provide you with."

"You want to give me a gun?" Hannah spoke slowly.

"Yeah. You can keep it on you all times while you're here, easily straps to the body, or you can keep it in a purse, whatever. But it's good for protection. Against the animals. It won't necessarily kill a bear, but it will a wolf. Even if you miss vital organs, it will slow it down or scare it off."

"You don't think it's a bit weird, you giving me a gun?"

"It's weird, I know, but it also might save your life. How many more nights are you staying?"

"Just the one."

"Okay, well perfect, you just need to keep it till tomorrow, then."

Colton's words sounded hollow even to his own ears. When he got his hands on those wolves he was going to make them pay. Were it not for them, he could have spent today charming her and casually flirting, a far more effective way of getting a woman's attention that gifting her firearms.

"I don't actually know how I feel about this. I'm kind of a person who tends to a gunshot wound, rather than one who inflicts it."

"I get that, really I do, but you have to be careful around here. Most adults, especially when they're in the woods, carry. It's just a way of life for people around these parts."

"I didn't notice you carrying anything." Hannah quipped. Colton wanted to laugh. He was about ten times more deadly than most weapons.

"I didn't want to frighten you, but I do, usually."

"I wouldn't know how to fire one of these anyhow. I'm much more likely to shoot myself in the toe."

"This is where target practice comes in. I can show you, if you want."

"I'm not sure about this."

"Do it for the town? Can you imagine what effect it would have on our tourism if a 'Beautiful Young Doctor Killed By Rogue Wolf' headline got out?"

She laughed a little, but reluctantly.

"Okay. I'll try. But know that you are one *strange* man, Colton Sterling."

"I get that all the time."

At last she took the pistol from him, aiming it at his chest by accident before he lowered it for her. They walked a bit farther into the forest, still within view of the cabin so that Hannah would be safe. Colton was pretty sure that all romantic intent, if she'd had any to begin with, would definitely be gone by now.

"Okay, let's just focus on a tree, and see how we do."

He slowly and carefully took her through the motions of loading the cartridges and then unlocking the safety.

"It's got a rubber grip, so that should help with recoil. To be honest, the Redhawk is always pretty smooth."

Hannah nodded, but at the same time looked hugely skeptical. Colton decided to drop the details and just get her comfortable with pulling the trigger.

"Okay, use both hands…raise it up, look down the sight…"

Colton stood behind her, gently lifting her arms to the right height. She was driving him *crazy*. He felt his bear tugging at him, desperate to claim her. The act of touching her, even over a substantial amount of layers of clothing, was like electricity shooting through his body. She was damn divine. The smell of her hair that gently brushed past his face in the breeze made him rock hard, his body frantic to mate with hers. He took a step back, avoiding the chance that she might back up into his groin and feel his longing.

He cleared his throat.

"Right, great, good position, now release, pull the trigger."

The gunshot echoed throughout the forest, sending napping birds fluttering out of their nests. The shot was a good one.

"Nice. You got it in the trunk."

"Did I? How can you see that?"

There was a very faint groove in the tree where the bullet landed. Too late, Colton realized that the human eye probably couldn't see it.

"You get used to knowing where a mark lands. Take a look."

Hannah went up to the tree and inspected the bark.

"I did! I did it!"

"Yep," Colton was bemused. For someone who didn't want to shoot anything she was a pretty enthusiastic student. "Want to try again?"

"Yes!"

She bounded back over. Colton didn't say anything. Hannah's face looked alive and beautiful, her cheeks and nose reddened by the drive, and the bright blue of her eyes shimmered with excitement.

They shot multiple rounds. Sometimes they hit their mark, sometimes they didn't. The more she aimed and fired, the more Colton relaxed. She wasn't bad at all. If it came to it, he was pretty confident that she could protect herself. Colton had a history of dating women who liked their men big, tough and capable, largely because they tended toward the helpless and incapable, far more comfortable picking out a pair of shoes than unclogging a sink drain, but Hannah wasn't like that. He found her straight-talking, and her obvious intellect refreshing. She may not like to ride too fast on a skidoo, but Colton felt that in genuine emergencies and high-risk situations, Hannah would be able to handle what was thrown at her.

Dusk settled in, and Colton felt confident enough in her ability to stop the lessons. As they walked slowly back to the cabin, Colton recalled the question that he'd needed to ask.

"Who are you visiting here, by the way?"

"Just a friend."

Great.

"Anyone I might know?" Colton cursed himself for sounding so desperate, and also for deceiving her. Trying to get information from her that she clearly wasn't comfortable divulging was making him furious.

"I doubt it."

Colton dropped the subject. The clan would tail her if she left the cabin tonight anyway; they had no choice.

"Are you doing anything tonight? I wondered if you wanted to have dinner?" Colton asked.

"I can't, I've got some business to discuss with my friend. Otherwise, I would have loved to, really."

Hannah stopped and looked up at him. Colton forgot whatever it was he was going to say as he took in her lips, eyes, the small silver necklace that nestled in the dip of her collarbone that made him want to kiss the delicate, exposed skin there.

"Maybe next time you're in Port Ursa."

"Yes." She sounded disappointed, and gave him a small smile. For her it was goodbye, and for Colton it was the start of a frustrating night and morning following her but keeping his distance. Damn whatever universal power presented him with his one true mate, only to take her back to Chicago where the likelihood of her return, or that she would remember Colton at all, would fade more every day.

He bent down toward her slowly, transfixed by those welcoming lips, hoping that they would rise to meet his. Instead her head ducked away, and she took a step back.

"Bye Colton."

He smiled and took a step back, "See you, Hannah."

11

She'd found the restaurant easily, too easily. She was about ten minutes early, and if her memory served her correctly, it was likely that Brad would be ten minutes late. The restaurant was nice, homey and warm. There was a fire roaring away in one corner of the room, and combined with the low-level lighting and the softly playing music the atmosphere was romantic and intimate.

Hannah half wished she were here with Colton tonight instead. She was still kicking herself for moving away from him at the last moment when they said goodbye. She couldn't be totally sure, but she thought he might have been about to kiss her. She'd moved out of the way partly because she was nervous, but partly because that kiss would have most likely led to more. She knew *she* wouldn't have stopped anything, and from her experience men weren't usually the ones to put the brakes on intimacy.

She was already falling for him. Her own insistence that she stay a maximum of one night had been put on hold by Brad. She knew that if something started with Colton, she'd want to stay longer. No way would one night be enough time with that body. Not only that, but she found herself frustrated that she didn't know more about him. She wanted to hear about what it was like growing up here, what his brothers were like, how he was running such a successful chain of stores at such a young age. He couldn't have been more than a few years older than her.

She sipped slowly at her glass of wine. Straight after Colton left, she'd taken a hot shower, when clearly a cold one would have been more beneficial to her current mood. Colton Sterling just wouldn't leave her headspace.

She was gazing out of the restaurant window when Brad approached. He'd gone to a lot of effort, she noticed. He was dressed in a black suit and a tie, and was clean-shaven. She rose to greet him, holding out her hand. Mistakenly, or perhaps deliberately misreading her signals, Brad dove in and kissed her on the cheek.

"You look amazing, Hannah."

"Thank you – nice suit."

He smiled at her and sat down. He eyed her glass of wine, seemingly pleased.

"We should order a bottle."

"Um, okay. Sure." Hannah never really drank more than one glass or two, but she didn't want to be a downer on the evening before it had begun.

He ordered wine from the waitress as she handed them dinner menus.

"I come here a lot. Do you mind if I order for you? I've got a pretty good idea of what you'd like."

"That's confident. Why not?"

Hannah put the menu back down, but not before she'd seen the prices. They were pretty steep by small town standards. Brad must be doing well to frequent this place. She was impressed. His garage may not have looked like much, but he was obviously working hard to keep it profitable. The Brad she'd known had been a bit of a slacker, she was pleased that his attitude had changed. It almost tempted her to tell him about her plans to open her own practice.

"How are you liking Port Ursa so far?"

"Loving it. It's so beautiful, and it's amazing to get actual fresh air. It's been a long time."

"Not desperate to get back to the city yet?"

Hannah laughed, "No, not desperate. It's just work that I need to get back for, otherwise I would have extended the trip."

"How's your family?"

"They're good. I haven't seen them in a while, but I still speak to mom about once a week, and dad almost as often. I spoke to your sister when I was tracking you down."

"Yeah, well. You know what she's like. I haven't seen her much."

Brad looked away, shutting that line of conversation down. Hannah regretted bringing it up. Family was always a bit of a sore spot for Brad. She knew better than that.

"So, you dating anyone in town?"

"No, I'm married remember?"

Brad smiled at her to show he was joking, but the comment threw Hannah. She took another sip of wine, hoping the waitress would return to take their order.

"Seriously though, the right woman must have escaped me. I'm not big on the dating scene."

"She'll come along," Hannah smiled, "Just a matter of time."

"Oh, I know."

Brad looked at her, his eyes meeting hers in an intense gaze. Small alarm bells started to ring, but Hannah ignored them. She was absolutely positive that Brad had zero interest in attempting to reconcile their relationship.

The waitress arrived, and Brad gave the order—seafood gumbo as an appetizer, and pan seared trout and Lobster brisket as an entrée, along with a lemon sorbet desert. Hannah had really been expecting a casual working dinner, maybe going over some of the finer points of the documentation. She hadn't been prepared for any extravagance on Brad's part.

"It's really nice of you to take the time to meet me. I appreciate it. Port Ursa is a pretty friendly place."

"Other locals been friendly, then?" Hannah could detect a slight edge to his voice.

"Sure. Everyone I've met. I helped a kid in a store yesterday. Her mother and the guy in the shop couldn't thank me enough. It was sweet."

Brad nodded.

"More wine?"

"I'm good for now, thank you."

He poured a glass for himself, looking satisfied as he took a deep gulp.

"Nice stuff. So, tell me about medical school. Was it all it was cracked up to be?"

"Honestly? I loved it–every minute. It was hard work, and I don't think I've slept a full eight hours in about six years, but It's been worth every second."

"And what now?"

Hannah deliberated. It was the perfect time to tell him about her plans. Anything else would be deceptive, but she still didn't feel comfortable telling him. She was also mildly embarrassed. If she told him now about the plans to open her own practice, she would need to explain about the money, and then he would understand the reason she was suddenly, after so long, interested in getting a divorce. It would sound crass, like she didn't trust him not to come along one day and take half of her assets.

"I'm going to wait and see. No firm plans yet. Keeping my options open."

"Right."

He gave her a tight smile.

"Did you ever think about me at all–during those years?"

Hannah was taken aback by the question. It was a pretty rapid conversation change, and she stumbled over her answer.

"Well...of course, sure. I often wondered how you were doing..." the sentence trailed off into silence.

"I thought about you a lot."

The waitress brought over the appetizer. It smelled mouthwatering, but Hannah wished they hadn't ordered three courses. She didn't understand what Brad's deal was. They had been apart for so long, their marriage had been a bit of a joke, and they'd barely given the false marriage a shot. Now it was almost like he was taking her out on a *date*, when she had purposely come into town to obtain a divorce.

"You must think a lot about Matt, too." Hannah tried to keep the topic on safer ground.

"Not as much as I thought about you."

"Brad-"

"I know what you're going to say," he interjected, "Don't worry about it. You were busy, I don't expect you to have given me a second thought."

"It wasn't like that, Brad."

"Sure. But we were good together, you and I."

"When we were at school, yes, we were. I loved hanging out with you, we had some really fun times."

"It was more than that. We had a connection."

Hannah almost choked on her wine. Brad's version of their relationship was not hers. She had cared for him, liked him a lot, but it had been a typical high school romance–a little bit intense at times, mainly because Brad had been the first guy she ever slept with, but it had been an immature, sweet relationship. Nothing more.

"Brad. We should really discuss the divorce papers. I'm sorry to hurry you, I know it's rude, but I need to be out of here on a flight tomorrow."

"No."

"*What?*"

"Hannah, listen, I want you to give us a shot. I've been thinking about it. We worked well together. We never gave the marriage a chance, and now we have an opportunity."

"When exactly did you think about this? After I came to see you yesterday? Brad, this is madness!"

Other diners were starting to look around and Hannah lowered her voice, "You haven't thought about this at *all*."

"I haven't stopped thinking about you since you went off to college."

"Bullshit. You didn't contact me once in all that time. "

"I wanted to! I just also didn't want to get in the way of your career."

Hannah knew he was lying. She had no idea why this was happening, or what exactly was going on in Brad's head, but she had heard enough to be absolutely furious with his behavior.

"So, you're really not going to sign the papers? Even if there's no way in hell that I'd be willing to give this another shot?"

"Hannah, calm down."

"Brad, I'm mad as hell at you right now. If you're not going to give me a logical explanation for all of this, I'm leaving."

"Don't."

Brad's hand reached out and clasped hers. She instantly tried to pull it back, but his grip tightened.

"Are you kidding me?"

"Hear me out— "

"Let *go* of my hand. *Now*."

Reluctantly he released her. Hannah grabbed her purse from the back of her chair.

"How much do I owe, roughly?"

"Hannah, you're being hysterical."

"Don't patronize me. I want to leave. How much do I owe?"

"It all comes down to money, doesn't it?"

Hannah paused, "What's that supposed to mean?"

"Nothing. I'll pay. "

"No, come on Brad, what do you mean?"

"The reason you left me—because you thought I'd be a hopeless drop out."

Hannah lowered herself back into the seat. She felt crushingly guilty, not really certain whether it was true or not. Had she left him because she knew she couldn't support the both of them? Perhaps.

"Brad, it's not like that. I just want to get on with my life, that's all. Really."

"I want to get on with my life, too, and I want you in it."

Hannah sighed, pushing her hair back from her forehead in frustration.

"I'm sorry Brad, I don't want that."

Brad stood up, leaving a wad of notes on the table.

"Let's get out of here."

Hannah nodded and walked toward the exit, her head spinning. She hadn't expected this to get so out of hand. The cold air hit her like a slap in the face as she entered the parking lot.

"Hannah," Brad gabbed her arm as she prepared to walk toward her car, "wait."

She spun around. Once again his grip was too tight, enraging her.

"Let go of me!"

He didn't. Using the grip he had on her arm he yanked her against him, pulling her up to his chest.

"Hannah, listen to me, I want us to be together!"

She didn't bother arguing with him this time. Clearly, he was in no mood to be reasonable. With the other arm, she shoved against his chest, forcibly. He hardly seemed to feel it. His grip tightened, and he grabbed her other arm, locking her in his grip completely.

"Get your hands off her."

The voice came from behind Hannah, but she recognized it. Colton Sterling.

12

"Fuck off, this is between me and my *wife*."

The word was viciously spat out, but even if it hadn't been, Colton would have recoiled. His *wife*?

Colton recognized Brad Crawford. He ran the local garage, and was reputed to be a nasty piece of work. Worse, he was an integral part of Jackson's pack. Simon, their current leader, considered Brad his pet lackey.

It all made sense to Colton now. Hannah was the target of a wolf attack because somehow she was *married* to one. Apparently, the relationship had turned sour, and Hannah had obviously done something to make Brad angry enough to attack her, and risk turning the standoff between the pack and the clan in to an all-out war.

"I said get your hands off her."

Colton kept his tone even. He wasn't going to rise to someone like Brad. He was a volatile enough creature as it was, without adding fuel to the fire.

"Mind your own business, Sterling."

Hannah took Brad's distraction as an opportunity to remove herself fully from his grip. She shoved at him, and this time he released her.

"Brad, go home. Enough is enough," Hannah's voice was firm.

Brad barely glanced in her direction. He was looking Colton up and down, his fists clenched at his sides. Colton just wanted to get Hannah out of there, take her home and make sure she was safe.

"You heard her. Leave, Brad."

"No!"

Colton froze. *Shit*. Brad's voice had come out feral, more than a normal man's should, and ended in an almost growl. He was about to turn.

"Calm down, Brad."

Colton stepped in front of Hannah, shielding her as best he could, should Brad decide to shift. If she were married to him, Hannah would know about his shifting abilities, but may not have ever seen it done in a rage before. For a human, it could be lethal.

"Come on, Colton. Too soft to take me?"

Colton didn't say a word.

"I heard you had the pack tracked. Seems like you've been paying a lot of attention to my wife," continued Brad, "Jackson's not happy."

Hannah looked at Colton in bewilderment. She clearly had no idea about any of the pack politics that she was inadvertently at the center of.

"Get to the truck," Colton spoke to her as calmly as he could.

Brad let out a growl. It was inhuman, and Hannah backed away, walking in the direction of her SUV. He was about to shift.

"Don't do it, Brad," Colton tried to pacify him. A large part of him was desperate to destroy Brad. His pack could have killed Hannah the morning she went running. He deserved to be put in the ground, but he didn't want Hannah around to see this; it wasn't safe.

Brad laughed, his facial features becoming sharper, elongating into a snout. He dropped onto all fours, his suit tearing into shreds as his body doubled in size. He growled at Colton, leaning back onto his haunches, ready to attack.

With one last glance at Hannah, who he could see standing at the far end of the lot, staring dumbfounded with amazement at her husband, Colton transformed. His body reared upward, and he roared, a tearing sound that shook the foundations of the restaurant.

In his primal form, the restraint that he'd tried to show had fallen away. He lusted for Brad's blood, wanting to tear him limb from limb for threatening his mate. A wolf, even one as ferocious and feral as Brad, was no match for a Kodiak grizzly.

Brad lunged at him, jaws open, salivating. Colton clubbed him aside. Brad slammed onto his back, sliding across the ground, then leapt back to his feet to attack again.

Colton knew Brad's fury would be insatiable, equally matched by his own. He lunged again, sideways on, and Colton bit at his hindquarter. Brad howled and then whimpered in pain. Still he kept coming.

Colton recognized him as the Wolf he'd attacked in the forest, the one who had gotten away alive. He didn't want to give him the same chance this time. Brad now aimed at Colton's underbelly, staying low on the ground. Colton lowered himself on all fours, protecting himself. He swiped again at Brad, this time his claws raking down the side of Brad's body.

Blood seeped through Brad's fur, trickling onto the parking lot. He made a move as if to attack Colton again, but as he retracted back onto his haunches a whimper escaped him. Colton saw the fear flash in the wolf's eyes. He was done. If he stopped now, he could live.

Brad's tail lowered between his legs, and he leapt forward, bypassing Colton and running off into the night.

Colton was relieved. Brad may deserve everything that had come his way, but now that the adrenaline was draining from his system, Colton was thankful that he hadn't had to kill the man. He was still furious, but there were better ways to settle this than more bloodshed. He would ask Joe to call a clan meeting tomorrow and discuss the situation. He still didn't understand the motive behind the attacks, but now at least he knew who was responsible, and he had a strong hunch that Brad was in this with Jackson. They would both be brought to justice by the clan.

There was nothing but silence in the empty parking lot. The

inhabitants of Port Ursa knew when to stay indoors and mind their own business. The restaurant clientele would have heard his roar, and carried on eating their fresh Alaskan fish, knowing that living in this part of the world had its own unique set of hazards.

Colton swiftly transformed back into his human form, and stood naked in the half-light of the night sky.

Whatever emotion Colton felt prior to shifting, always intensified once he was in bear form. Rage would become fury. Passion would become a ruling hunger. When he shifted back, it took a while for the climaxed emotions to become right-sized again. It had never been truer than tonight. He felt fury, white hot, prickling his skin. And lust. Intensified to the point of physical pain.

He marched across the parking lot, trying to quash his emotions before he faced Hannah. Unconcerned that he was stark naked, the physical manifestations of his inner lust and fury clearly evident.

"Get in my truck. I'm taking you home."

Taking her elbow firmly, but not tightly, he walked her to his truck. He didn't meet her eyes, or wait to listen to what she might have to say. In truth, it looked like Hannah was too shocked to say anything at all.

He opened the passenger door for her, and waited as she got in. Then he slammed it shut, and dug through a duffle in the bed of the truck for one of the spare sets of clothes he always carried with him. He pulled on a pair of jeans and a thermal, ignoring shoes and a jacket.

Once dressed, he climbed into the driver's seat, abruptly putting the truck into gear and setting off for Hannah's cabin.

As they drove, Colton didn't trust himself to speak. He knew he should say something, something reassuring and kind. She'd been through a lot tonight. But he was struggling to think of the right words, and didn't trust himself not to bad mouth her husband. Even after all that had happened tonight, Colton felt that would be inappropriate. He didn't understand their relationship, but it wasn't his place to say anything about it.

He'd seen Brad around town with many different women, come

tourist season, it was practically a different woman every night. He was a notorious flirt. Brad had also been living in Port Ursa for a while, and this was Hannah's first visit. Clearly they were estranged or something to that effect. He couldn't even begin to imagine what a woman like Hannah–bright, intelligent, sexy as hell, and ambitious, would have ever been doing with a loser like Brad. Seeing him manhandle her tonight had sent Colton off in a fury, but it wasn't a surprise. It was exactly how he would have expected Brad to treat a woman.

He was also assuming, rightly or wrongly, that Hannah knew about the shifter community. If she'd been married to Brad, then surely she would have known that he had certain abilities. Though the more he thought about it, and recalling her expression after she'd watched Brad shift, Colton couldn't actually be sure. She had looked absolutely terrified. He glanced over at her. Hannah was sitting stock still in the seat, hands clasped tightly in her lap and staring straight ahead. Maybe part of the problem between the two of them was Hannah's revulsion toward shifters, but Colton didn't want to believe that. It would kill him. He wished dearly that he knew more about how the mate bonding process worked because he felt so strongly toward her. Did that mean that the feelings were the same for her? Or could a shifter know his true mate, love her with everything he had, and she not return the affection or passion? He wasn't sure.

13

Even when the engine was cut, and Colton exited the car, Hannah didn't realize that they'd arrived at her cabin. What she'd just witnessed wasn't physically possible. It defied the purest laws of science—the practiced, principled laws that she'd based her entire career on, the laws and rules that she loved–chiefly because there was such limited grey area. It was black and white, divided into what was possible, and what was impossible. She couldn't count how many times a medical intervention had caused results deemed to be a 'miracle.' It was lovely that people thought so, but in her experience, it was never true. There was always a percentage of possibility, no matter how small, that could weigh in a person's favor. But a man turning into a wolf or a bear before her eyes? That was completely, categorically impossible. But, it had happened. Hannah felt as though her entire perception of reality had just been liquidated.

"Hannah?"

Colton was standing by the passenger door, waiting for her to get out. He was wearing clothes. She hadn't noticed that he'd put them back on. He looked completely normal. Normal, human, hot, sexy. All the things she'd thought him to be only hours ago. The fact that she'd seen him transform, shredding his clothes like the Incredible Hulk, into a huge, terrifying grizzly bear, seemed laughable now.

She exited the car cautiously. Looking up at him, she questioned her sanity. Had the fresh air gotten to her? Had high levels of oxygen, as opposed to the usual monoxide she must have inhaled everyday living in the city, given her strange hallucinations? Was it some intense and acute psychosomatic thing where thinking that her husband was threatening and underhand, like a wolf, and that Colton was warm, solid and big and cuddly like a bear, suddenly manifested itself in her reality?

She walked unsteadily to her door. She could feel the heat from Colton at her side even though he wasn't touching her. That had been another thing, she recalled, the bizarrely intense heat that constantly emanated from his body. Hypothetically, she thought, if someone *was* going to physically transform into another shape entirely, then the energy required would be astounding. Colton must walk around with a ball of nuclear fusion residing in him. No wonder he felt hot.

Hannah fumbled for her keys as they reached the door. Her body was on autopilot, familiar motions taking over while her brain scrambled itself.

"Hannah?"

Colton was standing at the doorway. She had assumed he was going to come in, explain what the hell was going on, but it didn't seem that way.

"Lock the door."

She was momentarily confused by the request, till it clicked. *Brad.* He might come back. Her wolf husband. The thought made her feel queasy. She didn't want him around her ever again. Not because of his seeming ability to transform (which she still doubted was wholly real), but the guilt trip, the grabbing, and the totally out-of-the-blue notion that they should be together made Hannah half furious and half afraid. Brad just didn't seem stable. And unstable people were dangerous.

She nodded at his request, closing the door when Colton made no move to come in. She double bolted it, the metal screeching from lack of oil.

Not really knowing what to do, she sat down on the bed. Staring at the empty fire grate. Her mind commanded her to get up and light it before she froze to death, but her body was unable to move.

Wine. There was a bottle that she'd placed in the cooler the evening she'd arrived. It had been purchased to honor the moment when she obtained the signed divorce papers from Brad. She'd imagined pouring a glass, and toasting to her future. Well, it was redundant now. Hannah didn't think she'd ever needed a drink more in the entirety of her life.

A few sips, and she felt able to light the fire. Every movement her body made, she quietly congratulated herself, urging herself on, the end goal to try and reach a sense of normalcy. Another sip, that resembled more of a gulp, and her mind drifted to Colton. She tried to focus her mind on analyzing who and what exactly he was, but it didn't work. All she could think about was the naked body, the beautiful, buff and muscled hard-body that had strode across the restaurant parking lot towards her, his junk hanging out all over the place. The man was extremely well hung. Even then, as her world was erupting into madness, that vision jolted her, pure unadulterated desire rippling through her.

It then occurred to her to wonder why he hadn't spoken in the car. It was she who was suffering extreme shock. Why hadn't he said a word? She was certain that it wasn't the revelation of the fact that she was married. Yes, they'd had a few moments since meeting that potentially could have led to something more, but any personal subjects hadn't really been brought up. Certainly nothing that would have led her to reveal that kind of information.

Perhaps he thought she had lied to him about the business meeting. To Hannah it hadn't been a lie, she had considered it such, but perhaps Colton got the wrong idea? She dismissed that. She didn't believe that Colton was that petty. *Why the hell hadn't he come inside?*

Earlier, she had been reluctant for anything to happen between them. That reluctance was fast fading. Tomorrow she'd be leaving

Alaska, and she knew without a shadow of doubt that she would regret not sharing a bed with Colton for a long, long time. She laughed at herself. Clearly the fact that Colton could transform into a bear, seemingly at will, had absolutely not dampened his desirability to her. If anything, it was the opposite.

She walked over to the window. Drawing aside the curtains, she looked out. Colton's truck was out there. She could make out his shadowy figure inside the cab. Hannah's stomach flipped. He was standing watch, making sure Brad didn't return.

Oh, hell no. If he was going to be her protector, then he was going to do it from inside of her cabin, with her. Her world had been turned inside out tonight. To hell with precaution and her feelings tomorrow. Hannah wanted Colton Sterling for as long as she could have him.

She grabbed the coverlet off the bed, and wrapped it around herself. With one last gulp from the wine glass to fortify herself, she stepped out of the cabin and walked toward Colton's truck.

14

Colton heard her approach before she knocked on the window. Her cheeks were flushed, and her eyes were still wide and uncomprehending. He opened the door, waiting for her to speak.

"Please come inside."

She had started shivering on the walk up to him, and wrapped the cover she was wearing more tightly around herself. Colton wanted to take her in his arms and share his body heat with her. He held back, still unsure as to what she truly wanted.

"Are you sure?"

"No."

He nodded. He was going to come inside anyway. He felt himself harden against his jeans. She might be somebody else's wife, but Hannah Cooper was *his* mate, and he was tired of trying to fight the chemistry between them.

He led the way back to the cabin.

"Can I get you a drink?" She asked.

"No."

Colton placed a hand on the small of her back, moving her closer to the fire.

"You're cold."

After a few minutes by the open flames, she shed the coverlet gratefully. Colton didn't say a word.

"Do you want to explain what happened back there?" Hannah asked eventually.

"I'm a shifter. Part of an old clan that's lived in the Port Ursa's territory for years. Your husband is also a shifter, but then I guess you already knew that."

"No. I did *not* know that."

"What?"

"I didn't know that," she repeated herself, looking up at Colton as if waiting for him to clarify what the hell he was talking about.

"I didn't realize. I thought as his wife, you would have known."

"No. I married Brad the summer we graduated from High School. In Vegas. It was a spur of the moment, crazy, reckless and stupid thing that we did. The moment we got back from the road trip, when the summer was over, I went off to college, and I never saw Brad again. Till yesterday."

"Oh."

"I came to get divorce papers signed. I recently came into a large inheritance, and I want to use it to open my own practice. My lawyer advised that I find Brad and get a legal divorce, to protect my assets should he ever come looking for me."

Things were starting to get a lot clearer for Colton. If Hannah was the beneficiary of an inheritance, then it could be why Brad and the pack were hunting her down.

"Did Brad know about the inheritance?"

"No," she hesitated, "not that I'm aware of."

"What do you mean?"

"Well, there was something he said—before we left the restaurant —about it always being about the money. I didn't know what he meant. But his behavior was so strange, wanting to get back with me. I really can't figure out why. Unless, somehow, he knew about the money. I don't know. It just doesn't seem like him, that behavior would be out of character."

Colton didn't say anything. Hannah had known Brad as a High School student. The behavior that Colton suspected Brad of, trying by any means to get that money, was completely typical of the Brad he knew.

"Why do you ask?"

"It's nothing. Just stay away from him," replied Colton.

"I'm leaving tomorrow."

"I know."

Colton took a step toward her. She was wearing a simple blouse, one that would have been commonplace on anyone but Hannah. Her breasts filled it out to bursting point, and Colton could see her nipples puckered beneath the cotton fabric.

He adverted his eyes from her chest, and met her gaze. The heat of the room seemed to intensify, blood pounding in Colton's body as he drowned in the dilated pupils of her blue eyes. Her breath was coming in perceptibly shorter gasps as Colton bent his head down toward her.

She didn't move away this time. He let his lip gently graze hers, enjoying her obvious reaction to him. His acute hearing easily detected her accelerated heart rate. He did it again. Colton could be patient, take this at a painfully slow pace, just to get Hannah to beg for him when the time came.

He ran his thumb along her jaw line, studying her. It was a face he would never forget. Those perfect rosebud lips, those flushed cheekbones, and the small smattering of freckles that bridged her nose. He leaned in and breathed her scent. He had never smelled anything like her, as if she had been made perfectly, just for him.

He kissed her. Starting slowly, lightly. Her lips parted in wanting, and he increased the pressure, his tongue emulating what he would eventually be doing between her thighs. She moaned softly against him, and Colton wrapped his arms around her, drawing her closer to his body, pressing his erection against the lower part of her stomach.

Hannah slid her arms around his back, bringing his body closer still. She was delicious, her mouth tasting like honey and cold Artic air. As their kiss deepened, the space between them vanished. Their bodies molded to one another in a perfect fit. Colton wanted to take his time. Hannah was moving against him, deepening the kiss. The friction caused by their closeness wasn't helping him slow things down.

He dragged his lips away from hers. Their breathing, in perfect unison, was heavy. Hannah's chest rose up and down rapidly causing the buttons on her blouse to stretch even more.

Colton couldn't wait any longer to undress her. From the moment he'd laid eyes on Hannah in Sterling Outfitters, all he'd wanted to do was discover intimately the rest of the body that drove him to distraction. He had already thought of a million different ways he wanted to touch her, what he was going to do when that perfectly rounded ass was within his reach.

He didn't have the patience to undo her buttons. With complete ease, he ripped the blouse apart. The buttons cascaded across the wooden floor, and the shirt hung open, revealing Hannah's full breasts wrapped in a white lacy bra. He drank in the view for a moment, noticing the almost pearlescent whiteness of her chest, the softness of her stomach. He took a step closer, but didn't touch her.

Colton fingered the button on her jeans. He undid it more carefully this time, and then slowly unzipped the fly. He tugged the jeans down over her thighs, pulling them down to her knees.

Standing back up, he kissed her again. Gently moving his lips against hers, licking her cupid's bow, tracing its shape with his tongue. As he did so, he trailed his hand between her breasts, down over her stomach till it reached the top of her panties. Hannah started to pant against him, her body jolting slightly at his touch.

He reached down further still, sliding his fingers over the satin and finding the damp patch between her thighs that was waiting for him. He smiled against her lips.

"I can't wait to taste you, Hannah."

Her body jolted more forcefully this time. Colton slipped his fingers under the satin, groaning deeply as he found the soft, silken layers of her entrance. He softly rubbed her small bud, loving the feeling of it becoming engorged against his finger. Hannah clenched onto him, moving her hips against the rhythm of his fingers, driving him on till she cried out softly, flooding his waiting palm.

Without pausing, Colton removed the rest of her blouse. He unclipped her bra, almost ejaculating at the sight of her heavy breasts coming loose, their nipples tight and hard. He bent down, taking her breast in his mouth, gently sucking on the dusky pink buds. Hannah entwined her fingers through his hair, drawing him closer, allowing him to take more of her breast in his mouth.

Without warning, Colton picked her up in his arms, carrying her, pressed against the length of his body, to the bed. He flung her down, her hair splaying outward as her head landed on the pillow. He kneeled up on the mattress, removing her jeans completely, and discarding them on the floor. Her body was lit by the fire, one side glowing, the other cast in shadow.

Hannah moved her long legs up toward her body, bending her knees. Colton gently took each foot in his hands, and firmly lowered them back down.

"Don't hide from me."

"You're not undressed," she whispered softly, as if he was denying her a gift.

"I know."

He smiled at her wickedly. He wouldn't give her what she wanted, and he wouldn't take all that he wanted.

Not until she begged.

15

Hannah could see the bulge pressing against his jeans. She wanted desperately for him to remove them, to have his hard, thick length inside her. Typically, in sexual situations, Hannah was the more dominant. She knew what she wanted, and as a doctor often on call, time was always of the essence. There was something about Colton, probably his animalistic nature, which made her feel as if she were being dominated. Completely. It was exhilarating, knowing that this man could do anything he wanted with her body, and she would not only let him, but every touch would be sheer ecstasy.

Colton parted her thighs, moving his body between her legs so that he was kneeling straight toward her. He was still for a moment, both hands clasped on her thighs, not permitting her to close them. He gazed at her wet panties till Hannah blushed.

He moved one of his hands upward, and without her realizing what he was doing, Colton tugged gently at the satin and the waistband elastic snapped in his hand. He removed them, looking down at her nakedness.

Colton leaned down onto his forearms, and trailed a finger lightly down the lips of her core. Hannah felt a hot flush spread from where his finger was touching to the rest of her body. He moved closer, and she felt his breath tantalizingly close to her skin. The next moment, he softly licked upward between her thighs, and then gently sucked at her bud in a languid rhythm. Hannah could feel another orgasm reaching up within her. His tongue explored deeper inside her, and Colton groaned softly, the sound reverberating within her body. He clenched her thighs tighter as he tongued her wetness. Hannah felt her abdomen flutter in response, her muscles involuntarily contracting in pleasure. She called out his name as she came, suddenly, waves of blackness washing over her till she didn't know where or who she was.

Colton stood up. With heavy lidded and sated eyes, Hannah watched as he removed his shirt. His torso was incredible. The contours of a well-defined six-pack made Hannah gulp, the long and lean muscles on his upper arms and shoulders looked like they had been carved from marble. He was an incredible man, thought Hannah. She'd never seen anything to equal him. She had spent years in medicine studying the human form, and here it was at its apex. The most perfect example of masculinity, and yet part animal. And tonight, he was hers.

He removed his jeans, unfastening the top button and then letting them fall to the floor. He stepped out of them slowly, his erection rock solid.

Hannah moved upward on the bed, making room for him. He knelt again on the mattress and yanked her back down. He flipped her body over, pushing her backside up toward him, till she could feel his erection against her bare skin.

"Hannah, you're amazing."

Colton murmured against her back, as he leaned forward and cupped her breasts in his hands. Without trying, his length found the warm opening, wet and waiting for him. He pushed in gently, as Hannah moved her body closer to receive him inside her.

He leaned back, trailing his hands down the sides of her body, coming to rest on her ass cheeks. He grabbed them firmly, pulling and kneading at their softness, his breath coming in heavy gasps.

One of his hands moved downward, skating over her hipbones, and then burying his fingers into her wetness, gently moving over her bud as he slid in and out of her. Hannah clenched around him, feeling the ribbing of his length against the muscles of her core. He was huge, pushing her body to its limit, riding the thin line between insatiable pleasure and pain.

Hannah felt another orgasm approaching, she tried to hold back and to come with him, wanting to be fully aware when he emptied himself inside her. But it was too much, his movements were speeding up as he searched for release, and Hannah couldn't hold off the inevitable. She came again, crying out.

"Please, Colton, please!"

He slammed her body into him, and Hannah felt a bolt of otherworldly pleasure shoot through her, making her gasp. She bit down on the pillow. The sensation made her body tremble, she wanted to cry, laugh, scream out, all at the same time.

Colton sped up his movements. His body was frantic, she could feel his grip on her intensify as if all his muscles were spasming, he started to pant, an animalistic sound that grew louder and louder. Hannah tried to widen her legs, pushing back into him, wanting her body to take everything his could possibly give.

He came with a roar, his body falling against hers, their sweat melding them together where they touched.

They lay still for a while, their breathing once again in sync, slowly regulating. Colton moved, dropping down onto one side of the bed and pulling Hannah toward him. She nestled into his body, her back against him, as he spanned his hand across her abdomen.

"Did I hurt you?" Colton spoke, his low, soft voice breaking the silence.

"The opposite."

"Good."

His hand continued to stay resting on her abdomen, it's heat soothing the loss she felt at the absence of him within her. Hannah moved her hand downward, covering his with her own.

"Tell me about being a bear, I think I'm ready to hear it now."

Colton laughed gently against her bare shoulder. He kissed her lightly there, before leaning back.

"Well, what do you want to know?"

"What is it? How do you do it?"

Hannah knew he was smiling. She pictured those sharp incisors that made him look so devilish, and leaned back closer into him.

"Okay," he started to move his hand lightly in a circular motion between her hips while he spoke, "That I don't really know. It's inherited, genetically, so I've always been this way. We don't usually come up against prying doctors, we heal rapidly."

Hannah laughed.

"I just don't understand it."

"Yeah, to be honest, I don't either. But it feels entirely natural to me. Sometimes my bear feels more natural than my human form, if that makes sense."

"No, it doesn't!"

Colton gently bit her shoulder, then inhaled the scent of her skin.

"You know, you smell like you were made for me. I wanted you the moment I saw you, I wanted this."

"It was the same for me, though based purely on your physical appearance."

"Not my winning personality?"

"No," Hannah gasped as he slid his fingers inside her, "that's just a bonus."

"I see."

He continued to move his fingers gently in and out of her, and Hannah flooded with wetness again, her head feeling light and floating as he drew out the waves of pleasure rushing though her body.

"Again?" She asked, feeling the unmistakable hardness against her back.

"We only have tonight, so, yes."

Hannah sighed with pleasure, hoping that dawn was a long way off.

16

Hannah awoke to the smell of fresh coffee. The percolator was churning away in the kitchenette, while Colton stood at the sink washing cups.

"Where did you get good coffee?" She asked.

"You're awake. Morning."

"Morning." She smiled at him sleepily, not wanting to move from the warmth of the bed.

"I get this stuff imported. Shipped straight to the Oufitters. I had my assistant run it by earlier. The coffee around here is appalling."

"It really is. I got some horrible stuff from the supermarket. You're my hero."

"I take it I've met another addict?"

"The biggest. We thrive in the medical profession, always an excuse."

He brought two steaming mugs over, and sat on the bed next to her. Hannah sipped the coffee gratefully.

"How are you feeling?" He asked.

"Well, right now I'm only choosing to remember the good bits."

"Keep it that way."

He leaned over and kissed her softly on the forehead.

"I have to go and take care of a couple of things. Are you leaving on the four o'clock?"

"Yes."

"Is there anything I can do to extend your trip?"

"No." Hannah took his hand, "But thank you. For everything."

Colton nodded. He smiled at her, but it didn't reach his eyes.

They didn't say goodbye to one another. Colton eventually rose from the bed, and rinsed his cup out under the faucet. Hannah covered herself up with the duvet, and walked him to the door. He kissed her once, briefly, tasting of coffee and sex. She didn't want to let him go.

COLTON DROVE to the main road, and then cut the engine. Picking up his phone he dialed Wyatt's number.

"Where have you been?" Wyatt didn't bother with formalities of greeting.

"With Hannah."

"I've been trying to get through to you all morning. We've got Brad here.

Joe hauled him in last night after your call."

"Good. I want a word with him. Keep him with you."

Colton hung up. He restarted the engine, and sped off to the Sterling warehouse down by the port. He wanted a chat with Brad, preferably in a sound proof room with no observers.

Tucker was waiting for him at the entrance.

"You alright?" he asked, taking in Colton's slightly disheveled state.

"I've been better. Where's Brad?"

"In the back. Wyatt's with him."

Colton nodded, making his way into the building. There were a couple of clan members dispersed throughout the space, waiting for shipments to come through. They all nodded in respect as Colton made his way to the back room.

Brad was sitting on an office chair, a glass of water in front of him on the table. Wyatt stood in the corner, patiently waiting for Colton's arrival.

"How is she?" he asked Colton.

"She's leaving. But she's okay."

Colton sat down in the chair opposite Brad. The man wouldn't make eye contact with him, staring stonily at the table top.

"He says it was all Jackson's idea," Wyatt sighed, "I'll leave you two to it. I'm sure you've got plenty to discuss."

He shut the door firmly behind him. Brad continued to look at the table.

"You been telling my brother fairytales, Brad?"

Brad looked up at him. His eyes were shadowed. Colton's guess was that he still hadn't healed from the night before. If he hadn't been able to sleep properly, then the recovery process would be slower. *Good.*

"Can I get a coffee?"

"Nope. Not till you start talking."

"I told your brothers everything I know."

"Great. Now you can tell me."

"Jesus." Brad rolled his eyes, trying to appear nonchalant. He wasn't fooling anyone. Colton could smell his fear.

"Is it true that Jackson's behind this? I find that hard to believe."

"It's the truth! Look, I got a call from my sister last week. She said Hannah had been calling, asking about me. I thought it was weird. Hannah hadn't contacted me since forever, so I asked her to do some investigating, find out what was going on. She bumped into Hannah's mom in the supermarket. Found out her uncle had died. Hannah's mom started talking about Hannah opening her own practice. You know how women like to chat. Can I get some coffee now?"

"Brad, continue the goddamn story. You're pissing me off more every second."

Brad huffed and then continued, "So, one night I was in the pub with Jackson. I start telling him about my wife, Hannah, and he tells me that we should get that money. I owe Jackson quite a bit."

Brad looked at the table, not able to meet Colton's eyes.

"You wouldn't understand," he continued sullenly.

"There's nothing to understand, Brad. You sold your wife out. Did you know that Jackson was going to have her *killed*?"

"No!" His voice had gone up a couple of octaves, and he was starting to sweat under the collar.

"That wasn't the *plan*. He said I should try and get back together with her when she arrived. That was the plan. I didn't know he was gonna try and hunt her down."

"That's funny, I remember you being in the forest that morning."

"That's not how it was! That other wolf was Steve Webb, Jackson had asked him to hunt her. When I picked up her scent, and then his, tearing across the forest after her, I tried to chase him down. Then I see you, a dammed grizzly, how the hell was I supposed to know you were protecting her?"

Brad crossed his arms and leaned back in his chair, "I don't care if you don't believe me. It's the truth."

"Then why wouldn't you sign the divorce papers? Her life was in danger at that point. What the hell were you thinking?"

"I needed the money. Seriously. Jackson's got me on a leash. I just thought...well - I thought we could give it a shot. Maybe we could make it work out. I should have known better."

"You should have behaved better," Colton corrected. He believed Brad was telling the truth. He'd heard rumors about Jackson's occasional side-line as a loan shark. It was how many, if not most, of his pack members stayed loyal. He owned their homes, their cars, large chunks of their business.

Colton slammed a paper file down on the desk.

"The divorce papers."

"You and Hannah have been getting friendly."

"Shut up and sign them."

"Or what?" The habitually cocky tone to Brad's voice was back. He'd already betrayed Jackson. It was starting to dawn on him that he didn't really have much left to loose.

"You sign them, I'll pay off your loan to Jackson, in cash. But I want you out of Port Ursa on the first flight tonight."

"Why? You think I'm competition, Colton?" Brad smirked at him.

Colton didn't deign to reply. He threw a pen onto the table, watching as it rolled toward Brad.

"Sign."

Brad sighed, and reluctantly picked up the pen. As soon as the ink touched the paper, Colton called Tucker in, asking him to withdraw funds from his personal account. Tucker asked no questions.

Once the papers were signed, Colton rose from the table.

"Stay here and you'll get your money, a coffee, and a goddamn plane ticket."

Brad nodded. He knew he was getting a generous deal. After what he'd told Colton and the others, he would be a wanted man in Port Ursa, better he walk out of here under the protection of the clan than take his chances with the pack. Under Jackson's rule, betrayal meant death.

17

Hannah returned to the cabin exhausted. She'd been for a long run, much further than she'd gone yesterday, and this time without an iPod and with a gun holstered at her waist. She felt pleased with herself. The lessons in Colton's wilderness 101 were paying off.

She took her time walking to the cabin door, stretching out her cramping legs with each step. Getting closer, she noticed a paper-wrapped parcel leaning against the door frame, with nothing but her name scrawled across the front.

Opening it, it took a few moments for her to register the contents. Her divorce papers, each page signed and initialed by Brad Crawford. A scrap of lined office paper fell to the floor as she thumbed through.

She recognized the penmanship before she read it:

I'm sorry for everything. I hope you make more of a success of your life than I have with mine. Brad.

She smiled at the words. *There* was the guy she'd known in high school. He might have been wild and impulsive, even stupid sometimes, but the boy back then had always had a good heart deep down. She felt sorry for Brad. It couldn't have been easy growing up, being what he was. Colton had obviously embraced his nature and grown up all the stronger for it, and had his brothers to help with that, but Brad would have most likely have dealt with it all alone.

She also knew that Colton was behind all this. Hannah felt profoundly grateful, so moved that he would go to this much trouble for a one-night stand. Clearly, by dropping them off undetected, he hadn't even expected a thank you. There weren't many men left like that in the world, she acknowledged. She had completely fallen for him, and the next few months would need to be dedicated to getting Colton out of her mind, but she would never regret meeting him. He was one in a million.

Hannah ran the shower, unsure what she would do for the rest of the day until her flight departed.

She had expected this moment, when she finally had the papers in her possession, to feel vastly different. She had everything that she wanted now. All the foundations were in place to start a new life and open up her own practice.

So why did she feel so hollow?

"Are you alright?"

Tucker and Colton stood at the water's edge, looking out over the navy blue of the Alaskan ridge. The wind had picked up following the balm of the morning, and they both had their coat collars up.

"Not really."

"You really believe she was your mate?" Tucker asked.

"I know she was. *Is*. It doesn't matter now."

"Come on Colton, we do business in Chicago, you'll see her again."

"Yeah. I know."

They turned and made their way up the coast, circling back to the warehouse. Colton jammed his hands in his pockets, flicking his car keys in agitation. Colton Sterling was rarely at a loss. Whatever problem he'd ever faced, small or large, he'd always found some way to apply an action–to negate the issue, work his way around it, come up with various strategies. It's what made him such a successful businessman. But, in this case, there was nothing he could do. He'd done everything in his power to ensure that Hannah could fulfill her dreams. It was the right thing to do, and what he found that he *wanted* to do. But helping her leave, because it was what she wanted, didn't take the pain out of losing her.

When they reached the warehouse, it was a hub of activity. A new shipment of supply goods had just come in. The spring and summer imports were always greater, to account for the tourist season. Almost the entire clan was working today in some capacity.

The old man that worked the reception at Burke's cabin was standing at the entrance, flipping through papers on a clipboard.

"Hannah left already?" Colton asked him, ready to lose his temper with the man if she hadn't. Jackson was still out there, and he didn't want to take any risks when they were almost home and dry.

"Nope. She's extended the cabin for a week. But I got my boy filling in for me. He'll look out for her."

"What?"

The old man looked surprised, and he repeated the information for Colton again, slowly.

"Where is she now?"

"Said she was looking for a realtor. I sent her to Sally."

"Hannah was looking for a realtor?"

The old man just looked at Colton like he'd lost his senses.

"That's what I said, yeah."

Colton nodded his thanks, hit his brother on the back in jubilation, and then tore off across the warehouse lot to his car.

It took an overly long conversation with Sally's assistant for her to divulge the information of Hannah's current location. Colton had never come so close to losing his patience. He eventually stormed out with a vague notion of their whereabouts, and hurried back to his car.

Colton felt like he'd been given a reprieve. He didn't want her leaving the island without Hannah knowing how he felt. He hoped that her looking in the area for real estate meant that she was considering some kind of summer home. If that was the case, then it was worth him saying something. Even if she didn't feel that same way about him, then at least he would know that he'd done everything he could to keep his mate in his life.

He slammed on the brakes of his truck. He could see Sally's distinct *Ursa Real Estate* branded car heading toward him. He jumped out and flagged her down.

She looked surprised to see him.

"You okay Colton?" She asked, winding down the window.

"Where's Hannah? I thought she was with you."

"She was, I left her at the Bayview Drive property to have a think."

"Great. Thanks."

Sally waved at him uncertainly as he dashed back to his truck. She'd never seen a Sterling behave so oddly and impassioned. They might all be as good looking as the devil, but they were reputed to be a bit of a controlled bunch. Sally shrugged and continued her drive back to the office, hoping that Colton didn't hassle her prospective buyer.

18

It was perfect. A thirty-four-acre lot, with a garage, greenhouse and studio attached. More than enough room to meet her needs. It was charming. The traditional wooden frame would need a good lick of paint, but the overall construction was sturdy. As a nice addition, the views were epic. Bayview drive was situated on a much higher level than the port. From the front of the house, she could see the winding roads all the way down to the water, and from the back porch, an endless vista of forest and mountain.

She was gazing at the front of the house, mentally designing the footpath, signage and imagining the whitewashed walls when she heard a truck pull up behind her.

"Hannah?"

She turned. Colton was exiting the truck. She smiled. She knew she'd be seeing him again soon enough, but having him arrive now, unexpectedly, took her breath away.

"Hey."

"What are you doing here?" Colton asked.

"Well...can I just caveat one thing, before I continue?"

"You can."

"Please don't think this is me, like, staying around, hoping for something more."

"Okay." Colton crossed his arms, waiting for her to continue. He didn't look particularly pleased by her words. His displeasure made Hannah hesitate before continuing.

"I was thinking, after I got the papers, which, thank you, by the way. Sorry I should have said that first. I'm so grateful, really."

"It's okay. Go on."

"Well, I was thinking about the time we met, the kid in the store. How he couldn't go to the doctors because the road was closed. And it got me thinking that, actually, for a town this size, there *should* really be a general practitioner…and maybe, better to go where I'm actually *needed*, than to a city where everyone is already well provided for."

"And I didn't come into the decision making process at all?"

"No!"

Hannah paused. It was a big fat lie. He was a large part of the decision, but she didn't want to put him under pressure. She was hoping if she moved here they could start dating, but she didn't want it to seem like she expected anything. On the other hand, it wouldn't do much good to be dishonest about it.

"Really?"

Hannah sighed at him. She kicked a pebble on the ground with her shoe, trying to find the words that could convey her interest in Colton without revealing the weighty truth of her feelings, the crazy, head-over-heels, impulsive feelings she had for him that even *she* didn't understand.

"Okay," he continued when Hannah didn't reply, "Let me tell you this. In the legends of our clan, going back over centuries, each shifter has one true mate. One person out there in the world somewhere that is perfectly matched for them." He rolled his eyes at her. "I thought it was a load of crap, to tell you truth. Until I met you. What I said earlier, about your smell, it's more than that. It's everything about you. Around you, always, my bear wants to break free. You call to it in a way that I don't understand. You call to *me*, in a way I don't understand. My entire life I have never been content. Happy, yes, but content, never. Like I was constantly searching for something that would temper the restlessness in me, and it's you. I don't think I can find peace without you Hannah. I'm in love with you. I will be in love with you always, no matter what you feel about me."

Hannah stood still, aware of the breeze making her hair dance around her face, the smell of the salt water being carried up from the coast. Knowing that for the rest of her life, she would remember this moment.

"I love you too, Colton. It hit me this morning, the realization that if I left, I would spend the rest of my life trying to get back here—to you."

Colton strode over and took her in his arms. He wound her hair up in his fist, holding her face up to his as he kissed her hello.

WYATT

A rare polar bear shifter in a clan of grizzly's, Wyatt is poised to assume the role of Alpha to the Sterling Shifter Clan. There's only one problem, all Alpha's must be mated and all Wyatt can seem to find is a string of horrendously bad dates.

With tensions running high between the warring Wolf Packs, the Sterling Clan needs Wyatt to step into his fated position as Alpha.

Always the innovative businessman, his brother Colton devises a plan:

Hire a mate!

1

The boy was tired and cold. The last meal he'd eaten was breakfast. It was oatmeal, which he didn't really like, but his mom always said it would make him healthy and strong, so he had to eat up.

His mom was washing up and singing a song when Simeon and his friends arrived. He was scared of Simeon. He had dark, dark eyes that always glinted as if he knew a secret you didn't. He didn't like children. Not even pup children.

He'd been sent to his room. His mom had smiled a really big smile and said he should be a good boy and go and play with his toys, but she was crying.

He hadn't been a good boy. From the top of the stairs he'd heard everything, the horrible whispered voice of Simeon, sounding like a snake, not a wolf. Then his mom had been screaming, screaming and screaming. It was so loud.

He'd run then. Out into the back garden.

But they'd caught him. He'd bitten one, one of the horrible men that Simeon liked to keep around him, who smelled like whiskey and cigarettes. He was wearing a leather coat, and when he bit it, it tasted like wax and salt water.

The man hit him really hard across the face.

"Thwack!"

His ears rang like bells, and the oatmeal all came back out.

Now he was here, and it was damp and horrible, and dark. It smelled like bad meat, like the Elk he'd found in the woods who'd been forgotten about or left by its killer, and sunk into the earth. It had looked like it was moving because of all the maggots. He remembered thinking that its eyes looked sad.

The door opened.

"Come on, you little shit. You're wanted upstairs."

It was the leather coat man. He had an ugly, scrunched up face and beady eyes. He clipped the boy on the ear. He flinched and then ran up the stairs, out of the cellar and into a large room.

"Look what we have here. Leslie, say hello to your son."

The boy lost his voice. His mom couldn't speak either. She was tied to a chair, and had a black cloth in her mouth. All her eye makeup was running down her cheeks. She was very frightened but the sounds that came out of her mouth were all muffled. She jerked in the chair.

"Leslie, stop moving." Simeon commanded.

Why wasn't she shifting? His mom was such a nice, beautiful wolf. She had red tinges in her brown hair that only came out when she was in sunlight. She was fast as well, she liked to run.

"I'm not doing this because I want to – I'm doing this as a lesson to all of you."

Simeon looked around the room. The boy noticed lots of other wolves; the whole Pack was standing around. Some were panting, like they were excited. Why weren't they helping his mom? Two of his friends were there too. They played Xbox together. When he looked at them, they lowered their heads.

"Leslie has betrayed the Pack. The strong bond that binds us – the bond of brotherhood and *trust*. She has sullied that. Dishonored you all," Simeon continued, "and it will not go unpunished."

Simeon was lying! His mom would never betray anybody; she was a good Pack member – everyone thought so. *Why wasn't anybody saying anything?*

Simeon walked up to his mom. He touched her lovely hair, stoking it. The boy wanted to kick him, to tear at him. He shouldn't be touching his mom.

"Leslie, I'm a benevolent man – I want to know what you think would be the more fitting punishment for your crime. Should I take out your throat, or shall it be your son's?"

He ripped the cloth down from her mouth. Her lips were red with blood, and it tricked down at the corners.

"Don't you *dare* fucking touch him! Don't you dare – you're a monster! You're a vile, inhuman monster!"

His mother was screaming again, and Simeon hit her hard on the back of the head. She whimpered and stopped screaming.

"Mommy?"

"Baby, it's going to be okay – just stay quiet darling, stay quiet for mommy." Her voice was scaring him. She didn't sound okay; he didn't think anything *was* going to be okay. Her eyes were wild. They didn't look like her eyes anymore.

"Shift and I will rip him to pieces, Leslie." Simeon's voice was soft.

"Let him go – please Simeon, I'm begging you – please let him go."

"Tell me what you told Drake, and I'll let him go."

His mom was breathing heavily, looking around the room for help. He wanted to tell her that he didn't think anyone was helping. They kept looking away. He *hated* them.

"I told him…I just told him about you, being nervous about Wyatt Sterling becoming Alpha…that you would do anything in your power to stop him. I told him about the properties…the new plans for Kodiak Island…that's all – I'm so sorry Simeon, please forgive me… please don't kill my son."

"Oh, Leslie, I am *so* displeased," Simeon sighed, "and what did he tell you? Can you impart any knowledge that might help you now?"

"Drake's coming for you, Simeon." His mom's voice was bitter now, bitter and twisted. "Your time is going to be over soon, that's what he promises. He's aligned with the Sterling Clan. They won't rest until you're in the ground."

"I see," Simeon whispered softly, "that's a terrible shame. You've told me nothing I don't already know. And now I think it's time for you to step off this mortal coil. Any last words for your son?"

His mom looked at him.

"I love you, baby. Never forget that I love you *so* much."

Simeon became a wolf. He was big and black and his eyes glinted yellow. He looked hungry. Then he couldn't see his mom anymore. Her chair got knocked backward onto the floor, and Simeon made crunching noises that were wet and meaty. Her legs were shaking in the air, up and down, up and down. Then they stopped moving. He thought of the Elk, and then he started screaming.

2

Relentless sheets of rain battered down on the pavement outside, washing away the debris of the city, making it gleam under neon lights and twinkling storefronts.

Haley flipped the collar of her Burberry trench coat, and tipped her umbrella forward as a shield against the onslaught. The streets were mostly empty, but raucous noises spilled from bars, and the city's homeless cowered in doorways, detected only by intermittent red tipped flares of cigarettes.

Eight months ago this part of the city would have been nothing more than a blur from a cab window for Haley. Now it was home.

She passed a derelict building and one of the fly posters caught her eye. It was soaked and peeling, but Haley could clearly make out the figure of a prima ballerina captured in the motion of an elegant Déboulé.

October 16 – December 21
La Bayader

CHOREOGRAPHER JUSTIN PECK

Introducing *Ela Rovimana* as Prima Ballerina

HAYLEY STARED AT IT, ignoring the damp seeping through inappropriately chosen suede boots. The corner of the poster had started to curl up, revealing a hint of faded paper beneath. Without thinking, Haley peeled back the top poster to reveal an almost identical one. Except in this version it was her own face staring back at her, poised and serene as she presented the camera with a genteel Écarté.

Hayley scrunched up both posters, leaving a long-ago gig advertisement from some obscure band remaining. That was better. She marched over to the nearest trashcan. Empty KFC styrofoam containers and crumpled papers spewed over the top as Haley pushed the paper down firmly into its depths.

She glanced the length of the street, checking to see if anyone had seen her act of pointless vandalism before hurrying on home.

HALEY DUG in her bag trying to locate her keys. She fumbled around, cursing under her breath and dropped the umbrella. Ignoring the sheet of rain that immediately drenched her hair and neck, she dug the key into the lock and sighed with relief as the door swung open into the warmth of her apartment building.

"Will you shut that 'brella? We got enough problems here without you bringing eight years of bad luck on my doorstep, Haley Dubois."

The African American woman glared down at her from the opposite end of the hallway.

"Hey May-May," she called, wrestling with the umbrella, "damn thing."

"Child, have you no sense of self-preservation? You look like you been swimming – and in such a fancy coat, too."

May-May tutted at her, the flamboyant earrings she always wore jangling loudly as she did so.

"I'm making tea. The spirits only know what you've got up there," she gestured upwards to Haley's apartment on the second floor, "you come in here and get warm."

Haley rolled her eyes at the woman. May-May's assumption was incorrect; Haley kept a warm, clean and cozy apartment with what little that she had – but she took the request at what it was, an offer of company. After another fruitless and dispiriting day, it's what Haley needed.

"Thanks May-May."

"Humph," the woman snorted with righteous indignation and marched back into her apartment, leaving the door open for Haley to follow.

Haley hung her coat over the rickety stand and made her way through the waterfall of beaded drapes to May-May's living room, sinking into a battered leather armchair.

A black cat immediately jumped onto her lap, and obnoxiously dug its face into Haley's stomach, flicking a tail in her face.

"Hey there, mister Prince."

He purred at her, digging his claws into her thighs to get comfy.

"He won't find a soft spot on you – bag of bones you are."

May-May came through rattling a tea set on her tray. She set it down on the coffee table, and it creaked beneath the weight.

"Your mamma was built like a coke bottle, she'd be turning in her grave at the sights of you – and with a child as well, Lord bless its soul."

She tutted again, and began pouring the tea. It smelled bitter and potent; May-May concocted her own herbal infusions, swearing that her teas, with the aid of her own home remedies, meant that she'd never had to visit a doctor in her life. Haley believed her, but suspected it was more that May-May had the constitution of an Ox and would be so insulted by any kind of illness or frailty, that she's probably managed to terrify any kind of malady into submission.

"So, what they say at the job center?"

Haley sighed, "nothing available at the moment, they'll keep in touch, etc. etc."

May-May nodded sagely.

"Tyler saying' the same thing. He got laid off from that construction delivery company, been two weeks and nothing."

Haley's face fell and May-May hurried to bolster her spirits.

"Mind – that boy's a few tools short of a toolbox, and you're a bright young thing. Be different for you; you'll be sittin' at a fancy reception desk somewhere, mark my words."

"Thanks May-May, I'm sure I will."

Haley took a sip of her tea. It warmed her straight through to the bone and Haley smiled softly in gratitude.

"Maybe time we did a reading." May-May mused.

She studied Haley intently. Reaching some unknown conclusion, she pursed her lips and nodded.

"Yep, I'll say it's time. Somethin' changing, somethin' coming – I can feel it."

"May-May, I'm too tired – it's been a long day."

Haley tried to protest, her eyes pleading with the old woman. May-May made a good living off Tarot card and palm readings; she got folks from all over North America visiting, eager to gain insight into the illicit of all promises – what the future held.

Haley never said it outright, but she didn't believe a word of the mystical hokum that May-May delivered. She had a suspicion that the old woman knew exactly how she felt, but as was May-May's way, she didn't give a damn about what others thought.

"My, My! A little bit of gratitude from you Dubois – I charge folks one-hundred dollars a pop for what I freely give to you," she clasped her hands together as if praying to the spirits for Haley's ungrateful soul.

"I'm sorry May-May" Haley tried to look abashed – but it was pretty much the same sequence they always performed, before May-May got her way.

"Always sorry, always sorry," she muttered, "now – get me my cards. Go on, top shelf." She waved her hands at the ornament-crowded dresser in the corner of the room.

Haley retrieved the deck, sticky with age and use, and placed them down in front of May-May.

She waved her hands over them, as if she were warming herself against an open fire.

"Oh, they powerful tonight – I can feel it."

The old woman's face lit up, and she gave Haley a big, toothy smile. It was infectious, and Haley grinned back at her despite her reticence – she loved making May-May happy.

She shuffled the cards slowly. Haley caught glimpses of the intricate hand-painted designs; elaborate gold leaf adorning depictions of mythical beasts, tall towers and handsome-looking Knights and steely Queens.

"We'll just do the major today – no need to look at the minors unless we have a specific question. Which," she eyed Haley beadily, "is rare in the disbelievers.

Hold the deck, Haley."

Haley did as she was told, clasping them to her chest as she'd been instructed countless times. The woman nodded, and held out her hand to take them back. She then placed five cards out on the table between them.

"Well, would you look at that – I was *right*."

Haley waited patiently for the woman to continue. She glanced at the 'death' card, the last card dealt, and felt decidedly uneasy.

May-May tapped her coral-pink manicured finger on the first card.

"Wheel of fortune – changing fate, what did I say? Your destiny's coming to pay you a visit, Haley Dubois, and not a moment too soon in my opinion."

She smacked her lips in satisfaction, "and right next to the star too – a bit of healin' and renewed hope, and a bit of travel too I'd say... Yep, look like you'll be getting out of here in no time."

May-May clapped her hands in glee, bangles jangling.

"Can't argue with the spirits, can't argue with the spirits!" She chucked. Haley was glad the cards were looking good, when May-

May didn't get the answers she was hoping for she tended to slump into a rotten mood that could last for weeks.

"Then, we got the Magician – he's a tricky one, it's tellin' you to watch that you ain't fooled. Take risks, but mind them. Tread carefully when all this change comes knocking at your door."

May-May wagged her finger at Haley, making sure the girl took heed of the card's warning.

"Yes, May-May – I'll watch out."

The old woman gave a grunt of disapproval, doubting the sincerity of Haley's words. Then her face brightened as she looked at the last two cards.

"The Lovers and Death – that's a winning combo if I ever saw one; you going to be lucky in love Haley Dubois!"

"*Hell* no," Haley shot back, "May-May, I'm avoiding men like the plague – do not tell me that I'm going to meet a handsome stranger, because I promise you, I'll run in the opposite direction. We do *not* need a man."

Haley gently rubbed her stomach, then patted her small, barely perceptible bump in reassurance.

"That baby need a daddy, Dubois. You don't let one bad apple ruin the whole bunch."

"May-May, I've had more bad apples than I can count. We're going to be fine on our own, aren't we blob?"

Haley peered down and smiled gently at the child growing inside her.

"This one's gonna be different, I can promise you that. You stick with him, and that baby of yours is goin' to grow up somewhere tropical, I can feel it in my bones."

"Tropical, *really*?" Haley couldn't hide her look of skepticism.

May-May pursed her lips in response, Haley thought she was going to get an earful, but the old woman took another card from the deck and placed it over the Lovers.

"Yep, different alright – this one gonna be the picture of temperance, moderation and self-control – you know anyone like that, miss high and mighty?"

Haley rolled her eyes.

"I didn't think so," May-May gave her a smug smile.

"Well, I'll call you from the Amazon the day I marry my monk," quipped Haley.

"Child – you not cheekin' me, you cheekin' the spirits. And they don't like that one bit."

Haley sighed, "sorry May-May, I'm just tired."

"I know you are baby girl. Alight," she shuffled the deck up, "that's enough for tonight. I'll let you get some rest."

"Thanks May-May."

The old woman walked with her to the door. Hayley had just stepped out into the corridor when May-May yelled at her to stop.

"Take this," she proffered today's paper in Haley's direction, "I got a good feelin' about the job page."

Haley smiled at the woman and took the paper. May-May might be a bit crazy sometimes, but there was no one on earth that watched Haley's back the way she did.

"Alight – night, May-May."

"Night child. Sleep well – it'll all be different soon. I promise you that."

She winked at Haley and then closed the front door.

Haley might not believe a word of the predictions that May-May made, but as she made her way up the stairs to her own apartment, was realized she was in a far better mood than she had been for weeks. *Positive thinking*, she reminded herself, that was the way forward.

3

"And so I said, Janet – that is a *fake*. Janet starts shaking her head, and all these people are looking round – because it's a classy joint, right? I said, show me the label. She starts pulling the bag away from me – she *knows*, but I grab it. It's a fake. The label's all wrong. *Fake Balenciaga*, at CORE? I mean – *honestly*. Some people, am I right?"

The woman drank noisily from her glass of red wine, tapping her bejeweled fingers against the glass as she did so.

"Some people have no *class*."

Wyatt nodded in agreement. Some people certainly didn't.

She pushed her scallops round on the plate, then dropped the fork down with a clatter. It resounded loudly around the half-empty restaurant.

"So, Wyatt – you the strong and silent type or what?"

She wiggled her eyebrows in what might have been construed as a suggestive manner.

"I can tell that you are - and just so you know," she took another gulp of wine, "that is *exactly* what I like - totally what I'm into. I dig it, right, who wants someone talking their ear off?"

"Mm Hmm." Wyatt nodded in agreement and tried to surreptitiously look at his wristwatch. He was being rude, he knew, but this was the tenth date this month that he'd been subjected to and it was, quite frankly, turning out to be the cherry on the top of a series of progressively more bizarre and unpleasant evenings.

"But," she continued, leaning forward over her plate and dangling her necklace in the scallop sauce, "You're single – so what's the deal? Gay? Too kinky for the average babe? Dead ex-wives in your closet?"

She laughed uproariously at her own joke, while Wyatt's eyes widened in disbelief.

"No, but seriously, what's the deal?"

She cocked her head to the side, feigning interest. Wyatt sighed. It was going to be a long night.

"Well, I guess I'm just a bit preoccupied with work, and…" he tried to come up with another vague reason to explain his single status, "I just haven't met the right woman."

She nodded sagely. Spearing one of her scallops, she pointed it in his direction.

"Workaholic. Could have told you that the moment you walked through the door."

She paused, as if waiting for applause.

"Wyatt – I know the pain of loneliness. But honey, you can't bury the pain in work. I know – I know where you're at. When Bob left me, he was my first husband," she shoved the scallop in her mouth, "Well, I just buried myself in work. I became the retailer *queen* of South Dallas. Did it make me happy? No Wyatt, it did not make me happy. What made me happy was the love of a good man – that was Jeremy, my second husband."

Suddenly she looked up from the table in the manner of a meerkat, and clicked her fingers at a passing waiter.

"More of this," she tapped her manicured nail on the rim of their empty Merlot.

"Jeremy passed," she crossed herself, "God rest his soul. But he taught me how to love again. And that *saved* me."

She placed her hand over Wyatt's.

"Let love in, Wyatt."

This is excruciating. He tried to politely pull his hand back, but she held on, staring into his eyes with all the zealousness of a fire and brimstone preacher.

Wyatt's cell buzzed in his pocket.

"Excuse me for a moment."

He hurriedly extracted his hands, and walked swiftly to the restroom. When the door was closed, he checked the screen.

"Colton – are you shitting me?" His tone was curter than he intended.

"Going that well?"

"What were you *thinking*?" He asked his brother, checking that all the stalls were empty.

"I'm sorry Wyatt, she seemed...you know, vibrant."

He could hear his brother trying to repress laughter.

"I'm going to kill you."

"Look – I'm trying, alright? Remember I have a vested interest in this. I thought an older woman might be refreshing, a bit more balanced."

Wyatt rolled his eyes in the bathroom mirror.

"Colton – she's about fifty. I'm thirty-one, how did you ever think that would work?"

"Well – she's had a lot of work done, she could pass for forty, easily."

Wyatt didn't deign to reply. He didn't want to bad-mouth the woman, it really wasn't his style, but he was utterly fed up with his brother's ludicrous attempts at matchmaking.

"Okay, Colton – we'll talk about this tomorrow. Right now I have to go and finish my date, and somehow make a clean exit without offending anyone."

"If anyone can do that, you can."

Wyatt wanted to hurl the phone across the room. He hung up abruptly. Turning on the faucet, he doused his face in the icy-cold Alaskan water.

. . .

"I ordered us a dessert to share."

The woman winked at him lasciviously.

"That's...great." Wyatt replied, seating himself back down.

"I didn't think you'd mind – you look like a guy that works out a *lot*."

She leaned forward on the table, pushing out her cleavage. She'd undone another button on her blouse, and Wyatt sighed inwardly. This was going to get awkward.

"I work out," she smiled and sat up straight pushing out her chest, "you can probably tell. It's so important. I do yoga, Pilates, soul cycle, the works. It's like, a *religion* for me, or something. Crazy right?"

She screeched with laughter, and Wyatt wondered if he'd missed something. A waiter approached with an elaborate dessert, and placed it down on the table with unnecessary flourish.

"Wow. That looks incredible," she screeched.

She poked at the plate's contents.

"Aw – wait!" She called back the waiter.

"Does this have nuts?"

The waiter paused briefly before replying, "Yes ma'am, it's the Butter Pecan Truffle you ordered."

"I *cannot* eat this. I have *serious* nut allergies."

She backed away from the dessert as if it were going to leap off the plate and attack her.

"I'm so sorry ma'am, is there anything else I can get you?"

"I don't think so. Not in a kitchen where you're using nuts – and not expressly stating that on the menu."

"Again, my sincere apologies."

"It's okay," Wyatt interrupted. He'd had enough.

"Can we just get the check, please."

"Right away sir."

His companion scowled.

"Wyatt – I'm going to the restroom."

She rose unsteadily to her feet, holding on to the chair for support. She tried to untangle her purse from the backrest, but it proved too difficult, and so she half dragged the chair across the restaurant floor till the straps finally came lose.

Wyatt massaged his temple with his thumb and forefinger. She was too drunk to drive back to her hotel. He'd have to persuade her to get into a cab.

The waiter came back with the check, and placed it in front of Wyatt.

"I'm so sorry about the dessert, sir."

"Don't worry about it."

"Did your mother enjoy herself?"

Wyatt suppressed a smirk.

"She's my date."

The waiter turned bright red, opened his mouth to say something and then thought better of it. Wyatt nodded in understanding. He placed his card down without checking the amount, and the waiter hurriedly swiped it through the system.

As much as he could happily throttle Colton right now, he understood the method behind his madness.

Wyatt was overdue assuming the Alpha position of the Clan. His uncle, Joe Sterling, was getting too old to carry on his duties as Alpha, particularly at a time when there was such a strong degree of civil unrest simmering in the underbelly of Port Ursa.

Clan law decreed that only a mated bear could take leadership, and though Wyatt was the likely choice as elder of the three brothers, he was unmated. Colton was the youngest of the three, and the only one with a mate; Hannah, Port Ursa's general practitioner who ran a small clinic in town. If Wyatt didn't find a mate soon, Colton would be called upon to take the Alpha position.

Wyatt idly peeled the label off the Merlot and ran its sticky paper between his fingers. He wondered if perhaps Colton taking the lead wasn't such a bad idea. His brother could be a complete hothead, often more ruled by emotion than logic, but Wyatt would always be there as a sounding board – all three brothers knew they worked best together as a team.

"Sir?"

Wyatt looked up to see a young waitress peering down at him.

"Yes?"

She blushed, taking in his stern features and impressive build.

"Your...err, date, is in the restroom..."

Wyatt smiled at her blandly, "Yes. Is there a problem?"

"I'm so sorry to trouble you, but she's passed out. I can't wake her."

He wanted to laugh. He'd been thinking that the night couldn't get any worse, but apparently it could.

"Right."

He stood up, smiling down at the waitress reassuringly. He was pretty sure that she wasn't paid enough for this type of drama.

"I'll sort it out. I might need a bit of help – what's your name?"

"Katie." She blushed again, and fiddled with her notepad.

"Okay Katie. Is she decent?" Wyatt asked as he guided her toward the restroom.

Katie scrunched up her face, "Sort of?"

"Can you make her decent? I'll wait out here – just call when you're done."

The girl nodded rapidly and scuttled off, the door swinging behind her. Wyatt sighed, and looked around the restaurant. It had emptied out, apart from one couple in the far corner practically eating one another's faces. The coast was more or less clear.

Katie peeked her head round the door.

"Good to go," she announced.

Wyatt took a deep breath and entered the ladies restroom. His date was slumped beneath the hand dryer, legs out, and the contents of her purse scattered across the floor. Vomit covered her blouse and skirt.

"I'm sorry – about that," Katie pointed toward the vomit, "I didn't know what to use..."

"No, don't be sorry, that's fine – I'll take care of it."

He knelt down and scooped his arms beneath her body. She was breathing steadily, her breath smelling like the inside of a brewery, but Wyatt was relieved that she didn't seem to be in any real danger.

"Okay, Katie – I'm going to lift her out. Will you hold the door for me, and then call a taxi? It's probably best if I take her outside, the cold air will do her good."

Katie nodded, after picking up the contents of the purse and handing it over to Wyatt, she skirted over to the door. Wyatt carried her easily; she wasn't lying about working out. The woman was practically emaciated.

With the help of Katie, he maneuvered her through the restaurant, and propped her up on a smokers' bench outside. Katie brought him a bottle of water.

"You're an angel – here." Wyatt handed her a fifty from his wallet.

"I couldn't, really, you've had a rough night as it is, sir," she protested.

"Katie – take the money. I couldn't have done it without you."

She timidly accepted the money.

"Thank you. The taxi is on its way."

Wyatt nodded his thanks. He wrapped his jacket round the woman, who was still sleeping peacefully in her drunken stupor. He buttoned it up, covering the vomit and hoped that the driver wouldn't notice.

He placed the bottle of water in one of the pockets. Somehow, someday, he was going to make Colton pay for this.

Big time.

4

The three men sat around a table in the back of Jackson's bar. The blinds were drawn, the air thick with cigar smoke.

"Come on, Colton – play your hand."

Tucker leaned back in his chair and smirked at his younger brother. Colton cocked an eyebrow and continued to idly chew on a toothpick while he studied his cards.

"Not feeling flush, brother?" Wyatt commented.

"Both of you lay off. I'm trying to concentrate."

Wyatt gave a snort of derision, "First time for everything."

Tucker placed his cards face down on the table; he was growing bored with the pace of the game.

"Hey, Wyatt – how did the date go?" He asked.

Colton groaned, "Wrong question."

Wyatt shot him a menacing look.

"It was a shit show. The most epic one yet. Colton has vowed to give up on his award-winningly terrible matchmaking, so something positive's come out of it."

Colton rolled his eyes.

"Shit. What you gonna do Wyatt?" Tucker looked mildly panicked.

"I thought maybe you wanted to try your luck?" Wyatt replied.

"Hell *no*. Not cut out for leadership."

"You're the one with the friendship with Drake," commented Colton, "It's a logical option if Wyatt can't mate."

"Careful with the 'can't' – it's more 'won't', I'm not fucking defective." Wyatt muttered. "But Colton's right, that friendship is our saving grace at the moment."

They were referring to Tucker's friendship with the Yupiq wolf Pack leader; an ex-army buddy of Tuckers who had recently succeeded to power.

"Right now he's the only one who can keep Simeon in check. Joe's been too soft on him, and one of us is going to need to step up and crush that monster."

"Well – it's not going to be me," Tucker staunchly replied, "Besides, Colton's the obvious choice."

He crushed his cigar into the ashtray. Both he and Wyatt looked expectantly at Colton.

"Oh come on – we all know I'd be the worst Alpha. Wyatt, neither Tucker nor I have your patience and moderation. I'd end up putting the whole Pack six feet under – which, incidentally, I'm itching to do already."

Colton had Simeon permanently at the top of his shit list, ever since the Pack leader had endangered his wife's life with the help of her ex-husband. He'd never been able to prove Simeon's involvement, and police were pretty much out of the question when it came to Pack and Clan politics, so Colton was biding his time till he could serve Simeon the justice he deserved.

"What about Lisa?" Tucker commented out of the blue.

His brothers looked at him blankly.

"Lucca's daughter. She's good looking, a shifter - she's great."

"Tucker," Wyatt sighed, "I went out with her two weeks ago. We're not compatible."

"Oh, yeah. Sorry man, I forgot."

"I've officially dated every shifter in Alaska, and a few from the lower 48," Wyatt clarified.

"So we continue with humans – it's no big deal," Tucker replied.

Colton sat up straight in his chair, "Hang on, Wyatt – do you think it's because of, you know, your bear?"

"What exactly do you mean?" Wyatt asked icily.

"Well – you're kind of unique in that respect, maybe we ought to be searching colder climates – like…Antarctica?"

Both Tucker and Wyatt looked at him as if he'd gone insane.

"Oh come on," he replied indignantly to their stares, "Wyatt – you're a fricken Polar Bear, there's probably some kind of ice maiden out there waiting for you to warm her up."

Wyatt felt tension building in his temples.

"Yeah, Colton – this is *exactly* why you're no longer on match-making duty." Wyatt heard a strange strangulated sound coming from Tucker, and turned to look at his brother. His face was bright red, tears of laughter pouring down his cheeks.

"Shit, I'm sorry Wyatt…" he took a shuddering breath trying to compose himself, "Jesus, Colton, you're something else."

Unable to contain himself any longer, Tucker burst out in gales of laughter. Wyatt smirked and punched his brother in the shoulder. Colton tried to look offended, but Tucker's merriment was infectious.

"Alright – bad idea." He held up his hands in surrender, "I'm going to think of something."

"No you're not." Wyatt interjected firmly.

Enough was enough. Wyatt had tried his best, but there was no use forcing it. He still had a several weeks before Joe officially resigned, and it was time to let fate run its course and let the cards fall where they may.

WYATT ARRIVED home much later that evening. He had a mild headache from the scotch, so he had walked rather than driven. The icy gales that flew up from the sea had helped clear his head, but putting the key in the door and opening his large, silent, dark home he had felt a pang of envy for Colton arriving home to his loving wife.

He'd never had any trouble finding willing women to keep him company, why finding a mate was proving impossible he had no idea. At the beginning of the process he'd almost enjoyed himself – it was fun; he may not have felt that any of the women he met were necessarily right for him, but they were always entertaining and attractive. It hadn't felt like a hardship. Then, after a few months of fruitless searching he'd started to berate himself for being too picky. Joe had started to put the pressure on, as had his brothers. It had become much less enjoyable, with Wyatt feeling obliged to take out whatever woman his brothers threw at him, no matter how unattractive he found them – physically or personality-wise.

Colton had suggested that Wyatt might be reluctant to commit, but he didn't think that was it. He had always *wanted* a wife and cubs, and had assumed that when the time was right it would just happen.

He understood now that it had been a naive thought. But he concluded that he'd rather spend the rest of his life single than go on another disastrous date.

5

"Hannah, you home?" Colton called from the hallway.

"Kitchen!"

Colton hung up his coat, wincing at the smell of Cigar smoke that clung to it. The light coming from the kitchen was warm and cozy, and he could hear the sounds of Hannah rifling through the cutlery draw.

"I'm reheating dinner for you," she called, "that okay?"

He stood in the doorway, admiring her figure from behind; the beautiful curvy body that he worshiped, with her luscious curves and plump backside. The novelty of coming home to her never wore off.

"Course – sorry I'm so late. Game dragged on."

She spun around to kiss him 'hello' and he enveloped her in his arms, gently stroking her hair.

"How's Wyatt doing?" She asked.

"Not great," Colton smirked, "Can't catch a break, that guy."

Hannah sighed at her husband, "You just need to give him a bit of time. It's too much pressure all of this – no wonder he can't find a mate."

"Yeah," Colton sat down at the dinner table, "but I think I've got an idea -"

"Colton," her tone held a warning, "Wyatt doesn't need whatever scheme is cooking in that head of yours, you'd do best to leave it be."

"Huh – you say that," protested Colton, "but if Wyatt doesn't come up with a mate, they're going to start looking at the only one of the Sterling family fortunate to have such a beautiful, accomplished and sexy-as-hell wife."

She rolled her eyes at him, and placed his dinner down on the table.

"Flattery will get you nowhere. Leave it be, Colton."

"Hear me out – what about placing an advertisement for someone to *play* the role of his companion – paid well, staying long enough to get Wyatt instated as Alpha, and then she can leave – we'll say she ran off with another man or got so bored of my taciturn brother that she left the country."

Hannah laughed out loud.

"Oh, that's fantastic – I can't imagine *anything* going wrong with that!"

"Love of my life – why do you doubt my brilliance?" Colton feigned hurt, clutching at his heart.

"It is completely flawed, and in addition to that, Wyatt would never go for it."

"He doesn't need to know till I find her. Then he'll see the method behind my madness."

"Please don't do this Colton," Hannah groaned.

"I have to. Time's running out. Joe's desperate to step down with all the Yupiq and Altik tensions. Damn wolves. I've got a good feeling about this, honestly."

Hannah sighed, Wyatt was going to be furious when he discovered what his brother was planning. But there was no stopping Colton once he had an idea. He was as stubborn as a mule. In business it was a wonderful thing to behold – he moved mountains to increase the wealth and power of the Sterling family, but when it came to matters of the heart, Colton's heavy-handed mergers and acquisitions approach just wasn't going to fly.

"Eat your dinner," she kissed him on the forehead, smiling at his familiar poker night smell of cigars and whiskey.

"I love you, Colton Sterling."

6

"What time you call this?"

May-May was in the hallway, nosing through the apartment building's postal boxes, her habitual weekend treat.

"You're going to get caught doing that one day, then you'll be sorry," Haley commented.

May-May sniffed in her direction, raising her eyebrows at Haley.

"Folks need checkin' up on. I'm naturally distrustful Haley Dubois, and it's a good thing too," she waved a piece of mail under Haley's nose, "Final notice for that noisy jack-ass musician up on nine – been suspicious of him from the start."

Haley struggled to keep a straight face. May-May was the absolute limit sometimes.

"Where you been?"

May-May folded her arms and glared at Haley.

"You reek of fancy perfume, and if I'm not mistaken, gone got your face painted like a no-good lady of the night. Hope you not been seein' that devil man."

"May-May! *Honestly*, no – I went for an interview at Macy's. I got collared by one of the make-up counters on my way out, then I had dinner with a friend."

"A friend, is it?"

May-May's eyes gleamed with suspicion.

"Yes, a *friend* – a female friend."

May-May snorted in derision.

"You look through that paper like I told you?" She asked.

Shit. She hadn't. It had completely slipped her mind.

"I'm doing it tonight, May-May."

May-May gasped and wrung her hands, "Lord! It's been over a week. Destiny come knocking on your door, clear as day, and you turn it away! Well, I never, Haley Dubois, ain't nothing the spirits can do for you now."

The old woman shook her head in complete bafflement at Haley's blatant disregard for her own future.

"I promise I'll look at it tonight – I promise."

Haley made her way up the steps, idly wondering when May-May would forgive her for this latest transgression. The last destiny-related misdemeanor had caused an entire week of mutterings, tuts and squinty-eyed looks thrown in her direction.

"She promises! She promises – fat lot of good it will do her now!"

May-May shuffled off back to her apartment, chatting away to the spirits and huffing theatrically at the impudent nature of young Haley Dubois.

THE KETTLE SCREECHED LOUDLY from the kitchen. Haley finished removing the last of the caked-on foundation, two tones too dark for her skin, and padded through to make tea.

While she waited for one of May-May's concoctions to brew, Haley flicked through the job section of the paper she'd discarded on the kitchen table over a week ago. Most of the short-term positions would probably be filled now, but she might have luck with some of the longer-term jobs that usually took a while to fill.

She spied one that looked promising,

AD SALES!
Join our go-getter team
$12k starting salary + benefits
No prior experience necessary!

SHE CIRCLED IT WITH A SHARPIE, determined to call them first thing tomorrow to see if they were still looking for someone. She gave a wry smile at the starting salary; it was a long time since she'd been paid as low as that, if ever.

Haley had gone straight from best student at the American Ballet Theatre to joining them as prima ballerina, leaving only for a two-year stint with the Bolshoi Theatre in Moscow – before she'd no longer been able to hack the insanely cold winters, and moved back home.

She scanned the rest of the page, ignoring the cleaning positions – she wasn't sure how long she'd be able to do that sort of work as her due date neared. She came across another advertisement that looked interesting, but she had to read it twice before fully understanding what exactly it was.

COMPANION NEEDED
Sensible, kind and adventurous applicant with GSOH
needed for three-month companion stint.
English speakers only.
$50,000 for duration.
Serious applicants only.

WELL, she thought, *the price is right.* There was an email address provided, but no other detail as to what the job involved. The use of the word 'Companion' suggested to Haley that the client was most likely elderly, though the mention of 'adventurous' was strange in that context. Unless, of course, it meant that the location – which was unspecified, was some far-off place. *Tropical perhaps?* Haley laughed to herself. If May-May turned out to be right, she would never again question the power of the spirits – and also buy her a nice house plant.

She didn't want to wait till tomorrow to reply to this one. Sitting down at the kitchen table, tea forgotten, Haley fired up her Mac Book.

Her inbox was shamefully empty; the fan mail she was used to receiving had dried up a few months ago. Now the only emails she got where marketing ads from expensive luxury brands she could no longer afford, and Viagra sale pitches.

Haley pondered over what to write. It seemed best to give them a bit of background on herself, maybe mention May-May as someone she looked after in the building – though Haley knew full well it was the other way round. It wouldn't hurt to stretch the truth a bit – especially since she was so desperate.

She wrote about her time in Moscow, which would indicate an adventurous spirit. Kind? Well, that would have to come across through the tone of the email and a well-chosen picture.

She flicked through her iPhoto collection. There were lots of her performing as well as black and white brochure portraits, but very few personal ones where she looked relaxed and happy.

Haley absent-mindedly chewed on the end of her pen. She checked a few friends on Facebook, seeing if they had any pics that were more appropriate. A few minutes later her search was successful – one of her old dancing partners had a picture of Haley in Paris, standing beneath the Eiffel Tower. She was laughing into the camera. Haley remembered it well; she'd been giddy on frothy cappuccinos and buttery croissants, a morning spent celebrating their final performance of Swan Lake at the Palais Garnier.

She attached it to the email. Drumming her fingers on the keys, she started to question the nature of the position. Perhaps it was worth mentioning what she *wasn't* willing to do – she recalled May-May's warning about being fooled. Was this opportunity too good to be true?

Before she could change her mind, she asked if the job required any form of sexual contact – and if so, she absolutely would *not* be a viable candidate for the job. She quickly reread the email and hit send.

Haley rose from the table, remembering her tea. She sighed; it was stone cold. She'd have to start again. Though it was far from a done deal, Haley couldn't help but daydream about the $50,000 check. It would cover her healthcare, new baby things – including a crib and stroller, and enough left over so that she wouldn't need to worry about getting a job as soon as little blob was born.

Maybe her luck *was* about to change.

7

Tucker parked his car away from the security lights of the ship yard. He could sense the tell-tale signs of the wolf's proximity as soon as he opened the truck door.

The ground was slushy with ice and a numbingly cold wind blew in off the port. Tucker walked past the warehouse entrance, and down the side alley that was part concealed by a brick wall. The wolf was waiting for him by the dumpsters. They reeked of day-old fish guts, even in this temperature.

"Hey Drake."

"Tucker, good to see you."

Drake stood in the shadows, his bulky frame covered with an old surplus jacket. A thick woolen hat covered his severe Army-regulation buzz-cut which he still maintained; Tucker had grown his out the moment he got the chance. Alaska was too harsh to shave anything.

"How are things going?" Tucker asked.

"Not great. We found a body in one of the abandoned warehouses by Airport Road. Leslie Lewis. She was an informant – been part of the Altik Pack for years, hated Simeon's leadership. Knew he wouldn't let her get away with leaving, so she did what good she could and came to us with intel. Got caught."

"Shit. I know Leslie – she's got a boy, right, where's he?"

Drake crossed his arms and looked down at the tips of his army boots.

"My place, for now. We found him next to the body. They'd just left him with her. The coroner said she'd been dead for two days before we found her."

"Fuck, Drake."

"Yeah. He hasn't spoken yet. Just sleeps."

Tucker felt sick.

"What's the plan?" He asked.

"We're ready. My Pack's chomping at the bit to take that fucker down, but I want to wait. I want to wait for the Clan to align with us," he looked up at Tucker, "Officially. This can't go wrong – we're going to get one chance to come at him, and I want it to be full-force, both Clan and Pack."

"I get it. But you know Joe's playing a game of his own. He won't move on this – wants to push Wyatt into taking Clan leadership."

"I heard. How long is this going to take – Wyatt wants it, right?" replied Drake.

"He does. Sort of – he's willing. But the Clan won't allow it unless he pair-bonds with a mate."

"Jesus," sighed Drake, "you Bears, so friggin' ritualistic. It's fucking *archaic*, man."

Tucker smirked at his friend's assessment, "Yeah – but it keeps the leader's mind on the job. Not hunting skirt."

"Sure," Drake rolled his eyes, "but when's Wyatt going to bond? We can't wait around forever, Simeon's coming for me – he'll take down Yupiq and then he'll come for you."

"I know. Colton's working on it. He'll come through."

"Shouldn't Wyatt be working on it?"

"Give him a break. He's dated every single woman in Port Ursa. This isn't really his thing."

Drake shook his head.

"Tucker – we need to get this show moving. Leslie would have spilled anything I told her with her child at stake. I didn't tell her much, but Simeon will know we're trying to align. He also knows he's number one on the Sterling family hit list after that thing with Colton and Hannah."

"I know. I'll keep the ball rolling – we're as eager for this as you are. We've just got to persuade the Clan it's the right thing to do. And only Wyatt can do that."

"Alright. I'll keep my ear to the ground, update you when I know anything."

"Same, brother."

They thumped one another on the back affectionately, and Tucker headed back to the parking lot the way he came.

8

Colton pressed his secretary's connection on his office phone.

"Jenna, please make sure no one disturbs me for the next hour."

"Yes, sir. Can I bring you a coffee?"

"No, I'm good – thanks."

He released the call button and shut the office blinds. He didn't want Wyatt coming in unannounced, as was so often his way.

The email account inbox he'd set up especially for his companion hire had about one hundred replies. He'd wished Hannah had been more enthusiastic about his scheme; he could really use her intuition going through the applicants.

Looking at the first reply, he laughed out loud, and then berated himself for not specifying the sex of the applicant – a rookie mistake. This was a muscly-looking personal trainer from Georgia. *Wow*. Not what Wyatt needed at all. Colton opened all the responses, swiftly deleting all the male respondents. That left about sixty per cent of the applicants, which was partly a relief, partly a worry as his pool of viable candidates was already much smaller.

After reading a few, Colton really started to panic. A lot of these women were under the impression that sex was involved. Countless pictures of nude women jumped out at him – all promising good times and mad skills in the bedroom. A few were way out of Wyatt's age range, and used to caring for the elderly. Colton couldn't stop laughing to himself – imagining eighty-year-old Mrs. Doris Withers from New England, who liked cats and crochet, stepping off the plane to be announced as Wyatt's new mate. It would certainly have comedic value.

Half an hour later, Colton was starting to lose heart. None of the applicants seemed truly suitable. There were a couple of actresses from LA that seemed likely, but when he saw their pictures they looked like plastic mannequins – over made-up, practically orange from tanning beds, and all stating that if the job entailed looking after an old person, no way would they be interested. He was sure they'd absolutely love Wyatt, but he couldn't put these wannabe starlets with his brother; it would be too cruel. Wyatt would hate it.

He was about to give up hope, when he opened an email from a Haley Dubois. The name sounded vaguely familiar, but when he opened her picture he didn't at all recognize the beautiful, relaxed and happy woman that smiled back at him. She *looked* perfect - he had no idea about his brother's preferred type, but that didn't really matter. She looked kind, which was the one thing his brother would appreciate above all else.

Reading her résumé, he smiled to himself. She was, or had been, a ballet dancer. Performance skills were going to be a plus. She also mentioned looking after an elderly lady in her building, which was perfect – she was obviously kind and caring to do such a thing without any financial reward.

He picked up the phone.

"Hannah?"

"Hi babe," she replied, "What's up?"

"I think I've found the perfect 'companion' for Wyatt – can I forward it to you?"

He could hear the groan on the end of the line.

"Colton, I didn't think you were actually going to pursue this idea…"

"Baby, honestly, it's a great idea – and I've got the perfect candidate. A ballet dancer from Manhattan. She's pretty, and looks kind."

There was a long pause. He could imagine his wife running her fingers through her hair in agitation. He smiled to himself.

"Okay," she sighed reluctantly, "but Colton – I really want you to think long and hard about this. Namely, the fact that you're in danger of turning someone's life upside down. There's no chance that a woman staying with Wyatt, and living in Port Ursa, is not going to come across a shifter. Then what?"

"That's not true! The Clan just needs to know that Wyatt's mated – she doesn't need to be a part of any ceremonies or meetings or anything – and they'll take our word for it because they *want* to; everyone wants Wyatt to be leader, we've just got to get through some red tape to keep it all legit."

"Have you even thought about this woman for one second? She's going to think the whole thing is crazy – a companion for a perfectly able bodied thirty-year-old? Come on, Colton."

He sighed in frustration. He hated it when his plans were doubted. This *could* work, he knew it.

"Baby – trust me. I get your point – and this is why we need to select an open-minded, kind looking woman. I really need your intuition…you're more of a people person than I am."

"Colton, *stop* trying to flatter me. Send the damn thing over and I'll get back to you later this afternoon, I need to get to the exam room."

Shit. She was angry. He was going to have to make this up to her somehow.

"Okay, thanks baby. I love you."

She huffed down the line.

"I know you do. I love you too."

Colton hung up. Hannah sounded resigned. He reminded himself that this was for the greater good – if Wyatt didn't find a mate and he had to step up, he and Hannah could wave goodbye to their freedom as a couple – no more jetting off on a last minute trip at the drop of a hat, no more Sunday mornings spent in bed with the newspaper and nothing to do but make love...the list went on. No *way* did he want to lose that.

He forwarded the email on, and then refocused his attentions on his increasing workload, finding it much easier to decipher legal documents pertaining to Sterling Outfitters and the shipping yard, than he did trying to gauge the suitability of Wyatt's potential mates.

Later that afternoon he received Hannah's reply via text.

SHE LOOKS LOVELY.
Still unsure about this.
W will NOT be happy.
XOXO

IT WAS ALL the conformation he needed.

Haley Dubois, welcome to Alaska. He started typing up a reply, and buzzed his secretary to book a flight.

9

Haley sat patiently in the lobby. The taxi driver had dropped her off at a huge, salt-aged warehouse overlooking the port. On seeing it, she had felt more than anxious – she had been expecting to be dropped off at someone's home, but the taxi driver had confirmed this was the destination.

Walking in through a set of sliding glass doors, she had been transported. Inside, the building was entirely unexpected. Beautiful pine paneling ran the length of the corridor, the light muted and warm thanks to exposed light bulbs hanging from thick black cords and the white-wash, exposed brick ceiling. Whoever had designed the interior had obviously taken cues from the industrial setting, but the overall effect was distinctly Scandinavian and naturally homely.

At the far end of the corridor Haley saw a reception desk, with a very attractive blond woman standing behind it, chattering merrily on the phone. She gave Haley a large smile as she approached, and gestured to the low fabric seating in front of her.

Haley sunk gratefully into the sofa, and waited for the woman to finish her conversation.

"Haley Dubois? You're here to see Colton Sterling?" She inquired.

"Yes, that's me."

"Great – he'll be ready for you in just a few moments – can I get you anything, tea, coffee?"

"Water would be great," she smiled at the receptionist. Haley could feel herself getting slightly dizzy. It was probably just the effort of the journey, and the mild anxiety that chewed at her stomach.

Moments later the receptionist came back with an ice-cold glass filled with water.

"Trust me – you won't taste anything better than Alaskan water." She beamed at Haley and returned to her post.

Haley sipped it gratefully and smiled at the woman – she was right; this stuff was delicious. It was so fresh and pure she could almost taste the slightly iron tang of minerals. She smiled to herself, exactly what she and her baby needed.

Haley hadn't mentioned her pregnancy in the correspondence with Colton. She was still hardly showing, and wore a bias cut dress to further obscure her figure. It was unlikely that she'd be showing over the next three months either – maybe a little, but by then it would be too late for them to send her away. And if she was looking after an elderly person, which she felt was becoming increasingly likely, then what harm would it do?

"Colton's ready for you now, shall I show you in?"

"Please."

Haley rose slowly, feeling a little blurry. She gave the receptionist a broad smile to cover her discomfort, and then followed her staccato heel clicks down the polished concrete corridor and through another set of sliding doors.

The receptionist stopped in front of a glass office in the corner of a large room that was filled to the brim with packing crates.

An incredibly handsome and friendly-looking man waved at them both from inside. The receptionist ushered Haley through the door and softly closed it behind her.

Colton offered her a chair.

"Thank you for coming all this way, Miss Dubois," he remarked cordially. Seeing her sit down in such a graceful manner and turn her large, slightly weary eyes toward him, there was something very familiar about her that he hadn't detected from the picture she'd sent.

"Please, call me Haley," her tone was equally professional, but warm.

"I have to say – you look familiar..." Colton looked at her askew, trying to place her face.

"Well, I've certainly never been to Alaska before!" She replied cheerfully.

Colton looked down at her résumé – reminding himself that she'd studied at the American Ballet Theatre. It clicked.

"Oh, you're Haley Dubois – the ballerina, am I correct? My wife and I saw you in New York on our last trip to the lower 48, it was The Tempest – you were incredible."

Colton saw her already pale face grow paler. His observation was swiftly followed by absolute amazement that New York's finest prima ballet star would be replying to his companion advertisement.

"Yes," her voice wavered slightly, "I'm glad you enjoyed the show."

Something wasn't quite right. Colton observed her more closely, trying to get a grasp on her scent. He hadn't noticed when she'd first walked in, but there was something amiss about her – as if she carried some other scent, or multiple scents, mixed in with the familiar notes of human.

He watched as Haley's hands fluttered near her abdomen. *Oh.* She was pregnant. That made a lot more sense.

"We did," he continued, trying to pick his words carefully. She had come all this way, but the arrangement couldn't work if she were pregnant with another man's child – he was already playing a risky game with the Clan leadership policies, no *way* would this wash.

"But Haley, I'm so sorry – I just don't think that a woman in your condition is going to be up for the job. I will of course pay you for your troubles – coming all the way out here..."

Haley rose to her feet. Her expression was bleak, but she nodded in understanding.

"That's quite alright, I should have said something. Thank you, Mr. Sterling, for your time."

She leaned forward to pick up her bag from the chair next to where she'd been sitting. Haley's vision clouded and black spots danced about the room.

"Oh!" She gasped, as the carpeted floor came up to greet her.

WYATT HAD ENTERED Colton's office to fetch the files on the commercial shipping acquisition. He'd seen that Colton was in some sort of meeting, but hadn't been able to wait.

Now he stood in the middle of Colton's office, with an incredibly beautiful woman slumped in his arms.

He'd gotten there just in time; Colton stood at the far end of the room in complete surprise while Wyatt just managed to grab her before she hit the floor.

"Colton – what the hell?"

Colton rushed around from behind his desk, "Shit – is she okay? She's pregnant – we need to get her to Hannah, now."

Wyatt cradled her closer to his chest. She was such a light thing, so small in his arms. Once again he found himself closing in on a woman's face to check if she was breathing. She was.

"Let's get her down to my truck. It will be quicker."

Holding the woman gently with one arm, he rummaged in his pocket with the other and threw Colton the keys.

As they made their way to the parking lot, Wyatt found he couldn't take his eyes off this tiny woman. He could tell her skin was naturally tan, but right now it was faded into a peaky whiteness with slight bruises under her eyes. Her hair was a dark raven black, currently tied up in a smart looking chignon that exposed her graceful neck.

"She's exhausted, Colton – this better not be your doing, who the hell is she anyway?" Wyatt asked as he maneuvered himself and the woman into the back seat of the truck.

"She's here on business. I don't really know her." Colton evaded the question, not yet willing to divulge his plan – which on reflection was looking more and more absurd. He should have listened to Hannah.

"Floor it, Colton."

It wasn't a long drive to Hannah's clinic, but for Wyatt the trip seemed to last a millennium. He found himself feeling unaccountably anxious about this unknown woman's welfare. The longer he held her, the more he found himself increasingly drawn to her scent; unable to take his eyes of her thick sweeping brows and the heavy lashes that shadowed her face. Her lips were full and perfectly shaped, with a delicate cupids bow on top, offset by a plumper bottom lip. They were an unusual pink – startlingly bright, and at first he thought she was wearing lipstick but he couldn't detect the usual waxy gloss of make-up.

"Seriously, Colton," he growled at his younger brother, "we need to get there."

"I'm going as fast as I can."

Wyatt shook his head. *What the hell was wrong with him? Why was he so tense all of a sudden?* He dragged his eyes away from the sleeping beauty held against him, and fixed his stare on the passing landscape. He felt a tug in his lower abdomen. Insistent, growing by the second. *Calm down!* He tried to steady his breathing.

"You alright, brother?" Colton peered back at him through the rear-view mirror.

"*Fine.*"

Wyatt felt his skin prickle all over. Colton kept staring at him, his expression concerned and confused.

"Keep your eyes on the damn road." Wyatt bit out.

His bear was itching to get out.

Wyatt was stunned. He had never before felt himself to be at the mercy of his shifting abilities – he had always been the one, especially compared with his two brothers, that had demonstrated complete and calculating control over his inner animal.

"Colton -"

"We're here – chill the fuck out Wyatt!"

Colton slammed down on the brakes, and hurried over to help Wyatt and the woman out of the truck. His brother's face was completely ashen, and Colton wasn't entirely sure who needed medical help more.

Hannah rushed out from the clinic, having been alerted by the screeching of truck tires across the parking lot.

"Colton – what's going on?"

"She fainted in my office. She's pregnant," he replied.

"Bring her in – Wyatt?" Hannah tried to catch her brother-in-law's attention, "Wyatt? Follow me."

Hannah shot Colton a confused look; Wyatt seemed so vacant. Colton shrugged; he had no idea what had gotten into his brother. They made their way up to the clinic, Wyatt following behind them in a daze, still clutching the woman.

"Is that her?" Hannah asked.

"Yes – he doesn't know," Colton spoke in hurried and hushed tones, trying to keep out of Wyatt's earshot.

"Colton, honestly!"

"I know – I know," he sighed.

As they entered the waiting room two nurses rushed forward with a gurney to take Haley. Wyatt didn't seem to want to let her go.

"Wyatt," Colton hissed, "put her *down!*"

He did so reluctantly, laying her down gently on the bed as if she were made of porcelain. The nurses immediately rushed her off out of sight, with Hannah hot on their heels.

THE TWO MEN sat sipping coffee in the waiting room. When Haley left, the dazed spell over Wyatt eased up too, and now he sat glaring at Colton over the rim of his paper cup.

"Hannah said – 'is that her', what did she mean by that, Colton?" Wyatt asked, breaking the silence.

"You heard that, then?" Colton sighed.

"I did. I have a really uneasy feeling about this Colton – and when I have an uneasy feeling, you are so often at the root of it, somewhere."

Colton could see Wyatt's jaw twitching. It was never a good sign.

"Well, I know you said I shouldn't match-make -"

Wyatt groaned loudly, and placed his coffee cup on the table, "Go on."

"But you know what's at stake here," he paused, watching the twitching muscle in Wyatt's jaw become more prominent.

"And so – I put an advertisement in a newspaper, not a local one, so the Clan would ever know – asking for a companion. For you. We pay her for three months, which gives you enough time to accept the Alpha position with a doting mate at your side, and then we make up some story about her cheating on you – breaking your heart, whatever...but you're still Clan Alpha – because we mate for life."

Colton actually looked mildly pleased with himself.

"But it didn't work, did it?" Wyatt folded his arms and leaned back in the plastic chair, "What actually happened is you brought a pregnant woman to Alaska in the middle of winter, endangering her and her unborn baby, and now here we are. Back to square one, but now with added complications."

Colton peered down into his coffee cup.

"Well – you seemed to like her," he mumbled.

Wyatt chose not to reply. He didn't understand what had happened in the truck. Perhaps some strange alpha male tendency when faced with a woman in distress. He rubbed his temples. Colton had really struck idiot gold this time.

"Colton – go back to the office. I need you to talk to Harry about the acquisition document; there's something wrong with what they've estimated for content insurance. Sort it out."

"I can wait here, Wyatt – this isn't your responsibility, it's mine."

"She is my responsibility. It's my situation that's got her into this mess. I'll see you later at my place, bring Tucker – we have business to discuss."

Colton nodded. He felt for his truck keys as he stood up, and then realized he only had Wyatt's.

Wyatt smirked at him, holding out his hand to grab them.

"Enjoy the walk, brother."

Colton muttered an obscenity under his breath and then stalked out.

10

Haley opened her eyes, slowly adjusting to the bright light that assaulted her. She was in a small room, lying on what appeared to be a hospital bed. Peering over her was a very attractive woman in her late twenties, with red hair and beautiful blue eyes that were looking down at her with a mixture of concern and warmth.

"Where am I?" Haley asked, her throat felt as dry as the desert, and she had an unappealing iron taste on her tongue.

"You're in Port Ursa – I'm doctor Hannah Cooper, you fainted. How are you feeling now?"

Haley took a moment to digest the information.

"Is the baby okay?"

"Absolutely fine," Hannah hurried to reassure her, "it's you I'm worried about!"

Haley nodded, perceptibly relaxing on hearing that her little blob was safe.

"I feel okay...how did I get here?"

Hannah smiled, "My husband – Colton, he and his brother drove you here. You were having a meeting with him," she prompted gently.

"Oh yes," Haley clenched her eyes shut in embarrassment, "The job interview. Oh *damn*."

"Don't worry about that now – you need to take it easy. You were seriously dehydrated when they brought you in," Hannah furrowed her brow, "it's not good for you or the baby."

"I think it was nerves; I should have drunk more water on the flight." Haley berated herself; she needed to take better care, for blob's sake.

"And you need to eat more – and get outdoors more, you live in Manhattan, right?"

"Yeah."

"Well, some fresh Alaskan air will do you a world of good," promised Hannah.

Haley nodded, privately thinking that she wouldn't be in Alaska much longer without the job offer, and there was little chance of her getting it now. She'd been so *stupid*.

"Wyatt's going to take you back to his place. He's my brother-in-law," Hannah amended, when she saw the confusion in Haley's eyes, "He's a very lovely man. You'll be in safe hands."

"I don't want to put anyone through any trouble," protested Haley.

"You won't be – he's happy to have you. All part of the job trial period," Hannah winked at Haley, "Don't you worry about a thing."

Haley nodded. She wasn't sure how comfortable she'd be staying at a stranger's house, but it was incredibly kind of them to take her in. Maybe once she was there she could start proving that she was perfectly capable – and more than able to be an elderly companion, or whatever it was that Colton needed.

After fetching her water and generally pampering Haley, Hannah left to go and see another patient.

Haley sat in the room, wishing that she could be discharged. She was already starting to feel restless, and she didn't particularly like being confined to a bed – especially not one at a doctor's office. They had given her a private room, and Haley tried not to think about the cost she was likely to incur for the treatment.

Someone knocked on the door. Thinking it was Hannah or a nurse, Haley hollered for them to come in.

An insanely handsome man – who certainly wasn't a nurse, walked in. He seemed to take up all the space in the small room, his presence was so vital, his physique so muscular and large that Haley couldn't stop staring at him.

"Hi," he said.

"Hi," she hesitated, "who are you?"

"I'm Wyatt. Colton's brother," he clarified.

"Oh."

He gave her a small smile, but he looked awkward and uncomfortable.

"I'll take you home once they discharge you."

Haley nodded, "Hannah – Doctor Cooper, said as much."

"Just wanted to introduce myself."

"I really hope I'm not putting you out, I have a room at the hotel already booked for tonight."

"I really think it would be better if you stayed with me." His tone was firm.

"Why?" Haley asked, still not comfortable with the arrangement.

He looked lost for a moment, and ran a thumb along his jawline in agitation. Haley got the impression that perhaps he was a man who wasn't used to having his commands questioned.

"Doctors orders," he finally muttered.

"Exactly!" Hannah exclaimed as she walked through the door, "Haley – honestly, as your Doctor while you're here in Port Ursa, I absolutely insist that you stay with Wyatt – he can give you the proper care and attention you need." She beamed up at Wyatt, who cocked an eyebrow in her direction – a clear warning for Doctor Cooper not to push her luck.

Haley realized that Wyatt was probably doing this against his will – or at the very least having his arm twisted by his sister-in-law. She sighed. This *was* going to be awkward.

"Agree to stay with Wyatt, and I'll discharge you." Hannah promised.

Haley didn't need to be told twice. She'd stay for one night and then get out of Wyatt's hair. She glanced in his direction and he gave her a small smile that looked more like a grimace.

"Okay. I'll stay. Thanks Wyatt." She muttered.

"I'll pull the truck round."

He stalked out of the room, and Haley turned to Hannah.

"He doesn't want me to stay with him – are you sure this is a good idea?" Haley asked, hoping that Doctor Cooper would see sense.

"It's an excellent idea. No questioning my professional opinion," she joked.

Haley sighed, "Fine. But would you do me one last favor? Will you tell your husband, tell Colton, that I'm perfectly capable of doing the job? That I just needed some fluids, or whatever?"

Hannah laughed, "Sure I can do that. I told you, stop worrying. I'll tell Colton you're the perfect candidate."

"Thanks Hannah – Doctor Cooper."

"Hannah's fine. Oh, and Haley?" she paused before walking out of the door, "I loved you in The Tempest – you were *amazing*. I cried the whole way through."

Haley smiled.

"Thanks Hannah. I'm glad."

The woman nodded and left. Haley rose from the bed and removed her gown. The clothes she arrived in were folded neatly on the chair beside her. She longed for a shower; she felt travel-weary and tired. The last thing she felt like doing was spending time with an intimidatingly handsome, taciturn man that didn't really want her around.

11

"I'm so sorry about all of this."

Haley gestured helplessly, irritated that she was still wrapped up in the wool blanket the Doctor had given her, like an old invalid.

"Don't mention it, really."

Wyatt Sterling kept his eyes on the road, barely glancing in her direction since they'd left the doctors. It was unnerving; Haley felt like she'd pissed him off somehow, but it also gave her the opportunity to study him surreptitiously without embarrassing herself.

Having travelled most of the world as a dancer, Haley could sometimes believe that she'd seen it all; suave men, richer that Croesus that showered gifts on principle dancers, exotic-looking lotharios intent on bedding the chorus, drunk yet talented and dashing orchestra players with warm, welcoming beds. She had started to think she was almost immune to the physical charms of the opposite sex, but that fallacy was ripped to shreds the moment she laid eyes on Wyatt Sterling.

Her usual type tended toward Romany gypsy men with subtle sex appeal – faintly malnourished and in need of looking after. As May-May continually reminded her, it was what had kept her love life in a state of continuous disrepair. Wyatt was the complete opposite; he towered over her for a start, easily six-four against her five-foot frame. He was also broad, filling out the white shirt he wore to almost bursting across the chest and shoulders. He'd rolled up the sleeves of his shirt, his blazer folded neatly over the back seat of the truck, and Haley became hypnotized by the flexing of the muscles and veins that ran along his forearm as he commanded the wheel.

Wyatt's appearance gave her the impression of a well-ordered, scrupulous man. His nails were cut short and squared, his hands in general were large, though not inelegant, and capable looking. His shirt was perfectly pressed, as were his suit pants. The only unruly thing about him was his hair; it was dirty blonde, but at the temples, shot through with white, which Haley found completely intriguing for his age – he couldn't have been much older than she was. His angular jaw was covered in thick stubble, which highlighted his full lips – currently set in an unwavering line.

He turned to look at her. Haley swiftly turned her head to face the window, blushing.

"Are you warm enough?"

"Oh, yes – thanks."

"We're almost there."

Haley nodded and took a deep breath.

"Look, I'm pretty sure that before I passed out Colton Sterling informed me I wouldn't be getting the job – because of the pregnancy. I just want to assure you, I am honestly as healthy as a horse – it was just the travel, I was dehydrated, that's all. I would really, really like another shot at it. Can I at least meet the client?"

"Don't worry about that right now."

Wyatt could feel color rushing to his cheekbones. *Shit, this was awkward.*

"But -" she began to protest.

"Really. You're coming to stay with me. I have a spare room," he looked agitated, "You just rest there tonight, and tomorrow we can talk about the job. Okay?"

"That's very kind of you," she replied meekly. She smarted from his abrupt tone before reminding herself that the intention of the offer was a kind one - she was being overly sensitive.

"What do you do, Wyatt?" She asked, trying to bring the conversation into safer territory.

"My brothers and I run an outdoor oufitter chain, and have recently expanded into a fishing interest – well, we will as soon as the lawyers stop arguing over the paper work," he smiled wryly, "That's in progress."

Haley digested the information, very aware that Wyatt's face had lifted at the mention of work – he was clearly a passionate man beneath the reserved veneer.

"What do you do? Well – before you applied for this job," he amended.

"I was a ballet dancer."

"Wow," he smiled at her properly this time, "I have a huge respect for your profession – grace under severe pain." He mock shuddered and Haley laughed.

"It's really not that bad. You get used to it. You know, after the first few broken toes."

He looked over at her in alarm. Haley smirked.

"Don't worry – I'm half joking."

"I guess you can't dance while pregnant, right?" He asked.

"No." Haley pursed her lips together. It was a good excuse; Wyatt didn't need to know her whole messy history.

He observed that the question had shut her down, and looked over at her with concern. She must have found it difficult to give up dancing. It was a pity that he couldn't help her out in some way. He idly thought of the possibilities of Colton's nutcase scheme, but dismissed it. It was a stupid idea. He also found himself *very* reluctant to have the beautiful, accomplished woman know that he couldn't find a mate via his own means.

"Here we are." Wyatt pulled up into the drive.

"Oh, it's beautiful." She exclaimed.

The house was huge, reaching at least three stories high and sprawling out from where they stood to the waterfront. They were fairly isolated here, and Haley, a born city girl, marveled at the peace and quiet that Wyatt would be privy to. It was built entirely from wooden beams, with a low sloping roof, which was currently covered in a thick layer of snow. All the rooms had huge, floor to ceiling glass windows so Haley could peek in nosily at every room as she stood gazing outside.

On the waterfront she could see a small jetty and a small two-seater seaplane idling on the water. *Oh.* It suddenly occurred to Haley that Wyatt might not live alone.

"Do you live with a...girlfriend, wife?" Haley tried keeping her voice level and nonplussed.

"No."

She nodded, turning her face away from his in the direction of the house so she didn't give her relief away. *Pull yourself together*! She mentally kicked herself.

She wasn't interested in Wyatt in that way at all, she had to remind herself – especially not in her condition, but if she'd had to see him being affectionate to an equally beautiful partner, it might have made her stay an uncomfortable one. She shrugged her thoughts off; she was only human. The man was a hot-blooded male god, and most women she knew would have secretly prayed for him to be single.

"Let me take that for you." He held out his hand for her bag.

"Really, it's fine. I'm good."

Haley was determined not to show another moment of weakness. Carrying her tote bag was a small, ineffectual start.

Wyatt opened the door and gestured for her to come inside. Haley sighed blissfully as the warmth of his home enveloped her, before marveling at how elegant and understated the décor was.

He showed her through to the open-plan living room, which adjoined a large, farmhouse kitchen. In the middle of the room stood an unlit fireplace which was completely open with a chute hovering above it. At the far end of both the living room and kitchen, sliding glass doors took up the entire wall. She could see out onto the ice-covered water, and beyond that the sloping land that made up a small cove.

"Can I get you something to drink?"

"If you have any herbal tea that would be great – though hot water if you don't is equally good." She replied, not wanting to put him to any further trouble.

"No – I have herbal tea. Hannah drinks it – the doctor you saw today."

"Colton's wife, right?"

"Yes."

"She's lovely."

Wyatt nodded his ascent. It was on the tip of his tongue to comment that she, too, was lovely – but thankfully his sanity returned before he could say anything so wholly inappropriate.

While he made the tea, he reflected on what a strange and bizarre effect Haley was having on him. She was beautiful, there was no doubt about it – and otherworldly graceful, but Wyatt had met plenty of beautiful woman. Perhaps none to equal Haley, in his opinion, but beauty rarely made him speechless, and never before had it had the same pull on his bear as Miss Dubois appeared to have.

He brought the tea back into the living room. She was perched uncomfortably on the sofa, as if afraid to fully relax.

"Here you go." He paused before continuing, "Please make yourself at home, Haley. You need to rest."

He sat down next to her on the sofa, keeping a substantial distance between them. She took the cup gratefully and clasped it in her hands.

"Are you cold?" He asked.

"No – really, I'm fine. I do need to call the hotel though – they have my bags."

"I'll take care of that for you. Wait here."

Haley tried to protest but Wyatt was off before she could say anything. A moment later she could hear him climbing the staircase, into another room.

Haley put the tea down and tried to relax. It was difficult, being in a handsome stranger's home, and not really knowing whether or not she would be considered for the companion job – if the brothers had already dismissed her as a viable candidate then Haley would feel like a complete charity case. She really hoped that wasn't going to happen.

As she leaned back on the sofa she felt a jolt in her stomach. She stared down in amazement. Another jolt, this time more insistent than the last. She placed her hands across her stomach, rubbing gently.

"Oh, hey there. I was wondering when you would show up, little blob." She smiled, hoping that she'd feel the sensation again. It was the first time that she'd felt the baby kick, and it completely blew her away. Her little blob felt more *real* all of a sudden, a small little human growing inside of her.

She was so transfixed she didn't hear Wyatt coming back down the stairs.

"Haley – are you okay?" His voice sounded taut and anxious.

She looked up, belatedly realizing that she'd been crying.

"Oh! – I'm so sorry," she wiped her cheeks abruptly, "Mommy moment – the baby kicked for the first time, it just took me by surprise, that's all."

Wyatt smiled broadly, and Haley was instantly dazzled by his good looks, more pronounced now that he wasn't so tight-lipped and stern.

"That's incredible – how did it feel?"

He sat down next to her, closer this time.

"Weird," she blushed, "It's so strange – having something growing inside of you. Oh!" she exclaimed, "It's doing it again! Here – feel."

Without thinking she had reached for Wyatt's hand and placed it on her abdomen.

The warmth of his hand, almost blazing hot, sated her whole body in an instant. His hand span covered the whole of her bump, and he held it there as the baby kicked away merrily beneath him.

"I can feel it," he whispered in reverence, "Shit. That's..." Wyatt's voice trailed off. He didn't know what it was. He suddenly felt strange about sharing such an intimate moment with a stranger. His breath hitched in his throat. Being so close to her was doing strange things to him. He was aroused, his blood pulsing in his ears as he felt himself growing erect. It was hugely inappropriate considering what they were doing, he chided himself, but he really couldn't help himself.

Haley looked at him. Her large blue eyes gazed into his, and she exhaled a tremoring breath. Something intense passed between them – the look was heated and wanting on both sides. Wyatt felt himself being pulled closer toward her, as if hypnotized.

His phone buzzed in his pants pocket. Wyatt pulled back abruptly, the spell broken. He reached down and switched the phone to silent.

"Sorry." He said automatically – not sure if he was apologizing for the interruption or what he had been about to do.

"I should have a shower, or something." Haley said brightly. Her face was flushed, and she couldn't quite meet his eyes.

"Good idea. I'll show you where everything is." He cleared his throat and stood up, shoving his hands in his pockets as if trying to restrain himself from touching her.

It was going to be another long night, for very, very different reasons, thought Wyatt.

12

"How is she?" Colton asked.

"She's fine." Wyatt replied curtly. He was still pissed as hell at his younger brother. They were sitting in the living room, going over the shipping documents while they waited for Tucker. The fire was blazing now, and the two of them shared a beer as they went over the fine print.

The doorbell rang and Wyatt rose to greet Tucker.

"Mind telling me why I'm carrying," he checked the label, "Haley Dubois' luggage?"

Tucker stood on the porch surrounded by three bags, looking mildly peeved.

"You can ask Colton. Come in – thanks for doing that."

Wyatt relieved him of the bags and placed them by the stairs, ready to take up to Haley when the meeting was over.

"Ah. Yeah – this has Colton Sterling scheme gone wrong written all over it," sniggered Tucker.

"His finest yet," muttered Wyatt, "We're in the living room."

Tucker sauntered on through.

"Before I have a good laugh, we need to discuss some Pack business." Tucker announced. He helped himself to a beer and popped it open.

"Any more news from Drake?" Wyatt asked.

"Nothing conclusive yet in regards to a planned attack – but one of their own Pack members, who was sharing intel with Drake, was found murdered."

"That's harsh."

Colton and Wyatt looked stunned. If Simeon was killing members of his own Pack, then it wouldn't be too long before an all-out war was launched.

Before Simon's rise to power the Altik Pack was far more temperate; they had always believed that the wolf shifter species was superior to humans, but they were more or less outwardly civil – they mostly kept to themselves, and inhabited the more remote parts of the world, avoiding mingling with humans to the best of their ability. The Yupiq Pack, the oldest shifter pack – born back when Alaska was an undiscovered land, and the America's were considered The New World, always treated humans as a species that needed to be protected and cared for: precious and innocent.

In the early days of Simeon's rise to power, he was markedly less temperate than most Altiks would stand for, and his behavior had only got more reactionary as time passed. Families that had been in Altik for generations started to divide – it was now not uncommon to have families spread across both Packs.

If Simeon was killing his own Pack members, then he would be killing the mothers, fathers, sons or daughters of Yupiq wolves. It seemed that war would be inevitable, and the Sterling Clan would be caught up in the fight.

"I'm going to speak to Joe. We need to offer complete support to Drake and the Yupiq Pack, or Port Ursa is going to turn into a bloody battlefield," said Wyatt.

"I'm really worried that Joe's going to try and duck out of this one," Colton eyed his brother wearily, "you know what he's like."

"If we go soft, we'll lose the respect of the Clan," muttered Tucker, "everything we have is built on that respect – and if we let Simeon roam free, then Port Ursa and beyond is going to be overrun by power hungry wolves."

"We know what the outcome will be," sighed Colton, "I just can't figure a way to stop it unless Joe stands strong."

"Or Wyatt starts being a bit more attractive to the opposite sex," smirked Tucker.

"Don't start that shit again."

"Alright, Wyatt - look you've got Haley upstairs, that's closer than you've ever got with another lady…"

Wyatt shot Colton a murderous look.

"I'm joking, I'm joking," he held out his hands in surrender, "*but what's the harm in taking her on? Giving her the job? She needs the money – she seems like a really nice woman, I'm sure she'll understand…*" Colton trailed off – partly out of surprise that Wyatt wasn't completely dismissing him out of hand.

"I am so confused – anyone want to fill me in?" Tucker interrupted.

"I put an ad in the newspaper – for a companion for Wyatt. She's come all this way, but she's pregnant." Colton replied.

Tucker took a sip of beer.

"I don't understand the problem. So what if she's pregnant. Doesn't matter, does it?"

"I'm starting to agree. Goddamn it, Wyatt – it's fifty thousand dollars, she's not going to mind going along with it – she's a performer for crying out loud." Colton replied.

"She's a ballet dancer, it's not the same thing!" burst out Wyatt, "and how the hell am I going to tell her I'm a shifter? You think about that, huh?"

"It makes *so* much sense now!"

All three brothers spun around at the sound of Haley's voice. Colton and Tucker were rendered speechless.

"You know what I am?" asked Wyatt, his voice hoarse.

"If you're a shifter, then yeah – I know what you are."

Her eyes were soft as she gazed at Wyatt, a small smile playing on her lips. Wyatt studied her. That scent of otherness he'd observed in the car - he'd put it down to the baby, but perhaps that wasn't the whole story.

He narrowed his eyes, trying to suppress a grin.

"I don't smell fur."

"Nope," Haley replied with a glint of laughter in her eye, "no fur."

"I see."

Tucker looked at Colton, and cocked one of his eyebrows in a silent question. Colton rolled his in response.

"We'll just leave you two to it." Colton headed toward the door, "Come on Tucker."

"Nice to meet you, Haley Dubois." Tucker bowed his head slightly in a form of greeting, and then followed Colton out of the room.

"Nice to meet you too," Haley called out after him.

Wyatt heard the door slam shut, and Colton loudly singing his own praises as his brothers made their way down the drive.

Wyatt hadn't moved an inch.

"Are you going to tell me what you are?" he asked.

"Maybe."

"*Maybe?*"

"Later, I think. Are you a bear? I bet you are," she asked, her eyes gleaming.

"That doesn't seem right," Wyatt crossed his arms, "You know what I am. Surely it's only fair...?"

Haley shrugged, "Life's not fair, Wyatt Sterling."

"I disagree, Haley Dubois."

She laughed out loud.

"Enough. I will tell you – eventually. But I'm famished, as your companion, I think I should cook your dinner."

"Hang on – who said you got the job?"

Haley stopped mid stride, and looked up at Wyatt in shock and dismay.

"Kidding."

"Hilarious," she shot back dryly, "I can see I'll have my work cut out for me."

"You can count on it, Miss Dubois."

Wyatt watched her pad gracefully through to the kitchen, her hair now tumbling loose round her shoulders and wearing one of his t-shirts as a dress, so oversized it came to her knees. She looked utterly delectable.

Wyatt felt as if he'd just been shot through the heart with cupid's arrow.

13

Joe was sitting in his trailer, the blinds drawn low with an NHL game playing on mute. Wyatt sighed at the disarray; plates still piled up in the sink, dirty mugs dotted about and an unpleasant smell coming from the stove.

"Jesus Joe, this place hasn't been cleaned in weeks – where's Macy?"

"Sent her away, don't like strangers touching my stuff."

He took a drag on his cigarette and eyed Wyatt beadily from his easy chair.

"Macy's not a stranger," Wyatt sighed, "Why do you live like this?"

"Don't be starting shit with me, Wyatt. I'll live how I want to live – and you can take your fancy-pants condos, your big mansions, your sports cars, and shove 'em up your backside."

"I'm worried about your health Joe, just living in one of the new developments on Birch Drive would be an improvement – nothing fancy about them."

"Huh," he took a swig of beer; "the IRS would be over me like a rash, no thank you."

Wyatt rolled his eyes. Joe had started to get intensely paranoid in his old age, convinced that the government was going to take away his millions – though as far as Wyatt could make out, it wouldn't make a damn bit of difference. Joe's cash, which came from high-yield shares in all of the Sterling businesses, just sat in his bank account, untouched.

"But I'm guessing you didn't come over here to tell me shit you already told me – what's up?"

"We need to talk about Simeon. He needs to be shut down, and Drake needs our support to do it. I want to publicly side with the Yupiq Pack now, before it's too late."

Joe exhaled an expletive, and switched off the TV set.

"Wyatt – we don't get mixed up in Pack politics, we keep the peace."

"There's not going to be any peace if Simeon gains more power and overthrows the Yupiq Pack. People will die, Joe. And the Clan alone won't have the power to stop him."

"You're overestimating that mongrel."

"I'm not. He is deadly and brutal – and he's going to destroy everything that stands in his path."

Wyatt ran a hand through his unwieldy hair, wanting to knock some sense into Joe.

"I say we stay out of it." Joe looked smug, "and if you don't like my decision as Clan leader, then you know what to do about it – same god damn thing I've been wanting you to do for the past five years."

Wyatt sat in silence for a moment, trying to reign in his temper.

"Joe," he spoke softly, "Please don't tell me that you're using this...*situation* as leverage to get me to take over as Alpha."

Joe smiled blandly at his nephew, "Now why would I go and do a thing like that?"

"Fuck sake Joe – you're playing with fire! People will die – people have already died."

"I heard about the woman," Joe replied.

"So you know – this is going to tear this town apart."

"So do the right thing," he looked at Wyatt straight on, "I heard you've got a lovely lady staying with you. Make her your mate. Do whatever needs to be done, and take over the Clan. They need you Wyatt. We all need you."

"Or what?" Wyatt knew he was being blackmailed, he just wanted to hear Joe come right out and say it his face.

"Or you know where I stand. The Clan will do nothing."

"You're an asshole Joe."

He smirked and took another swig of beer, "Yeah, but I'm an old asshole holding all the cards.

Now unless you're going to shut up and watch the game with me, get the hell out of my trailer."

He switched the game back on, dismissing Wyatt.

14

Wyatt's knuckles were white as he gripped the steering wheel. Joe had always been wily and manipulative, but he'd taken it too far this time. The Sterling family, starting with Wyatt's father, had built this town from the ground up. They stood to lose everything in the face of Simeon's grab for power.

Wyatt had been in two minds about presenting the Clan with Haley as his mate; he didn't like deceiving them, and it seemed grossly unfair to Haley to get caught up in all this when she'd come to Port Ursa expecting to be looking after an elderly person.

It also seemed like a gross parody of what he truly wanted. He was convinced that Haley was his true mate – the call of his bear in the truck on the way to the clinic, and the way he felt whenever she was near. At dinner he'd barely been able to talk to her. It sounded a lot like how Colton had explained his first experiences when meeting Hannah – his claimed mate. He had no idea if Haley felt the same way, but if there was any chance that she did, he didn't want to present her to the Clan under false pretenses – he wanted to wait until they were truly mated.

Which, he sighed, was all well and good – but they were running out of time.

Wyatt pulled up to the house, smiling softly as he saw that the lights were on, making his arrival home cozier and more inviting than it ever had been before.

When he cut the glare of the headlights, he saw Haley sitting on the porch, wrapped up in a blanket from head to toe – she looked like an Eskimo and Wyatt marveled at how Haley could wear the most ridiculous things and still look so utterly divine. She took his breath away.

He locked the truck and walked toward her, unable to hide the smile erupting at the corners of his lips.

"Cold, Haley?"

"Freezing to death."

"Then what are you doing out here?"

"Hannah said I should get fresh air. So here I am – outside, possibly dying from pneumonia."

"So dramatic," Wyatt smirked, "is this a Prima ballerina thing that I should watch out for?"

Haley snorted with derision.

"You ain't seen *nothing* yet Wyatt Sterling."

"High maintenance, huh?"

"The highest." Haley's eyes shone with suppressed laughter, "Can you handle it?"

Wyatt leaned back on the porch bench, and crossed his arms in mock contemplation.

"I thought you were meant to be *my* companion. Shouldn't I be the high maintenance one?"

"You should be far more thorough in your reference checks," she replied.

Wyatt burst out laughing.

"I can handle you, Haley Dubois."

The easy and playful atmosphere they'd created suddenly became charged with tension. Wyatt unconsciously licked his lips, his mouth dry. Haley's face flooded with heat.

"Do you think so?" she whispered.

"I know so."

15

"I've got a better idea, follow me."

Wyatt rose from the porch and gestured to Haley to follow him back into the house. She complied, wondering where he was taking her. She'd been serious about the fresh air – after blob's kicking last night, she was determined to follow Doctor Cooper's advice to the letter.

He strode over to the sliding back doors at the far end of the living room.

"There are heaters out here, and it looks out over the water." He announced, flicking a series of switches concealed beneath the doorframe.

Four space heaters roared to life, and Haley stepped out into the significantly less chilly fresh air.

"Oh, Wyatt – this is perfect, thank you." She smiled up at him, "are you going to join me?"

"I am. I just need to change first." He was still dressed in the dark navy suit and white shirt he'd worn to the office that morning. Haley thought he looked absolutely delicious, but she just nodded and made herself comfortable on the wicker sofa.

She relaxed, finally able to stop shivering so aggressively, and stared up at the night sky. She'd never seen anything like it. The moon hung heavy and full over the water, its beams rippling across the surface. But it was the stars that stole the evening show.

Wyatt reappeared. He was wearing jeans and a faded grey hoodie. Haley smiled. He looked so much younger and much less intimidating dressed like this - but still just as smoking hot as he did in more formal apparel. Perhaps more so.

"Better?" he asked. Haley was floored, before belatedly realizing that he was referring to the heaters, not his appearance.

Oh. "Perfect."

"How was your afternoon?"

"Relaxing. I didn't do much – I explored your house, poked my nose where it didn't belong..." she gave him a side-long glance.

"Oh really. That's quite an abuse of my hospitality, Dubois."

"Yep," she countered cheerfully, "I'm not even sorry."

"Well, you know what they say about curiosity..."

She laughed. "Nope, not a cat shifter."

Wyatt sighed, "Am I ever going to know what creature's hiding within you?"

"Hmm, still undecided. It's fairly *unusual*, I'd imagine – particularly in these parts."

"The plot thickens," Wyatt arched an eyebrow in her direction, "I'm guessing it's an animal that's far more comfortable in a warmer climate?"

"How did you guess?" She teased.

"Well," he tugged at the wool blanket still enveloping her, "This was my first clue."

Haley smiled. She wished she hadn't brought it out with her; Wyatt's arm lightly grazed it every time he moved, sending heat rushing through her. She wanted it out of the way, closer to his touch.

"In my defense, it's the middle of winter in Alaska – this is next level cold."

"I'll take your word for it. I can't say I ever really feel it."

"That a bear thing, I take it?"

"It is. It's also a growing up in Alaska thing – your body adjusts."

Haley nodded. She couldn't imagine ever getting used to the temperature here. She was wearing two layers of thermals and still felt like a popsicle.

"It's not just your shifter that I'm curious about." Wyatt announced, going back to their original subject. Haley sighed inwardly. She had known this was coming, ever since Colton and Hannah had remarked that they'd seen her perform. She'd seen the curiosity alight in their eyes, understandably wondering what on earth a prima ballerina was doing applying for a companion post advertised on the help wanted pages of a newspaper.

"What do you want to know?"

"Nothing that you don't want to tell me." He turned to her, "Haley, if you don't want to say anything you don't have to – I'm just here if you need to talk."

She looked up into his eyes. They were completely sincere, without a hint of impending judgement. She turned back to face the water. If she was going to tell her story it would be easier if she didn't get lost in his gaze.

"Well – I guess the long and short of it is, I fell for the wrong man." Haley shrugged, "Without realizing that he could destroy my career at the drop of a hat. Or, I guess, knowing that, but going right ahead and falling for him anyway."

She wrapped the blanket more tightly around her, hugging herself. It was still painful; it probably always would be.

"He was, is, the director of the American Ballet Institute. As charming as they come - and ruthless. He was the one who pushed me to become the Prima, another girl was in the running, but she had a complete nervous breakdown and left the Institute before the decision was made. They promoted me. Deep down I knew he was behind it somehow, but I was so blown away by my good fortune that I ignored it. We started having an affair, he was married – to a retired dancer; she lived in Paris. Her family was incredibly wealthy, he always claimed it was a union of convenience. Can you believe I fell for that? I should have known better. I should have behaved better."

Haley couldn't bear to look at Wyatt; she was so ashamed of her actions. She'd been young and in love, but that didn't excuse what she'd done.

"Please don't judge me," she whispered.

"Are you kidding?" Wyatt sounded furious, and Haley turned to face him – bracing herself for the onslaught of derision.

"He clearly took advantage of you, took advantage of his position. Haley, you have nothing to feel guilty about. Don't you dare beat yourself up over this. He's not worth it."

Relief flooded her. Wyatt didn't think any less of her. *Thank God.* She didn't agree with his assessment that he'd taken advantage of her – she couldn't abdicate responsibility for her mistakes, and what she'd done vastly opposed her sense of right and wrong; she'd lacked integrity, lost her sense of self and needed to face the consequences from that – a heavy guilt that would always be a part of her. The only positive thing to come out of it was her own little blob. She rubbed her stomach over the wool blanket, as if it to let it know that it wasn't a part of her regret.

"It's kind of you to say that." She murmured.

"It's not kind – it's the truth. I take it he also removed you from the Institute?"

Haley half-laughed, "The second he found out I was pregnant. Bam," she clicked her fingers, "I was out on my butt. I had a small savings, got an apartment and the rest kept me going, but it was time to find a job that I could keep while I was pregnant. I found the companion offer in a paper – and here I am."

"I'm glad you're here."

Wyatt turned to look at her. She lowered her gaze, but he reached out his hand and placed it gently but firmly on her cheek, drawing her face back up to meet his.

"I mean it Haley. You have nothing to be ashamed of."

"I'm glad I'm here too," she whispered.

Wyatt leaned his head forward and kissed her softly on the lips.

"Wyatt -" she broke away. "Kiss me. Properly."

He drew her face back into his, and she wrapped her fingers up into his hair as she drowned in his kiss.

"Can you feel that?" he asked, whispering softly into her skin.

"Yes. I can feel it everywhere."

Fire ran through her veins, coursing along with her pounding blood. Her skin hummed with electric volts. Wyatt trailed his fingers up the nape of her neck, gently rubbing her hairline. It sent shivers coursing through her body, so intense it was almost agony.

"Take me to bed, please Wyatt, I need to feel you."

Wyatt nodded. He picked her up, carrying her in his arms the same way he'd first held her. She ran her hands over his chest, feeling the hard muscle moving beneath her palms as he navigated his way to his bedroom.

He gently placed Haley back on her feet, removing the blanket and dragging her deeper into his kiss. Wyatt felt like he'd come home. Her scent and touch enveloped him completely, blinding him to everything except the tones of her skin, the waterfall of black hair running down her back, the large, stormy eyes that became the axis of his earth.

"Will you freeze to death if I remove your thermals?"

She laughed into his collarbone, gently biting his skin in response to his teasing. Wyatt exhaled a fragmented breath at her touch.

He ran his hands down her sides, tugging at the bottom of her layers and then lifting them up over her head. She stretched her arms up to help him free her, her breasts lifting upward as she did so. Wyatt lowered his head, taking her nipple in his mouth and sucking gently. Haley felt her abdomen muscles clench tightly in response and gasped.

Wyatt removed his mouth and ran his palms over her breasts; his weather beaten skin grazing her softness, making Haley lightheaded with lust and wanting. He kneeled at her feet, pulling down her leggings and panties, deftly pushing the fabric off each of her feet, kissing them softly as he did so.

He looked up, his eyes full of worship and lust as he surveyed Haley's body. She was magnificent.

Haley placed her hands over her slightly protruding stomach.

"Does it weird you out?" she asked, misreading his expression.

"Absolutely not! You're gorgeous, you look hot as hell." He replied, smirking.

"Oh." Haley blushed. She hadn't expected that.

He leaned forward and kissed her on the thigh. It sent a shot of electricity right up into her sex. Haley started to pant. Wyatt trailed kisses further up her leg toward the apex of her thighs.

He stopped, just before reaching the top, and stood up.

"You need to get on the bed Haley, I don't want you fainting on me again."

"Cocky," she admonished.

"Very."

Haley gracefully climbed onto the bed. Wyatt stood where he was, just watching her, taking in her long, supple limbs, her gorgeous backside as toned as a professional dancers, but filling out beautifully with baby weight.

Wyatt felt his erection grow heavier, becoming painful as his body sought to be sated. He walked slowly toward the bed. Haley didn't take her eyes off him.

"You're fully dressed – it seems a little unfair," she murmured.

He shrugged, "I can fix that."

He pulled his hoodie off over his head, leaving his hair in complete disarray. Haley felt her throat run dry as he dropped the hoodie on the floor and the muscles in his arms flexed and rippled. He was so broad; the muscles in his shoulders taught and solid, narrowing down to a six pack that tremored with each labored breath that he took. His jeans hung off his hips, exposing a tantalizing happy trail that Haley wanted to follow down into the contents of his boxer briefs.

Wyatt undid the top button of his jeans, and unzipped his fly. His jeans dropped down to the floor, and he deftly stepped out of them. Haley gulped at seeing his boxer-clad bulge. He looked *huge*.

"We'll go slow," he said, his voice hoarse, as he saw Haley's reaction.

She nodded.

"Wyatt – I need you to know, I've never told a...partner this," she hesitated, blushing furiously, "I'm a flamingo shifter. I wanted you to know."

"What?"

"I know – it's so...strange. I guess." She chewed on her lip anxiously, waiting for him to say something.

"That's fucking incredible!"

Wyatt's face lit up, a huge smile completely transforming his expression. He looked so young in that moment, a completely beguiling innocence that Haley couldn't help but laugh at.

"I would have told you sooner if I'd known I'd get that reaction."

"Jesus Haley, how could I not think that's amazing? A flamingo. Baby, you're *extraordinary*."

Haley felt her stomach turn to jelly at the endearment, warmth flooding her body. Wyatt came and kneeled on the bed. He wrapped his hands in her hair, drawing her face toward him and caught her lips in an intense, passionate kiss that caused Haley's body to hunger for his impatiently.

He forced her upward on her knees, cupping the cheeks of her backside in his hands. He groaned, "your body...*fuck*."

He lay her back on the bedcovers, grabbing her ankles and pushing her legs apart. He ran his hands up her calves and thighs, stilling her spasms of excitement and embarrassment that he was seeing her so intimately.

He reached down to the apex of her thighs, and kissed her pubic bone, then trailed his mouth down to her center. He licked the silken soft folds of skin, then sucked gently on her clitoris as Haley flooded his mouth with wetness. He grabbed her thighs and pulled her more deeply into his mouth. Haley felt the onset weightlessness and full-body shudder of her orgasm. She cried out Wyatt's name, and then it crashed around her, sending her senses reeling and rolling, riding waves of endless pleasure.

Wyatt removed his boxers, his erection springing free. Haley sat up on her elbows gazing at his hardness, her breath catching in her throat as a red flush spread across her body.

"Are you sure this is okay?" Wyatt asked breathlessly as he placed his hand across her stomach.

"Yes, we just need to be gentle," she whispered.

Wyatt cocked an eyebrow at her, "Don't worry about that – I want to feel every inch of you." His eyes were hooded with lust, and Haley felt a surge of desire that sent her head spinning.

He leaned forward, wrapping one hand around her hair, the other entwined in her fingers. She felt the head of his penis push insistently at her entrance. She gasped as inch by inch he made his way inside her, the muscles of her core already slick and expanding to welcome him.

She raised her hips to meet him, and he retracted slowly before pushing back inside her. As a natural rhythm asserted itself Haley moaned and clutched his hand tighter in hers.

Wyatt desperately wanted to remain in control; he was half afraid of transforming, or loosing himself in her so completely that he went too hard and hurt her. His entire body trembled with the effort of holding back. He gritted his teeth, panting into her neck as his lips softly grazed her skin and their perspiration combined into salty dew that smelled of sex and warmth.

"It's okay, Wyatt – let go, please, let go – I know it's going to be okay," Haley exhaled.

He didn't need to be told twice. Their pace sped up, her hips rising up to meet his thrusts. He leaned upward and buried his face in Haley's hair, spread across the pillow. She clutched and clawed at his muscled buttocks, driving him more deeply into her.

Haley felt the second orgasm build within her, one that reached into the tips of her fingers and down to her toes. It reached a climax, and Haley inhaled a gulp of air as her body lost itself in his.

As it was subsiding, she felt a bright, electric volt start to build from her stomach, as if she was about to shift. She briefly felt a flutter of anxiety at the fear of shifting while she was pregnant, but it passed, and instead of shifting the sensation just ran throughout every artery and vein in her body; healing, reviving and filling her with Wyatt.

She felt Wyatt's body tense and the muscles in his back contract, then with a deep, reverberating growl of her name, he let go, pulsing jets filling her with his seed. His body jerked, and he clung to her. She heard him take a sharp inhale of breath, and then moan against her. She knew it wasn't just her that had felt the strange sensation.

Haley looked into Wyatt's eyes and saw her own expression mirrored there; the understanding that she had found her true mate, the one soul that could bond with hers completely, in every way possible; two halves of one.

She smiled softly, "Did you know?" she asked.

"I thought so. Now I know."

Haley nodded, wrapping herself closer into his blazingly hot body as he stroked her hair.

Wyatt didn't sleep that night. He lay still, watching Haley in her sleep, knowing that he held the most precious being on earth in his arms.

16

Haley woke up alone in Wyatt's bed. The sheets were twisted and crumpled around her, bright white sunlight filtered through half closed blinds. She smiled softly to herself, stretching luxuriously as she inhaled the scent of Wyatt all around her and heard the soft padding of his footsteps downstairs.

She retrieved her leggings and thermals, neatly folded on an armchair by the side of the window.

When Haley had explored the house yesterday, she had tried to be respectful of Wyatt's room – only peeking her head around the door and not fully venturing inside. Now she was eager to explore, to find the objects and belongings that marked this extraordinary man.

She wandered over to the opposite side of the bed, finding a battered Bukowski novel face down on the side table. In the library yesterday she'd found a far-reaching assortment of novels from a myriad of genres, but it appeared that the hard-boiled American was a favorite. She smiled.

Opposite the bed was a large hanging photograph that had very briefly caught her attention last night as they dozed off. She gazed at it now, realizing that it depicted the Port Ursa coast; dark, moody with a raw beauty that spoke to Mother Nature's ferocity.

Haley heard his footsteps again, and the sound of a pan being knocked around. She wanted to go down and join him, but she couldn't help but peek into the closet first. It was huge, taking up a whole wall – but practically empty when she opened its doors. A dozen suits hung formally and some hoodies, alongside a row of folded jeans and another shelf full of sport clothes. *Well*, Haley smirked to herself, *not much of a surprise he works out.*

Satisfied she had been thorough, she made her way downstairs. Wyatt was clearly a man she wouldn't get to know through his belongings – he was a sparse and orderly individual, one that might appear cold to some, and would to Haley had he not sent her soaring into a seventh heaven last night. *Her mate.* She clutched herself gleefully at the treasured fact; the most ridiculously sexy, good-looking man she'd ever laid eyes on, and he was her mate.

She walked through to the kitchen. Wyatt was standing at the oven wearing nothing but a pair of low-slung sweat pants.

A bolt of desire shot through her abdomen, desecrating the sated, hazy feeling that she'd woken up with. She wanted him again.

He turned round to face her, his eyes lazily roaming over her figure in appreciation.

"Morning baby."

"Morning," she smiled, crossing the kitchen. He wrapped her in a bear hug as she ran her fingers up the taut muscles of his back. *Heaven.*

"Pancakes?"

"Please!" She eyed the contents of the pan, and inhaled deeply as she caught the scent of bacon on the griddle.

"Again, you're ruining my ability to do my job as your companion," she mock scolded him.

"You're under doctor's orders to relax, and anyway, I disagree – I'm feeling very, very well-cared for."

His lips melted into hers, first softly coaxing then deepening into a more urgent kiss that left them both gasping for breath, and Wyatt's desire pressed against her stomach.

"Enough, or I'll ruin your breakfast," he murmured.

She laughed and broke their embrace only to move behind him and wrap her arms round his waist while he attended to the food. After a moment, Haley felt that she should probably leave him alone, but as she moved to take her arms away he took hold of them with one hand, locking her to him.

She nuzzled the soft skin of his back, sighing contentedly.

Wyatt served up the pancakes and bacon with a steaming pot of freshly brewed coffee, and they sat perched on stools around the marble kitchen island.

"This is delicious." Haley praised him as she dug in with a ravenous hunger. When there was no reply, she looked up to see Wyatt's gaze fixed upon her.

"What?" she smiled uncertainly.

"I'm amazed – at this," he gestured at the two of them, "Finding you. And under such unlikely circumstances."

"I know." Haley whispered softly, "I can't believe it either."

Wyatt suddenly looked disgruntled, and Haley raised her eyebrows in surprise at his expression.

"I will *never* hear the end of this from Colton."

Haley burst out laughing. It was clear from the short time she'd known Colton and Wyatt that the two brothers didn't always see eye to eye.

"I take it this was all his idea?" She asked.

"Of course. It was a last resort after I died a thousand deaths on some truly awful dates, which I will entertain you with another time."

"I can't wait," Haley's eyes gleamed. She would treasure every single moment that she got to spend with Wyatt, whatever they were doing. *For how long?* The question came unbidden into her mind, and she swiftly dismissed it.

"So, baby momma, tell me about shifting while pregnant - not something I know much about." Wyatt asked.

"Basically I can't," Haley replied, "It could harm the baby –the amniotic sack, especially in the later stages. Not to mention the energy that it takes to shift, energy that is necessary to sustain a growing, developing baby"

"I can't wait to see you, your flamingo, after that baby's born." Wyatt smiled broadly at her, his eyes alight with excitement.

"Do you mean that?" Haley asked quietly.

"That I want to see you shift? Of course." Wyatt looked confused.

"No – I mean, that you want me to be around after the baby's born."

Wyatt looked taken aback. He put down his coffee cup and reached for Haley's hand. He ran a thumb down her index finger, rubbing her skin softly. Neither of them spoke.

Wyatt felt tongue tied, irritated at his inability to formulate a sentence. He'd closed million dollar deals without breaking a sweat, was soon to be Alpha of his Clan and command what equated to a small, yet powerful army. And here he was, unable to tell his mate what he truly wanted.

"Haley...You are my mate. Do you think, that after the miracle of finding you, I would *ever* let you go?"

Haley's breath hitched in her throat. Warmth flooded her entire body.

"I wasn't...sure – I didn't know if it meant as much to you..." she trailed off on seeing his eyes blaze with a mixture of anger and lust.

"It means *everything* to me. Not just because of the Clan, not just because I find you mind-blowingly sexy," he smirked at her, "But because I know that we belong to one another – last night, what I felt being with you, making love to you, it was fundamentally altering."

"Me too," Haley replied in wonder, "I feel different today. I can't put my finger on it. As if I'm *whole*, and no longer lost."

She blushed in embarrassment at her words, yet she meant everything she said, but it seemed so strange to be talking like this to a man she felt she knew, yet didn't know at all – as if she'd seen his soul before knowing how he liked his eggs. *Weird.*

"I know it's strange – now. But it won't be soon. And as soon as it's not strange, I would like to officially claim you as mine."

Haley smiled broadly across at him, deliriously happy and also squirming with anticipation in her seat at the idea of truly mating with Wyatt.

Most shifter pair-bonds were created through a bite, each one marking their partner often during climax, a bite deep enough to leave a scar; physically marking them as belonging to one another, but the act also left a scent that would indicate to other shifters that they were taken, that they belonged to another in an unbreakable, life-long union.

"Yes." Haley replied, simply.

Wyatt moved toward her swiftly, picking her up from her chair, he lifted her upward and wrapped her body around his. She squealed in surprise, and then wove her fingers into his hair kissing him deeply.

"Haley Dubois, you are *mine*."

"Always," she whispered into his ear.

Their half-eaten breakfasts were left unattended as Wyatt carried her back up to his bedroom and made love to her again, softly and gently as the morning light danced around them.

"I NEED to go into the office and go over a few things with my brothers." Wyatt lay on his side holding Haley naked in his arms, his legs wrapped around her, encasing her body completely with his.

Haley nodded, brushing her face against his chest.

"Then I thought we could go into town and get some baby things...we need to prepare a nursery," he leaned down and gently nibbled on her earlobe, "I have a room in mind, but will leave the decorating to you – it's really not my strong suit."

"Oh, Wyatt," Haley suddenly felt guilty, she'd come into this man's life like a wrecking ball, "You're taking a lot on – you know that right, a mother and a baby?"

Her earlobe received a sharp bite of admonishment.

"Haley, I can't wait for the baby to arrive – and I happen to be completely enchanted and head-over-heels for its mother. I've always wanted to have a family, just never thought I'd find the one that was meant for me."

"Okay," Haley laughed, relieved and back in her cocoon of contentment, "Just making sure."

"Be sure. I'll pick you up when I'm back from the office – and then I was thinking I could take you out for dinner tonight?"

"I would love that. Thank you, Wyatt."

"Good." He slowly untangled himself and stood up, retrieving clothes from his closet. Haley smiled to herself as she saw Wyatt's naked body in all its glory. She would *never* tire of that view.

17

Haley pulled on her boots. They weren't the most practical for the Alaskan weather, but they were the only pair she had to bring with her that weren't buttery-soft suede. At least her coat was mildly practical; it was a fur lined parka that she'd bought in Moscow, up till this trip it had been shoved into the back of her closet and hadn't seen the light of day for years. She was grateful for it now.

As she opened the back door, icy winds smacked her in the face, pulling at her hair. Haley shivered and sighed, but stepped out.

"This is for you, little blob. I sure hope you appreciate it." She rubbed her stomach with mitted hands.

Haley walked down to the water edge, admiring the seaplane that had frozen at its base in the water. She looked forward to summer when Wyatt might take her out on it, and they could skim the waters of the North Pacific. Little blob would be born by then.

She took a tentative step onto the jetty. It creaked loudly under her weight, ice cracking like glass around its spindly legs. *Perhaps not.* She hastily took a step back onto the frost-covered grass.

Haley trudged up and down, her feet feeling like ice blocks and her breath coming out in curls of condensation smoke.

She jumped up and down on the spot, persuading herself to stay out for just five more minutes before going to get a cup of hot tea. *God damn this weather.*

It would take some getting used to. It was the only thing that she hadn't mentioned to Wyatt when the subject of her shifter animal came up. Flamingos didn't fare well in the cold, and neither did Haley. And yet here she was, in one of the coldest climates on the planet, where her shifter mate had built an empire and ruled a Clan. She wouldn't ask him to live somewhere else, it would be impossible for him – but could she really remain here? All year round?

Haley started to walk back toward the house. It was a question she didn't want to dwell on, not right now.

As she stomped her feet on the porch to shake off the ice, her phone buzzed in her pocket. She was mildly startled – her phone reception out here had been laughable the moment she arrived.

Checking the caller ID, she was even more surprised to see May-May's name popping up.

"May-May? Hi!"

"Haley, that you?" The line was fuzzy, but she could just make out May-May's agitated tone as if from the end of a long tunnel.

"It's me May-May! It's so nice to hear your voice, are you okay?"

"I'm fine girl – it's you that's not." The line crackled.

"What? May-May hang on – I'm going to get to a better spot."

Haley stepped back off the porch and back to the water's edge where she thought there might be less interference.

"Can you hear me May-May?"

"Haley – listen to me. You're in danger girl."

"May-May, what are you taking about? I've got so much to tell you – the cards were right; I *have* met a man -"

"Haley Dubois, stop your jabberin'! I know what been going on, I'm not a psychic for nothin' – and I'm telling you, I did a card reading for you this morning, and something dark is comin' your way Haley, something dark, evil and black."

"May-May, stop it, you're scaring me." Haley tried to sound firm; May-May sometimes got a little erratic – claiming to see spirits, crossing herself when she bumped into certain people on the street. Haley wouldn't stand for it.

"You should be scared! Haley, I mean it – somethin' coming for you. Where are you now? Where's that polar bear man of yours?"

"I'm outside the house, May-May – everything's fine. Wyatt's at a meeting, he'll be back soon, we're going to look for stuff for the nursery, isn't that great?"

"Haley – don't go back into the house. Get into the truck, and get the hell outta there." May-May's voice sounded frantic, "Please Haley –"

The phone went dead.

"May-May? Can you hear me?" Haley tried to call back, but the signal on her phone showed no reception bars.

Damn. Haley could feel her heart palpitating. May-May had scared her. She closed her eyes and took a deep breath, listening to the stillness around her. Moments ago it had been peaceful, now it was eerily quiet.

That crazy-ass woman! Haley stomped on the porch again, determined to go back inside and end this nonsense. She was letting her imagination run away with her, and it was ridiculous. How the hell she'd even known Wyatt was a shifter was a complete mystery.

She shoved her boots and coat off, leaving them by the door and slammed it shut. The warmth of the house, and the smell of their breakfast comforted her. There was nothing to be afraid of, she was safe, and warm, and May-May was a batty old lady with too much time on her hands.

Haley flicked the kettle on, and went in search of a mug. She wondered if Wyatt had a stereo somewhere; the silence of the house was starting to become deafening. Every sound she made seemed amplified, every creak, groan and electric hum of the house made her tense. *You are being stupid!*

Haley tried to shake off the unwelcome anxiety, but her heartbeat wasn't calming. This anxiety wasn't good for the baby. She needed to get outside and into civilization. Wyatt would probably think she was a crazy woman, but if her, and her baby's health, was at stake then it was worth it.

Wyatt had left in the truck this morning, but he still had an SUV parked outside in the drive. It was a better option than wandering off in the cold – it was too isolated here for that. She just needed to find the keys.

She checked by the house phone and the table in the foyer, but found nothing. On her snooping afternoon, Haley had stumbled on the basement entrance – it hadn't held much interest for her, it looked more like a workshop, smelling of dust and faint traces of gasoline. If Wyatt didn't use the SUV all that much, then the keys might be down there.

In her current state of mind, a trip to the basement didn't sound too appealing, but it was means to an end then she would just pull herself together and do what needed to be done.

She located the door. It was stiff, and she shoved against it. It creaked loudly as it swung open, and Haley had to pause for a moment to calm herself down. *You are behaving like a child!* She scolded herself.

She pulled on the light switch hanging by the entrance, relieved that she didn't have to walk down into the darkness. A naked power-saver bulb lit the room dimly, casting shadows where bits of machinery lay against the walls and a couple of larder fridges stood humming away.

She started to walk down the stairs, heading for the worktop that had various keys dangling from nails above it. One of them was sure to be the SUV key. She began to sing softly, stringing together nonsense words, telling herself it was to reassure her little blob. *Yeah, right.*

She inspected the keys, finding two that had Ford key chains. One of these might be it. She placed them both in the pocket of the sweater she was wearing, and turned to walk back up the stairs.

Leaning against part of the wall by the banister was a large sheet of metal. Haley jumped on seeing her own reflection in it. She rolled her eyes at her stupidity, feeling calmer with the keys in her pocket.

As she was walking past it, she saw a black figure moving in the corner of the room. Her stomach plummeted. She lost control of her legs, as if they would collapse beneath her. Frozen with fear she couldn't run forward, she couldn't turn around, she could only look at her silent, distorted scream of horror in the reflection of the metal and the figure moving closer toward her.

Her senses jolted. *Run!*

Before she could act on her command, a damp cloth was forcefully shoved across her mouth and nose. She struggled against the arm that gripped her, inhaling the noxious fumes of the cloth in rapid breaths. The room started to blur, swimming softly in front of her vision before everything went black.

Her last thought was of Wyatt and the smile he'd given her last night as he'd placed his palm across little blob.

18

"Thanks for coming." Wyatt nodded at Joe as the old man joined them at the table.

"What you lookin' so smug about?" inquired Joe, disgruntled as always to be taken away from his easy chair and trailer.

"I'm taking the position. I'm announcing my bid for Alpha in the next few weeks." Wyatt announced to the room.

Tucker cheered loudly and whopped, Colton just sat in the chair looking self-satisfied.

"*Finally*," Joe retorted. He relaxed back in the chair as if a huge weight had been taken off his shoulders. It had been a long time coming, but clearly Wyatt had finally got his act together.

"I need to give Haley some time to feel ready for the pair-bond, it's too soon to do it now – we need to wait a few weeks. That okay with everyone?"

Wyatt turned to Tucker; he was the one with the line to Drake.

"Should be fine," agreed Tucker, "Been quiet on that front lately."

Colton cleared his throat, smirking as he waited for Wyatt to acknowledge his orchestration of a perfect plan. Wyatt cocked an eyebrow at him and pursed his lips. His reluctance made the moment all the sweeter for Colton.

"Yeah, alright – you got a lucky break." Wyatt murmured in his direction.

"*What?* You should be thanking me brother, loudly, and with feeling."

"Hell, Colton – you just got lucky. It was a miracle that Haley responded to your ad. I'm not crediting you with a miracle."

"Jesus. If that's all the thanks I'm gonna get..." he trailed off, rolling his eyes. At least Hannah would be pleased with him that it had all worked out well.

"I take it it's going well then – you calling her a miracle and all." Tucker smiled, lightly teasing his elder brother.

Wyatt smirked. He wasn't going to divulge the details of his relationship with these morons. He had, however, asked the receptionist to bring through some champagne. He *was* grateful to Colton and Tucker for helping him the last few months, there was just no way on earth that he'd let Colton know it.

When the sharp rap on the door came, Wyatt thought it was the champagne. He was as surprised as the rest of them when Drake walked through the door.

"Sorry to interrupt. I need to talk to you."

He looked at Wyatt. Drake's usual mask of indifference had slipped. He looked panicked, and as if he'd driven here in a hurry – truck keys still clutched in his hand.

"What's up?" Wyatt asked.

"I think Simeon's been watching your house. Word is that you've got a new mate there, one that's going to be your ticket to Clan leadership."

Wyatt's stomach lurched. *Haley.*

"How the fuck?" Wyatt burst out.

"I don't know. Don't know the details – but, where is she? Simeon's going to stop at nothing to block your rise to Alpha."

Wyatt didn't need to hear another word. *Why the hell had he left her at home?* He started running toward the door, his brothers calling out after him.

"Let him go." Drake commanded.

"We need to go too." Colton replied, jumping up from his chair.

"I think I know where they might be taking her – but I'm not sure. I'll point you in the general direction and you'll have to start tracking from there."

"Then why the hell you let Wyatt go off on a wild goose chase?" Colton asked him angrily.

"Because I'm hoping that I got here in time. She could be at home for all I know. I've just got a really uneasy feeling about this."

Tucker nodded, "Thanks, Drake. We appreciate it." He turned to Colton, "We need to talk about security afterwards – there must be a leak somewhere in the Clan."

Colton nodded.

"Joe, go and alert the rest of the Clan. I want them all on standby," said Colton, "This could escalate quickly if we don't get to Haley in time."

It was a sobering thought. The three men left the office at a half run, down the corridor to their waiting vehicles. The receptionist looked stunned and flustered as they stormed past her, a bottle of chilled champagne on her tray.

"We need to drive up to Pavlutsky Point. We'll park out of sight and then track," Drake shouted over his shoulder.

"Wait," Tucker commanded, "Drake – you should go and talk to your Pack. If Simeon sees you helping us out, and his plan's successful, the first thing he's going to do is come after you. Let me and Colton handle it from here."

Drake nodded, "Appreciate it. Alright. Good luck."

Tucker nodded and then ran to his truck. Colton got in the passenger seat, and they sped off.

19

As soon as he opened the truck door to step out, the rank odor of wolf hit him. They had been here.

He ran to the front door, yelling Haley's name. It was locked. He fumbled for his keys, noticing his shaking hands. Forcing the key into the door he yanked it open. The house was still. The only sound he could hear was the blood rushing in his own ears.

"Haley!" he yelled again. Nothing but silence.

He searched the house, looking for evidence – a smashed window, a forced door. Nothing. He paused. He needed to follow the scent, not wildly lose his head running in circles.

Closing his eyes, he tried to summon his primal instincts to the fore. *Haley*. He could smell her fear. It pervaded the house, making it strong enough to track. He could sense wafts of it mixing in with the smell of fried bacon in the kitchen, sullying their cozy breakfast scene only hours earlier, but the most potent concentration came from the hallway. The basement.

He ran down the stairs. Here. It had happened here. Beneath the reek of wolf, he could smell pure, undiluted fear. His heart broke. She had been so afraid, so, so afraid. And he hadn't been here to stop it.

He could also smell a strong element of chloroform. His blood boiled over and rage drenched him. He would annihilate the men that took her.

Wyatt ran from the house. Outside he could see what he'd missed before, a shattered window by the ground – one large enough for someone to crawl through. He could see footprints in the snow, and followed them down to the bottom of the drive. They had carried her. *Where the fuck were they now?*

He could see no sign of a vehicle – there would be tire marks somewhere on the road. Which meant that they were on foot. The tarmac had been salted countless times over the winter so he couldn't make out any footprints, but he could just about grasp the scent.

He looked around. *Focus.* On the other side of the road the land dipped sharply down to the port; there was nothing for miles – and it was a truly long trek to get down to the water. He scanned the landscape, only noting a flat slope covered in ice and snow. If they'd gone that way he'd be able to see prints.

The only other alternative was going up; a few miles from his house the journey up to Pavlutsky Point began, a steep incline that led to the cliff edge, then a sharp drop straight into the ocean. *They're going to kill her.*

A sharp, technicolor image flashed through his mind; a graceful body, long hair as black as a ravens, falling, falling through the white sky, spinning and dancing in the wind before it hit the icy depths of the ocean.

Wyatt started to run.

He willed himself to shift. Usually the small primal tug within him would take a few seconds to spread throughout his body. This time it was instant; his bear wanted to be unleashed, wanted to rescue his mate. His human fear, rage and bloodlust were amplified as his animal form shook off the reservations of humanity and let instinct take over.

As soon as he reached the start of the incline, he saw snow mobile tracks marked in the snow. He emitted a low growl. It would mean they were travelling faster than he would have hoped, but they'd also made it easy for Wyatt to trail them.

His paws pounded the icy earth breaking the ground as his claws acted like ice picks, making the incline easier for him than it would be on his enemies – the drag on the machines would slow them down. He moved swiftly, his size no disadvantage to his speed, as his brute strength tore against the oncoming wind.

It wasn't long before he spotted them in the distance. They were still driving, not yet at the precipice. He increased his pace. They wouldn't be able to drive all the way to the edge of the cliff; they would have to get off and walk soon – the shifting rock level made it impossible to get to any other way but on foot. That would be his advantage.

Soon he was so close he was inhaling their gasoline. One of the men turned around, yelling to his partner as he saw Wyatt. They were almost at the edge. Wyatt wanted their attention now.

He rose onto his hindquarters, the snow-white fur of his polar bear quivering. Lifting his muzzle to the sky he roared. The ground trembled beneath him as the reverberations shook the mountain, ice breaking in deference to the sound of fury and vengeance echoing across the wilderness, the cry of one of Alaska's most ancient and majestic creatures.

Two of the men yanked their snowmobiles to a halt. The third, carrying the limp form of his mate, carried on.

They shifted, becoming two snarling, wretched and malnourished wolves. They blocked his path to Haley, circling him slowly, keeping their front haunches low on the ground, ready to leap.

Wyatt didn't have time to wait for their brutal, short attacks designed to wear him down by repeating to launch then retreat in quick succession. He wanted blood.

He leapt forward, pinning one of the wolves down with his claws outstretched. It whimpered beneath him, and then latched its teeth into his front leg. Wyatt slammed his paw down on the head of the wolf, loosening his grip. Wyatt launched his muzzle down to the wolf's neck, ready to rip out its throat.

Before he could finish the beast off, the second wolf leapt onto Wyatt's back, tearing into the muscles at his shoulder blades. Wyatt reared backward, trying to fling the creature off. As he did so, the wolf beneath him followed him upward, jaw parted, trying to get his teeth into Wyatt's neck.

Wyatt spun; avoiding the open jaws of the wolf in front and launched himself on the one behind him. Wyatt had knocked him to the ground, and he lay on his back, panting. Wyatt swiped his face with outstretched claws. The wolf whimpered and lay still.

The other wolf began to circle him again. Wyatt had hoped that he would retreat with his fellow pack member; if the wolf got the proper treatment now, he would probably survive. As Wyatt looked into the creature's eyes, he realized it was a foolish hope. This wolf wanted Wyatt dead.

He didn't have any time. The human carrying Haley's body had now disembarked from the snowmobile and was making his way to the edge of the cliff. He couldn't afford to let his panic make him clumsy.

The wolf jumped. Flying through the air toward him, claws outstretched, his jaw wide and rabid-looking in its hunger.

Standing on his hind legs, Wyatt welcomed the dog into his embrace. Its claws dug into his chest tearing at his skin and fur. His jaw plunged into Wyatt's shoulder, biting deeply, crimson blood erupting onto Wyatt's white fur.

Wyatt ducked his head down and in one fluid motion he ripped the muscle, flesh and jugular out of the wolf's neck. It sunk to the icy ground, blood pooling around it.

Wyatt thundered toward the cliff edge.

Haley was still in the human's arms. The wind was ferocious now, whipping at the pair as they approached the precipice, the kidnapper lowered his torso and bent his knees in order to struggle onward to his destination. Wyatt was going to be too late.

With his sight set so firmly on his mate, he didn't notice the black shapes approaching the ridge from the left side of the mountain. They had been moving slowly, keeping their trail by the snowdrift formations that edged the cliff. Keeping their eyes on their prey.

The human stopped dead in his tracks. Wyatt thought he had

reached the edge, and bellowed out a roar of agony and torment. He pushed himself to increase his pace, blood seeping out of him with every movement his muscles made.

Two Kodiak grizzly's surrounded the human. They stood between him and the cliffs edge, pawing hungrily at the ground.

Wyatt could see them now. Even from a distance, with the icy snow that half obscured the landscape, Wyatt would recognize those bears anywhere. His brothers had arrived.

The man backed away from the edge. He clung onto the woman's body, looking around him wildly. The polar bear was fast approaching from behind him, and there was nowhere left to run.

He placed the woman on the snow, lifting his arms up in surrender. One of the bears launched themselves at him, knocking the man down and pinning him to the ground. He was wearing a balaclava and black mountain gear, unrecognizable to the bear that surveyed his face.

Wyatt arrived and shifted back into human form in agony. His shoulder blade had practically been torn from his body, and his chest was mutilated and seeping with blood. Unconcerned with his own injuries, he flung himself down to Haley, picking her up with the less damaged of his arms. He cradled her to his chest.

"Haley? Haley? Wake up, baby – wake up."

His voice was low and urgent. His fingers gently caressed her sleeping face, willing her eyes to open. He held her tighter, thinking about how cold she'd be.

Colton had shifted back into human form, and was tying the man – knocked out cold, to the back of his snowmobile. Tucker remained as his grizzly, pacing the ground as he waited for a sign of life from his brother's mate.

"Baby, please wake up...I need you Haley, don't leave me."

Wyatt knew that the amount of chloroform needed to knock her out for this long, could also do permanent damage, or kill her... and the baby. He could hear a faint pulse at her neck, but it seemed to be fading, not strengthening.

"I love you Haley, I don't want to do this without you."

Her eyes fluttered open. Wyatt's heart constricted, waiting.

"Wyatt?" she murmured, "I'm so cold."

He almost laughed in relief. He held her closer, trying to project as much of his body heat into her as he could.

"I know baby; we're going to take you home now. You're safe. It's going to be okay."

She nodded gently, her eyes not really focusing, and eventually they fell shut again.

"We need to get her back, now," commanded Wyatt, "I don't think I can shift again. Tucker, take her on your back – run like hell to the house. Colton – call Hannah, get her to my place."

"What do you want to do with this?" Colton gestured to the man. He'd removed his balaclava, exposing the face that none of the group recognized. "I think he's a gun for hire," said Colton.

"We'll tie him up in the basement for now, then get him to Joe. I recognized the men back there – this is Simeon's Pack."

"We're going to war."

Wyatt lifted Haley's body onto the back of his brother, ensuring she was lying flat to benefit from Tucker's body heat.

"Take her home," he said, "you're carrying the most precious thing in the world to me. Remember that."

Tucker growled loudly in understanding and set off swiftly down the mountain.

20

Little blob was officially named Leila Dubois. She was born on the first day of March, a happy, healthy baby that weighed six and a half pounds. The moment she'd opened her stormy grey eyes and waved her impossibly small fist in the air, Haley had loved her with every fiber of her being.

Wyatt couldn't hide his pride and joy at being a father; he would gaze for hours at Leila, carry her around the ward whispering sweet nothings into her ear, telling her how he would take her and her mother on the seaplane and they'd travel for miles across the ocean, watching the sun set.

From the moment that Haley had found out she was pregnant, she'd expected to give birth in an anonymous Manhattan hospital room, the only visitor perhaps being May-May. The idea had saddened her; she had no family left in the world, and given her job, she had travelled too much to form many tight friendships.

Leila's birthday couldn't have been more different from what she'd pictured. Wyatt was with her the entire time, driving her to Hannah's clinic when her water broke, never leaving her side for the twelve hours they had to wait until Leila was ready to emerge into the world.

Then the visitors came; her new family. Tucker was the most awkward, tentative about holding Leila until Wyatt sat him down and forced the infant into his arms. He'd quite obviously melted at the sight of her, and held her like a precious jewel. Haley would never forget what Tucker did for her when he carried her home for miles on his back that day – not once jolting her, keeping the cold at bay. She would be forever grateful to him.

Hannah and Colton were avid fans of Leila; every spare moment Hannah had was spent in Haley's room, holding the baby, cooing at it softly. She would also cluck around Haley like a mother hen, and the two women had become inseparable.

Drake also came by to visit, holding on to a wild eyed boy who didn't speak much, but who clearly loved Hannah – gazing at the Doctor intently whenever she was near. He was also a gem with Leila – a born baby soother, holding on to her tightly whenever she cried, almost instantly stemming her tears. It was remarkable.

The only person she missed was May-May. She had called her a few hours after giving birth, but not been able to get through.

At last, Haley had been sent home. Wyatt insisted on carrying both her and Leila out to the truck, which already had a baby seat strapped in the back, and a catchall filled to the brim with baby paraphernalia.

"Have I ever told you what an amazing man you are, Wyatt Sterling?" Haley announced; surveying the car and recognizing all the effort he'd gone to. He was going to make such an amazing father.

"Spurred on by my incredible mate," he replied wryly, "I was very average before you came along."

Haley snorted with derision. *Yeah, right.*

"So, I've got a special surprise for you when we get home."

"What?" Haley cried, "Wyatt – you've been completely spoiling me, you'll just bring out the high maintenance monster within me; we discussed this – remember?"

"I do remember," he retorted, "and I told you I could more than handle it. So hush. If I want to spoil you, I damn well will."

Haley rolled her eyes and laughed.

"You're incorrigible."

"That I am. How's Leila?"

Haley smiled softly at the little girl in her car carrier.

"She's fast asleep. I think she likes car rides."

"Good to know," replied Wyatt, smiling, "but we're home already."

He pulled into the driveway.

"Are you warm enough?" He asked Haley as she stepped out of the truck.

"Why – are we going on a trek? I'll be warm inside."

"I want you to follow me, come."

He took Leila in his arms and took Haley by the hand. They walked down to the water's edge, and further along to the other side of the house.

Where there had been nothing but grass and an old outhouse used to store coal and firewood, there was now an absolutely enormous glass and wood building that resembled a large atrium.

Haley looked over at Wyatt in disbelief; she couldn't understand what it was.

"Go in!" He laughed at her, gesturing toward the door.

She opened the glass door and stepped inside.

The heat hit her in unrelenting waves, and Haley was transported to an exotic, tropical jungle.

Palm trees of various types and sizes surrounded a large, shallow pool covered with bright pink lotus flowers. Every available surface was covered in tropical plants; gaudy Anthurums, Birds of Paradise, bright red Ecuadorian roses, perfectly white and waxy Gardenias, Musas, Calatheas, Orchids of various colors, the list went on. Haley could do nothing but stare open-mouthed as she gazed on with wonder.

"It's home fit for a Flamingo, isn't it?" Wyatt asked quietly.

"You did all this for me?" Haley's voice cracked. She could barely get the words out.

"You and Leila, my two favorite Flamingos, yes. I know you were worried about living here all year round – and for Leila's sake too.

This will be your warm spot, I will always promise you summer, Haley, even in the dead of winter."

Haley turned to him, tears building up in the corners of her eyes. She was speechless with gratitude. She could only fling her arms around him, thanking her lucky stars for Wyatt coming into her life.

"I love you Wyatt," she whispered against him.

"I love you too, baby."

"This is perfect," she broke away, encompassing the magnificence of the room with her gesture.

"Do you think May-May will approve?"

"What?" Haley asked.

"May-May. She's on the first flight out tomorrow, I thought you might want some help with Leila – you know, like a grandma-type thing."

"You did that, too?"

"Shit, yes – is that okay? I thought you would like her being here…" Wyatt stumbled into silence. He couldn't read Haley's expression.

"I don't know what to say. You've made me so happy, Wyatt. Everything about you…everything you do for me…"

Wyatt exhaled with relief. "Haley – let's not forget I almost got you killed. I love doing things for you, and I have a lot to make up for."

"That's complete bologna – you saved me. Not just from Simeon's men, but from being unhappy, alone and without a family. I have all that now – and it's because of you."

Wyatt cupped her jaw with his hand, holding Leila gently between them. He bent down and kissed her lips, the softest, sweetest kiss that held so much promise of the life that lay before them.

TUCKER

Olivia Harris is recovering from a nightmare. Most days she's certain she will never be mentally healthy enough to rejoin the human race. Suffering from PTSD and experiencing severe anxiety attacks, she returns to her native Alaska to live in semi-seclusion in the little cabin she inherited from her father.

Tucker Sterling struggles with a restless, unsettled bear that he is unable to tame. Nothing soothes his bear, not the six years he spent in the army's Delta Force unit, not the multitude of nameless, faceless, women who share his bed, nothing, until Liv Harris returns to Port Ursa.

But, Liv has changed and Tucker is determined to find out what happened to her and how he can help even if it means sacrificing everything for the woman he loves.

1

Tucker came to a standstill in front of his brother Wyatt. He was panting hard, his heavily muscled chest heaving. The eight laps he'd done around the forest behind Longview Drive had given his bear a good run, hopefully released some of the restless agitation it constantly felt. He grabbed at the pair of old jeans and t-shirt still folded neatly next to the barrier where he'd left them. He'd just done a forced change-back, overpowering his bear's desire to continue running. His lungs were at the bursting point. Wyatt, in comparison, looked like he'd just stepped out of a J. Crew catalogue.

"You need a water or something? Ambulance?" Wyatt asked dryly.

Tucker shook his head, and leaned against the barriers that surrounded the cliff edge. The sea was ferocious today, smacking aggressively against the fishing boats that populated the harbor.

"What's up?" Tucker asked when he finally got his breath back.

"Nothing much," Wyatt shrugged, "Just wanted to check in. Missed you at dinner last night."

Oh shit. Wyatt and his wife, Haley, had invited him over for dinner - along with his younger brother Colton and Colton's wife, Hannah. He had planned to attend, but his date for the evening fell through, and he hadn't relished attending another couples evening as the only single man.

"Sorry, man."

"It's fine. But Haley has it in her head that you didn't come because you feel awkward now that me and Colton are mated."

Great. Tucker sighed, and then recovered his usual good humor.

"It would be fine if Haley and Hannah didn't incessantly tell me that I need to settle down and find a mate. Really not my thing - I'm perfectly happy."

"Uh-huh," Wyatt's mouth scrunched up in a smirk, "I hate to tell you, you don't make a very compelling case for yourself, bro."

Tucker grunted, "Why's that? Because Haley and Hannah don't think *anyone's* good enough for me? I *love* the women I date. They're great..."

"But they never last more than a week."

"That's why I *love* them!"

Wyatt laughed, "Alright, whatever. Just go by the house and see Haley. She made your favorite."

"I will."

Both brothers leaned against the rail, their backs turned away from the strong sea winds. Tucker gazed up Longview Drive, which wound its way up the mountain, and then petered off into the forest beyond. It was one of the most populated roads in Port Ursa, but the brick houses were steadily replaced by smaller wooden cabins the closer the road got to the forest. The last cabin on the road, too far off into the distance to see from their vantage point, had stood abandoned for over six years. In the past month, Tucker had noticed various construction vehicles driving up to it, and a team of local contractors working on the place.

As if reading his mind, Wyatt asked, "You ever hear from her?"

"No."

"Never? I thought with all that construction going on she might have gotten back in touch."

Tucker didn't reply.

"I just remember the two of you being close as kids," Wyatt commented, "You followed her around *everywhere*."

"Just let it go - I said no." Tucker turned back to face the sea. He hated looking at that house. Hated it so much that every time he went for a run he was unaccountably drawn to it, his bear searching through the forest beyond for something, a scent, a feeling, a faint flicker of a memory that always remained just out of his grasp. He would never tell his brother, or anyone else for that matter, that he spent hours alone in the forest in the special place they'd once shared.

Wyatt was looking at him with concern.

"You alright?" He asked.

"Yeah, I'm good. I'll beg forgiveness from Haley later today. Sorry I missed it."

Wyatt shrugged the apology off. He flicked up the collar on his coat and turned to make his way back to his truck. Tucker gestured a half-hearted salute.

As soon as truck rounded the corner, Tucker kicked one of the cliff barriers in frustration. He knew Wyatt would be worried about him now. He crossed his arms over his chest, legs spread in a wide stance as he stared out over the raging sea. His brothers kept a close eye on him, looking out for telltale signs that his military service had left internal scars, signs that he wasn't quite adjusting to civilian life.

It had been two years since he'd returned from the military. Not just the military, but the Army's special ops unit, Delta Force. When he'd enlisted in the Army, Tucker had hoped that it would fill the void inside, the hollow empty feeling that caused his bear to be ever restless and unsettled. He and his buddy Drake, a wolf shifter had signed up together. Because they both had special shifter abilities which allowed them each a unique set of skills, they were quickly recruited for clandestine military operations.

The military had suited Tucker well enough, but the void inside never left. After 6 years, he requested a discharge with the hope that a return home to the slower, more tranquil pace of Alaska would help his bear find peace.

Alaskan life did have a steady, easy quality he appreciated, and he loved being close to his brothers, but the hollow feeling remained a constant, and his bear was forever unsettled.

Why the hell did he cringe inside every time Wyatt or Colton mentioned *her*? Why did it rile him so much? And, why did they think he still cared about someone he hadn't seen in almost fifteen years? *They'd been children for Christ's sake.*

Tucker started the walk down the port towards his office where he could have a hot shower and fresh change of clothes. He would bury himself in work for the next few hours and then go and visit Haley and his new niece and try to beg forgiveness and, if he was lucky, leftovers.

2

Doctor Young shifted in his seat. The tick of his desk clock resonated; it had ceased to represent a measure of time, Olivia felt like she could have been listening to it for a single minute or twenty.

"Olivia? You seem distracted."

Olivia stared at her thumbnail. Her nails were polished in a creamy violet. It wasn't her color, but the nail polish was part of her new self-care routine, devised by herself and Doctor Young- small steps and actions geared toward boosting her self-esteem. But, things like nail polish, long baths and solo outings to the movies were like tiny band-aids attempting to seal the gaping hole of emptiness inside.

"I just feel a bit overwhelmed at the moment."

Doctor Young nodded.

"It's understandable, Olivia. This is a big step for you. I think most people would be overwhelmed, let alone people who have been through the extreme experiences that you have."

Olivia sighed.

"Did you look into support groups out there as we discussed?"

"I did. I couldn't find anything."

He scribbled something in his pad. Olivia looked at it pointedly.

"I'm making a note to see if there are any therapy professionals in the area. I think, at least in the beginning, you should have a point of contact that you can communicate with face to face."

Olivia looked down at the floor.

"I was hoping that this would be a fresh start."

"It will be. But there's no reason for you to have to do it alone. It helps to have someone to talk to. Do you know anyone out there? Any friends from your childhood?"

She felt a tug on her heartstrings as a pair of dark brown eyes flickered into her conscience. *Tucker.* But, surely he was long gone by now.

"No."

Doctor Young had observed the pause.

"No?" He queried.

"None that I remember... It was so long ago. I can't even remember the cold. They say you never forget the cold, that it's so chilling, so bone-deep that it stays with you forever, but I have. I have forgotten it. I suppose it doesn't matter since I'll get a refresher course in frigidly icy weather soon enough." She was rambling, trying to shift her thoughts from *him* before Dr. Young read her mind or something.

The closeness, the bond she and Tucker had shared was nothing more than a cherished memory for her. He probably hadn't even thought of her in years. *They'd been children for Christ's sake.*

"Well, since this is our last session, Olivia, I must caution you. I understand your need for more tranquil, more..." Dr. Young hesitated, "... remote surroundings. I realize that your life here in Shreveport, your surroundings, are not serving you."

She had come to Shreveport six months ago under a new identity, *Jane Hardwick,* hoping for a fresh start, much like she was hoping for one now. She'd even gotten herself a part-time job at Bert's Shoe Emporium in the city center. The job turned out to be a complete bust, though. It lasted a week before the fears, anxieties and panic attacks that plagued her made it impossible to withstand crowds or speak to strangers. At times she had difficulty even leaving her apartment.

"I must caution you," Dr. Young continued, "To be extra careful not to isolate yourself up there in Port Ursa. You need to start making friends, rejoining the human race. It is an important part of your recovery, and not to be ignored. It should be easier for you to leave the house knowing you won't be faced with large crowds. Continue to force yourself to take baby steps outside of your comfort zone, Olivia."

The doctor scribbled more notes down, but Olivia was lost in thought. By this time tomorrow she would be on a plane back to Port Ursa, all her belongings in a single suitcase. She would be reclaiming her true self—something she and Doctor Young had discussed at length. No more *Jane Hardwick*. The chances of anyone finding her in the extreme northwest arm of the Americas, in its largest and least densely populated state, were slim. Slim enough for her to be able to take back her identity, and start to begin a new life.

She'd been twelve the last time she'd been in Port Ursa, Alaska. She could only remember fragments. She could remember the wallpaper in the cabin, a faded pink floral pattern, the snow, blankets of blue-white that covered everything in the winter, the muted crunch of it underfoot, and the tree house that was her haven, *their* haven, hers and Tucker's sanctuary. And, she could remember *him*.

"I'm excited. Nervous, but excited." Olivia broke the silence. It was a way of saying thank you. However grey and unsure she might feel today, she was a far cry from the wreck of a human she'd been the first day she'd arrived. It had been a month before she'd been able to look Doctor Young in the eye. She knew he was immensely proud of her for her continued progress, and she found herself eager for that pride, wanting to be deserving of it.

"I'll make some new friends." Olivia's voice was tentative, but it contained hope.

"I'm very glad to hear it, Olivia. I'm sure you will. If you continue to work on opening up to people, you'll find meaningful and rewarding relationships anywhere. Even Alaska." Doctor Young laughed at his own joke.

Olivia managed a weak smile in return.

"Have contractors started making the place habitable?"

"Yes. I get updates from the team out there. It's all ready."

A small buzz from his desk phone indicated that their time was up.

"Well, Olivia. It's been wonderful getting to know you. You have my phone number, do call if you need to. And I wish you the best of luck in your future, which I know will be bright."

Olivia attempted to say thank you, but the words stuck in her throat. Whatever she said would feel insignificant in the face of all Doctor Young had done for her. Impulsively, she wrapped the man in a hug, clutching at him briefly before releasing him, stunned and embarrassed in equal measure.

But Doctor Young smiled broadly, thrilled at her gesture. He opened the door to his office, and she stepped out into the dingy reception area where Doctor Young's sweet but scatter-brained secretary grinned, showing lipstick on her teeth.

"Last session! We'll miss you, Jane," she called out, waving enthusiastically from behind her desk.

"Thanks Muriel, I'll miss y'all too." Olivia smiled at her before she turned to follow the stairs down past the near-empty salon and out the main entrance where the sun was beating down on the pavement with a thick, heavy intensity.

Olivia braced herself for the heat which was riding in ribbons off the asphalt. She was still in the habit of wearing long sleeved tops and pants, whatever the weather. As she swung open the heavy door at the bottom of the stairs, she heard Dr. Young holler down to her.

"Go grab your life, Olivia."

3

Tucker gave in to his bear and started his morning run across the island. The run was mandatory. If he didn't run his bear and run him hard, the damn thing would be clawing the hell out of his insides, fighting with him to get out all day long. He knew his bear was damaged, he'd known for a long time. His bear was always searching. He could temporarily appease it with a woman's company and a quick roll in the hay, but only temporarily. This morning was bad, his bear was so damn restless, so searching, he needed to head to the spot, the one place that would serve to calm him for a few hours.

Their place, the treehouse where he and Liv had spent hours together. It had been their secret sanctuary. When he returned to Port Ursa two years ago, and found the old structure dilapidated and falling apart, his bear insisted he build it back up. He added new lumber, secured the foundation, and restrung the rope ladder. He visited the place regularly, so regularly, in fact, that he kept a blanket and a change of clothes up there. When his bear was particularly out of sorts, it helped to soothe the beast.

As he'd neared the area, he caught a faint scent in the air. A familiar one that seemed to waft through the trees, vines and undergrowth all these years later. The scent that his bear was always drawn to, always chasing down only to find that it was a memory and as intangible as mist. Today, the memory of the scent was stronger. It almost seemed real rather than merely an ephemeral vapor teasing him from the depths of his mental recall. His mind played tricks on him sometimes out here. Today, he was certain that seeing all the construction around the old cabin overstimulated that part of his mind.

4

The contractors were finally finished. The last scrap of wood, dust and general debris had been cleared away before dusk yesterday. Now, Olivia stood in the middle of a spotless and near-empty kitchen, listening to the hum of the new refrigerator echo around the cabin. She would eventually call her mother, but not yet. She wasn't sure how her mother would react to the news that Olivia was in Alaska, and she wasn't ready to have *that* conversation yet. Besides, she was still angry.

Olivia and her mother used to be close, until the day that Olivia was contacted, out of the blue, by an attorney representing her father's estate. He had passed away and left her a small sum of money and the old family cabin in Alaska. At the time, Olivia hadn't seen nor heard from father in nine years.

Confused and surprised by his uncharacteristic generosity, Olivia questioned her mother. That's when the truth came out. Her mother finally admitted that the man hadn't *intentionally* cut Olivia out of his life, as she'd been led to believe. He simply had no way of finding her. Olivia's mother had blocked all contact, allowing Olivia to continue to believe that she'd been abandoned by her father. The news had been devastating to Oliva.

It wasn't only her dad that had been extricated from Olivia's life, it had been Tucker, too. Tucker, who had always been her rock, her shoulder to lean on was ripped from her. She remembered how difficult it had been for her, a bold and unruly wild-child, used to running free in the Alaskan wilderness to fit in with a peer group whose favorite hangout was the mall. While Olivia had been learning to hunt, set traps, and prepare for long, harsh winters, the other girls her age busied themselves with keeping up with popular clothing brands and new makeup trends.

Olivia had stuck out like a sore thumb that first year. She'd desperately wanted to talk to Tucker. She'd written to him several times, but eventually stopped after the silence from his end became too painful. During *the* conversation with her mother, she learned that her mother had neglected to mail her letters, and had disposed of the letters that Tucker had sent her.

Yes, her heart ached for what her mother had done, robbing her of a relationship with her dad, a friendship that she'd desperately needed at the time, but it ached more for her father. What must he have felt to have his only child taken from him?

She'd spent the day yesterday boxing up her father's things. Boxes were now piled on top of one another in the back room. Out of sight, but still haunting her. They were the possessions of a man she hardly knew, yet at the same time evoked old memories.

He had kept so many of her things. Favorite childrens books, battered and worn with love, toys that she'd completely forgotten about, and a small jewelry box with a dancing ballerina. He'd even kept shells that she had collected as a child from the port. Then there were the photographs. Handfuls of old photographs, her father and mother on their wedding day, another of Olivia as a baby in her mother's arms, and then one of her in her father's arms. Photos of her in the front of the cabin, pointing a twig at the camera - demanding something. Birthdays, all of them, until the year she and her mother left. Olivia blowing out a single candle when she turned one, wearing a bright yellow dress. Then blowing out twelve. She looked so *happy*. Her cheeks plump even then, her smile wide and genuine. That would have been the last year she spent in Alaska.

She had asked for the wallpaper to be taken down before she arrived. From the pictures the relator had emailed, she could see that her father hadn't changed much in the way of decoration over the years. The cabin now smelled of fresh paint, walls now a plain yet warm off-white. She had decided to toss the furniture. It was old and looked mildew stained. She'd ordered a few items; a bed, sofa, armchair, kitchen table and chairs from a reasonably priced furniture store in Anchorage and had them shipped over to the island. It had cost her a pretty penny, but today she was glad she'd done it. All she needed now were a few homey touches, wall decorations, curtains to make the place looked lived-in.

Yes, the cabin would serve its purpose. She was particularly pleased with the open fireplace. She couldn't remember even *seeing* one since she left Alaska, and the prospect of cold nights spent huddled up by the roaring flames with a book and a glass of wine seemed like absolute heaven.

Olivia already felt more content than she had in a long time. It would be strange living back here and adjusting to the harsh climate and back-to-basics lifestyle, but it was what she needed. She had to have some space to get her head on straight without being constantly surrounded by crowds and people.

She reached for her heavy fur-lined parka, on her way out to assess the back clearing. She grabbed the handgun from the entrance table, recalling the warnings about the high bear and wolf population. It wasn't currently mating season, but it was better to be safe than sorry.

She stomped around the frosty grass outside. Icy blasts from the sea hit her full force. As cold as the air was up here, it was also fresh. Olivia remembered that from her childhood. Air pure and clean, unsullied by city pollution. She made her way to the back of the house, her hands firmly shoved into her pockets to keep warm.

The backyard was littered with a few rusted buckets and an old gas can, the end of a torn, frayed clothesline swayed gently in the breeze. The grass was wild and overgrown, and what was left of the small patio off the back door was covered in weeds, many of the paving stones broken. Fixing it would be a summer job, certainly not one she needed to bother with now.

She was drawn inexplicably to the edge of the clearing by the hint of a distant memory. Stepping over the chicken wire fence, she followed the small familiar path towards the tree line. How many times in her life had she walked this trail? Every step felt vaguely familiar, but the view had changed. She remembered how the grass used to come up to her shoulders. Now it grazed her thighs. The forest loomed ahead, impossibly large, another world entirely. It seemed almost reassuring. Those Sitka Spruces and Alder trees felt like old familiar friends standing watch, braving the constant battering from the sea winds and offering respite within the forest depths.

Tucker. His name slammed into her conscience as she reached for the cold bark of the nearest spruce. Her feet kept taking her along an imaginary path, one that echoed of familiarity. As she neared her destination, memories flooded her.

She could see him, hair in wild, unkempt tufts, running through the undergrowth in scuffed track shoes and tattered jeans, calling out her name. The leaves damp underfoot, their laughter echoing for miles. His impatience, "You're too slow, hurry up Liv! I want to show you!" Crouching down, eyes earnest and his breath coming out like smoke, warming her face. Mud-stained hands, pulling at moss and uncovering three bright blue eggs in a nest. Removing his sweatshirt, then covering the eggs to keep them warm.

She didn't know that boy anymore. And, she wasn't that girl anymore. Both were long gone, a faded memory. She made her way further through the trees into the forest, appreciating the warmth, a relief from the wind. Olivia wondered if Tucker even lived in Alaska anymore. Probably not. His father had run a local shop, a camping supply store. Olivia had seen Sterling Outfitters chain stores pop up all over the place in the last five years. The Sterling brothers had obviously done very well at transforming a little outdoor goods store in Hole-in-the-wall, Alaska to a popular national retailer of outdoor recreation equipment. It would be unlikely that Tucker Sterling would still live around here. He would be filthy rich, the whole world his oyster. He was probably living in California somewhere, married to a svelte blonde and enjoying afternoon dips in their infinity pool with their beautiful blonde children.

Olivia laughed out loud at her assumption. The sound startled her, its ringing bouncing off the trees and causing heavy thumps of snow to cascade down in the distance. *Is that snow?* She could hear something heavy hitting the floor, making rustles in the undergrowth.

She paused, holding her breath. Rather than fading out, the sound was getting louder. She felt her hand grip the gun in her pocket, not on a command from her, but through instinct taking over. There was something approaching. Perhaps whatever it was would pass her by, unnerved by her human scent.

She could tell by the sound of its approach that whatever animal it was, it was large. Wolves made little noise when they ran, so she could count them out. There was only one animal that was large enough to be making the ground rumble beneath her feet. She waited, statue-still, for its approach.

A grizzly. It launched itself over a fallen tree not ten feet away from where Olivia stood, and came to a standstill. Its large eyes met hers, and for all its ferocious majesty, in that moment the grizzly looked as stunned and horrified as she was.

Olivia reached for her gun. *Don't shut down. Don't shut down.* Her left eyelid twitched rapidly and her vision blurred. She tried to remain focused on the bear, watching it study her in the silence of the forest. She was going to have a panic attack. The familiar sensations built up within her, and as she tried to retrieve her gun, black spots danced across the forest floor, obscuring the predator till he was nothing but a distant flickering image, and the world went black.

5

Tucker searched the cupboards and found an old tea kettle tucked away in the far corner of the one above the sink. It was covered in lime scale, but it was usable. He waited patiently for the water to boil on the stove. Liv hadn't moved. He still couldn't believe it was her.

Looking down at her, wrapped snugly in every blanket he could find in the cabin, he felt a wave of melancholy creep over him. In sleep, her eyes looked pinched, with dark shadows beneath them, and her complexion was far too pale. Physically he couldn't smell any illness, and didn't notice anything else amiss. When he'd removed the parka to make her more comfortable, he'd seen the voluptuous curves of her figure, the full breasts that strained against her thermals, a full, round backside. She was thick and curvy, like she'd always been, but now her figure had matured. No, there was *nothing* wrong with her physically. In fact, little Livvy had grown into a gorgeous woman. But something *was* wrong.

Just then, she whimpered softly in her sleep. Her brows were drawn together. Something was definitely wrong, but Tucker had a strong suspicion that her torments were internal. Even in a deep sleep, she looked as if she were haunted by ghosts.

He knew that look. He'd seen men in the Army who appeared, for all intents and purposes normal; able to share a joke and a smoke, telling tales and popping open a can of Bud like they hadn't a care in the world. But at night their screams echoed across the barracks. Twisting and turning in their army-issue bunks, they fought faceless terrors, immutable memories that they white-washed during the day, but at night their consciences would hunt these images down, replaying them, reliving them in technicolor.

What demons haunted his Livvy Harris? In his memories of her, she was wild and free. A girl who was quick to accept a dare, easy to laugh, always had a twinkle in her eye. This Liv was anything but free. She looked caged.

THE KETTLE SCREECHED and shattered the silence. Liv sat bolt upright on the sofa. She turned toward Tucker, her eyes wide and frightened. He could smell the fear coming off her in thick waves.

"Liv - it's just me, Tucker, remember?"

Her expression calmed slightly, but her body still visibly trembled.

"Tucker?" She asked, uncomprehendingly.

"Yeah. Hey." He slowly moved toward the fireplace, and took a seat in the armchair facing her.

"What are you... I thought I saw..." She hesitated, "something in the woods, a bear."

She kept studying him,

"I found you passed out cold on the ground."

Tucker was uncomfortable lying, but it was half true anyway.

"Thank you."

"Not a problem. How are you feeling?"

She looked down at herself, as if checking for injuries. Realizing that everything was okay she shoved the blankets aside.

"I'm... um... fine. So... you still lived here, then?" Her voice was soft, and as sweet as Tucker remembered. It had been a long time since he'd heard Liv's voice. It was like balm.

"Yeah," he smiled at her, "Still here. Well, I travel a lot for business. I help run Sterling Outfitters, and we've got a fishing charter, too."

"It is good to see you." Her fingers fiddled nervously with the blankets. "It's been like what, ten years?"

"Fifteen" Tucker replied.

"Wow. That's a long time."

"Yeah."

Tucker wanted to kick himself. His answers sounded curt even to his own ears. Was he angry with her? For what, leaving her old life behind? He was being irrational. Oddly, the restlessness that was a constant with his bear was gone, but it had been replaced with something else, something more urgent and uncomfortable.

"How are your brothers?" She asked.

"They're good. Wyatt's married, got a baby. Colton's married to the local doctor, Hannah."

Liv smiled, "Port Ursa has a doctor? That's new. I remember getting my appendix removed. I had to be flown over to the mainland. Most exciting moment of my childhood."

"I remember it well," Tucker laughed, "I thought you were *dying*, you hollered so loud."

"It was painful! I'd like to see you handle it any better."

"Huh, I'm much tougher than you, Livalot"

"*Livalot*?" She giggled softly, "I haven't heard that in years. How on earth do you still remember?"

'Livalot' had been his pet name for her. He couldn't exactly remember how it came about, but it had suited her loud, outgoing personality. Back then. This Liv had barely cracked a smile, she wouldn't even hold eye contact with him.

He waved off her question and replied lightly, "Some stuff is easy to remember. I boiled water for tea. I'll make you some"

He rose from the chair. As he did so, he noticed one of the blankets sliding down to the floor. He reached forward to pick it up, his arm outstretched. Liv flinched backward.

"Whoa, I'm not going to bite." Tucker said the last words gently, but stepped backward, his hands raised in a gesture of surrender.

"S...sorry. Just a bit shaken up, that's all, after the woods."

He nodded. She'd had a panic attack in the woods, literally collapsing in fear. Damn, he should have been more attentive, he berated himself.

"Lie back down, I'll get that tea."

He moved over toward the kitchen, and watched her settle back down into the sofa. He re-boiled the water, removing the kettle from the stove before it made any more noise, and hunted around for tea bags. The crackling of the wood in the fire made the cabin feel cozy, and he thought Liv might have dozed off she was so quiet. When he looked over he saw her staring, mesmerized, into the flames.

He brought the tea over, holding it out toward her. She didn't notice his approach, so he spoke her name, "Liv?"

She spun around on the sofa, startled. Her arm flew out and knocked the tea out of Tucker's hand. It fell and smashed onto the floor.

"Oh my God!" She jumped up off the sofa, backing away from Tucker. Her eyes looked wild, flitting about the room—the door, the windows, and finally on the broken cup on the floor.

"My fault," Tucker held out a hand to stop her from approaching and stepping on the broken china, "I'll get a mop."

"No," she protested, "Please don't. Can you...can you just leave? Please. I'm sorry, Tucker, obviously I'm not in the right frame of mind for guests."

Her voice betrayed a shortness of breath, and her chest rose rapidly as the words flew from her mouth in a hurried tirade. He was worried about her. Three times now she had reacted with unprecedented fear, her body shooting straight into breakdown mode. This behavior wasn't normal.

"Okay, Liv," he spoke softly, holding his hands up in a placating gesture as he backed away toward the door, "I'll leave. It's alright. Take it easy."

She looked as if she were either about to collapse on the floor or break down crying. It physically pained him to leave her in this state. He wanted to wrap her in his arms and assure her that nothing bad would happen to her, that he would stay and protect her. But, the last thing he wanted to do was panic her further by insisting he stay.

"I'm just going to write down my number," he grabbed a pen and paper from the small table by the door, "So you can reach me if you need to. Okay?"

She just stared at him wide eyed, frozen to the spot. Hurriedly he scribbled his information down and waved her goodbye before shutting the door quietly behind him.

Standing in the bitterly cold air outside her house, Tucker took stock of what had just happened. It was a miracle and a blessing that Liv Harris was back in Port Ursa, but his Liv was *not* alright.

He wanted to know why.

6

He's somewhere in the house. I can feel him, and smell him. Somewhere, but I can't see him. The walls keep moving, jittering and flickering like florescent strip lighting. I'm stumbling, there must be something wrong with my legs; they keep thinking I'm walking upstairs, but the surface is flat so I stumble and slump into a wall.

If I could only see him, then I'd be able to get away. I could run, but if I don't know where he is, I can't run and I can't hide. Every shadow is his. I stumble into our bedroom, except it doesn't quite look like our bedroom. The arrangement is all wrong, and the walls are white. In our actual bedroom, the walls are painted a light dove grey, a color I picked out because I thought it was soothing. The bed sheets are white, but there's blood on them. Only on my side. Blood pooling in an indent of the pillow, and spread across the sheets. In some places, it's fresh and a bright crimson and in others it's dark and stale. It will be a nightmare to get out in the wash. He won't be happy about that.

I'm somewhere else now. In the utility room with the washer and dryer. I remember this! This was the first time. I'm watching myself from the ceiling. It's strange because I've never seen the top of my head before, it doesn't really look like me. This woman has a nice tan; she's wearing an old pair of jeans and a white tank top. She's pretty, wiping sweat off her brow. It's a warm day outside, the sun's filtering in through one of the small windows at the top of the room. I'm not surprised she's warm, the machinery makes this room warm even in winter.

He walks in. He's bigger than I remember. He's drunk, I can tell by the way he stands against the door frame. He's got his belt buckle undone, and his shirt hangs sloppily out of his pants. My heartbeat is accelerating; I know what's coming. The girl below me doesn't. She's smiling at him. He's leering at her. I know that she thinks she's going to get lucky. His voice is low and soft. She doesn't yet know that's a danger sign, stupid girl thinks it's an invitation.

Bam. He's backhanded her across the jaw. She's fallen backwards, and hit her spine on the corner of the washing machine. She falls on the floor. He says something else, I can't remember what it was now, and then he kicks her in the stomach. He's only wearing office loafers, so it's not that bad.

She lies there for a long time after he's gone. She is crying quietly. I want to laugh at her, this is nothing! She thinks she might have lost the baby. She hasn't, it's fine. She'll lose it later, in about two months because she broke a plate.

It's a different day. A different time. It's sunny, again, but I'm wearing lots of layers. I don't remember being hot in them, ever. Layers of cotton and cashmere, lovely and soft and warm. I had a very generous expense account, and it was always being topped up so I could buy whatever I wanted. And I did. I spent lots of time on shopping sites, searching for hours, reading all the product details in full, imagining how each piece would feel next to my skin. Then it would arrive in the mail, carefully wrapped in folds of pink tissue, sometimes with lovely thick bows of velvet, and I would think that maybe this item would make me different. I would be better, sexier and more confident, like the model in the picture. I wouldn't make so many mistakes, and we'd be happy. I could be happy.

On this day, I'm wearing a long jacket, and beneath that is a powdery blue sweater, the softest of them all. I was coming back from a follow up appointment at the doctors after my miscarriage. It hadn't been a good day. It's never a good day when people talk to me. They ask too many questions, especially doctors.

When he kisses me, I don't taste Jim Beam. I thought I was okay. His arms snake around my body, lightly. He's being careful not to hurt me. I'm so pleased. I think he's been shocked by the loss of our child, and that he's changed, he's trying to be loving and we're going back in time to holding hands when we walk along the waterfront at dusk and eat from trendy street vendors and we kiss like teenagers and laugh. He takes me upstairs, guiding me by the hand. My layers come off. I'm embarrassed by my bruises. I try and cover my body with my arms, but he gently separates my limbs and lays me down on the bed.

He leaves me there, and walks into the next room, promising that he'll be back. I try to feel sexy, I try to clear my mind and think about our bodies, and imagine that mine is different. *Three cracked ribs, a broken collarbone, you had internal bleeding when you came in, ugh.* I can't get Doctor Winslow's voice out of my head. *If you ever want your nose to look the way it did, you'll need reconstructive surgery.* Go away! I'm trying to feel sexy. We're trying to make a fresh start. The doctor is making it impossible with all his warnings.

He walks back in. He's got something in his hand. They're cuffs. Metal. I can tell that he's excited, so I try and be excited too. He takes my arms and puts them over my head. Stretching this way hurts. I think there's something wrong with my arm socket.

He climbs on top of me. He starts rubbing me between my legs. *There are both old and new lacerations on your cervix, and you have severe genital bruising.* It hurts, and I grit my teeth. He thinks I am enjoying myself and rubs harder. The handcuffs are locked. The pain is quite intense now, and I remind myself that it's just old wounds, we are starting again.

He pinches me, beneath my breast. I think he's being playful. The second one is harder. His breathing becomes more labored. He's smiling down at me. I look up at him, and he slaps me, hard, across the face.

It took a really long time for him to run out of energy that afternoon. I guess it was because he was sober, I don't know. It was the last time that I bought anything pretty off the shopping sites.

I am standing in a morgue. My body is laid out on a metal tabletop. My skin is so white it's almost luminous. My eyes are closed, at rest. This image makes me smile. I look beautiful. My hair is fanned out around me, it's back to the lush thickness I used to have. As I stare at my white skin, marks start *to appear. Deep blue and purple bruises, covering my face, my torso, legs and arms. There's a few marks around my neck, those don't look very pretty. But they dim and fade as I keep watching; a light show on my corpse. A little baby is crying, softly, somewhere.*

OLIVIA WOKE WITH A START. Jumping off the sofa, she rushed through the cabin to the bathroom and heaved in the toilet. Nothing came out but bile. She hadn't eaten anything since last night. She chastised herself. The nightmares were worse when she didn't eat regular meals. Leaning her forehead against the cool bathroom tiles, she struggled to catch her breath.

In PTSD recovery terms, today had not gone well. She should call Doctor Young and speak to him. She should put in some productive action like looking for another local therapist or some support groups on the mainland. Physically she was far from danger. Hundreds of miles from her past, but mentally she had little control over what her subconscious chose to hold on to.

Olivia rose from the bathroom floor. Splashing her face with the icy Alaskan water, she forced herself into the present moment. Food. That was self-care step one, according to Doctor Young. She'd been to the market yesterday, stocking the fridge with tons of fresh vegetables and meat. As she made her way back into the kitchen, she noticed the fire dying out in the hearth. She had slept most of the day. Outside, the colors of a twilight sky were splashing purple and blue hazes across the room.

She felt a wave of guilt and embarrassment at the way she'd treated Tucker. No doubt the guy would turn tail and run the opposite direction as fast as he could the next time he saw her. He should, too. She was bad news. Totally messed up. Besides, he wasn't the boy she'd once known anymore. He probably had a wife or girlfriend in Port Ursa, an entire life that she knew nothing about. A life, she recalled, she had barely asked him about.

She chopped the vegetables at the sink, taking out her frustration on carrots and potatoes. The setting sun made the trees that circled the house appear almost black. She admired the sky from the window, and found herself enjoying the stillness for the first time since her arrival.

A slight movement at the tree line made her do a doubletake. At the edge, just inside the clearing, a monstrous black shape was shadowed by the trees. Olivia froze. There was no mistaking it. A grizzly. Probably the biggest one she'd ever seen. She watched for several minutes, straining her eyes, before determining with a good degree of certainty that it was, in fact, the same grizzly she'd encountered earlier in the woods. It yawned. It yawned, exposing a ferocious-looking set of fangs, followed by a tongue flickering out and licking the end of its nose. It shifted slightly, lowering its haunches as if getting into a more comfortable position.

Watching the large beast, Olivia was overcome with a sense of peace that she hadn't felt in a very long time. As tranquility settled over her, she felt in no immediate danger from the bear. It certainly didn't look like it had any great desire to beat down her cabin door to make a snack out of her. If anything, it was the picture of serenity, calmly minding its own business while she watched.

Oddly enough, she hadn't thought about what might have transpired between the time when she'd passed out in the woods in front of a giant grizzly bear, and the moment Tucker found her unconscious and brought her to the cabin. What she did know was that if the bear had wanted to eat her, it certainly would have. In fact, she would have been its easiest meal of the year, falling to the ground at its feet.

She studied the bear some more. No, he looked to her more like... a guard dog. She snickered at the thought. A guard bear. But, sitting out there at the edge of the clearing, looking around languidly, the bear reminded her more of a domesticated, rather than a wild, animal.

It was wishful thinking on her part, a bit fantasy, a bit whimsy, yet Olivia couldn't help but smile at the thought of her own personal 'guardian grizzly'.

If only it could protect her from her own nightmares.

7

Sterling Outfitters was jam packed. The weather forecast called for a clear spell that would hit this coming Friday and last the entire weekend. Hordes of mainland tourists would plan to spend the weekend bird watching, hiking and whale spotting off the Port Ursa coast. The more affluent of these visitors hunted eagerly for the latest in high-tech equipment to better enjoy the experience.

Tucker avoided the front entrance. Shopping crowds gave him a headache. He went through the warehouse entrance instead, which backed onto the shipping port. Pulling open the runner door, he was met by Colton chatting with a supplier, both standing next to a four-man tent.

"Get a load of this Tucker, a two second open, brand new guy line system, lightest in its class and feather-light aluminum poles. It's incredible."

Colton barely glanced at his brother as he spoke, so fascinated was he by the Geodesic tent design. Colton got pretty passionate about all things camping, as they all did, but whenever Colton had the chance to geek out over new specs, he could spend hours lost to the world.

"Nice," replied Tucker. He was distracted, and in no real mood to engage in a lengthy debate about the attributes of the latest tent designs. The supplier looked like he was more than happy to indulge Colton, so he left them to it.

Wyatt was in the warehouse office. It had one entrance, which allowed access to the warehouse space, and one that took them straight through to the shop floor. Wyatt had the latter shut firmly. He too avoided the mayhem of shopping crowds like the plague.

Wyatt looked up from the pile of invoices scattered across the desk, his expression quickly turning to surprise as he took in Tucker's uncharacteristically disheveled appearance. Tucker was usually meticulously groomed, a military habit that was virtually unbreakable. This morning, he looked like he'd slept in last night's clothes, and he sported a thick layer of stubble across his chin and jaw.

"Y' alright?" he inquired, "Cause you look like shit."

"Thanks brother," Tucker replied, "How's Haley and the baby?" He swiftly changed the subject as he sat himself down awkwardly on one of the office chairs.

"They're fine...as you know, because you saw them a few days ago." Wyatt dropped his pen and leaned back in his chair, giving Tucker his full attention.

"Do you wanna tell me what's going on, Tuck?"

"Nothing, really." Tucker blew out a long, slow breath, "I saw Liv Harris yesterday. She's living at her old man's place on the top of Longview Drive."

"Whoa... is that place even habitable? I thought it was falling-down derelict."

"It is now. She's had a lot of work done to it," Tucker shrugged, "It looks good."

"She alright?" Wyatt asked gently. It had been a long time since any of them had seen Olivia Harris. It had obviously shaken Tucker.

"Yeah. She's...okay."

Tucker hesitated. His brother wouldn't be too impressed when he found out that Tucker had tracked her down in bear form and scared the living crap out of her.

"I kind of worry about her up there by herself."

Wyatt nodded, "I understand the concern but the wolves have been behaving themselves since Drake took over. As far as I'm aware, there's not much else to worry about other than the occasional wild coyote, and they wouldn't venture any further than the backyard at nighttime. You know that."

"Yeah. I don't know, she seems kinda... jumpy," Tucker replied. *Jumpy*, Tucker thought to himself, *was an understatement.* He'd seen downright terror in her eyes.

"She's probably just forgotten what it's like up here. The cold, the quiet. It's not for the faint hearted. Haley still gets anxious when she's left in the house alone at night."

Haley had been a New Yorker before coming to Port Ursa and marrying Wyatt. It had taken her a long time to adjust, not just to the cold, but the wilderness and its prevailing silence.

"I can put on a watch up there if you like," continued Wyatt, "It wouldn't be any trouble."

"No, man, it's all good. I got it covered."

Wyatt reappraised Tucker's appearance. Clearly his brother had been keeping an eye on Olivia throughout the night. As the oldest of the brothers, Wyatt could recall the bond shared between Tucker and Olivia when they were younger. Wherever Olivia was, Tucker had never been far behind and vice versa - where one was, the other would follow. Wyatt had been a bit jealous of their tight friendship growing up. Before Colton came along he sometimes felt that Olivia had taken away his playmate, and with no younger brother to boss around, Wyatt had often been left alone to bury his head in a book and find other ways to entertain himself. He also remembered the hell that Tucker went through when she left. Olivia had hardly said goodbye - here one day, gone the next. His brother had taken it hard. Now, looking at the past from an adult perspective, and one who had recently bonded with his own mate, Wyatt wondered if there wasn't more to the situation. Could Tucker have found his mate in Liv? It was too young for a shifter to bond, normally, but he'd heard stories that said it was possible.

"Alright. But let me know if you need anything. I'm glad she's back," replied Wyatt.

"Yeah, me too. Nice to see her."

"She changed much?" Wyatt asked, curious as to why Tucker didn't seem too enthusiastic at her return.

"Yes and no. She's just grown up, I guess."

"Who's grown up?" Colton poked his head around the door, catching the end of the conversation, "Certainly not you, Tucker."

Tucker rolled his eyes at his younger brother, "Olivia Harris. She's back in Port Ursa."

"Yeah, I know. I got a snow mobile delivery this morning with her name on it at the Harris address. Threw me a bit."

"Is it ready to go?" Tucker asked, rising hastily from his chair.

Colton raised his eyebrows in surprise, "Err, yeah. What the hell happened to you, man? You're supposed to sleep on top of the mattress, not under it... and a shave wouldn't hurt, either."

"I'll deliver it." Tucker tried to sound off-hand, but he was undermined by Wyatt's smirk.

"Oh, I get it," Colton's eyes lit up, "Tucker's going to add another notch to his bedpost. Nice one, bro."

"Shut the fuck up, Colt. You don't know what the hell you're talking about." Tucker grumbled as he strode from the room.

He found a snowmobile ready for delivery alongside the back of the warehouse. It looked like it had seen better days—last century. He checked the label. The label read Olivia Harris. *Oh, hell no. No way.*

"Colton?" Tucker shouted to the empty expanse of warehouse.

"Yeah?"

"C'mere a sec."

He waited for Colton to make his way through the piles of supplies.

"What's up?"

"This," he kicked the snowmobile, "It's a pile of junk."

"Still runs. It's gotten the twice-over. It may look like a steaming pile of cow dung, but all working parts are up to safety spec. It's what she wanted, third hand, cheapest we had." Colton replied defensively.

Tucker walked over to the newest model - an *Expedition Le,* perfect for track and snow riding, with unequalled precision and the safest in its class.

"Hands off that one. It's for a Russian oligarch coming to watch Narwhals next week. Don't even think about it," Colton warned, his eyes narrowing.

"Colton, order another one. It will be here in a few days. I'm taking this for Liv. Put it on my bill."

His brother looked at him if he'd lost his mind.

"Are you fucking serious? She'll be fine on that one!" Colton protested.

"No. No, she won't, because she's not going anywhere near that one." Tucker's stern tone left zero room for argument.

"I'm charging you for shipping costs of that one, *and* the new one."

Tucker sighed, "Whatever, man."

"Jesus," Colton snapped irritably, "It's not like you to go to such lengths to get your dick wet."

Tucker ignored him. Wondering, not for the first time, how the lovely and caring Hannah ever put up with her dickhead of a husband.

8

Olivia spent the morning walking the clearing around her cabin. Distinctive bear tracks made a neat circle around the circumference of the property, as if the bear had been patrolling the perimeter throughout the night. A light dusting of snow made his paw prints obvious, along with evidence of him going back around them time and time again.

Olivia wondered if maybe it was some sort of predatory behavior, marking out the territory of the prey he later planned to attack, but she dismissed the thought. She'd never heard of such behavior from a bear, and her instincts remained set on the idea that this bear was her guardian, not her predator.

Idly she contemplated leaving food out. She had a few steaks in the freezer, but judging by the size of the bear it wasn't having any problems getting sustenance. The tracks were some of the biggest bear paw prints she'd ever seen.

Coming in from the cold, she knelt to rekindle the fire while weighing her options for the day's activities. There were a couple things left to do around the house, the cupboards needed to be cleaned out for one. But she was also conscious of spending too much time alone in the cabin. She'd promised Doctor Young she wouldn't isolate herself. Maybe it would be better for her to go into town and have a look around, see how much the place had changed. She might even run into Tucker. The thought sent little butterflies of excitement flittering around in her stomach, but her excitement was swiftly dampened by the memories of her behavior yesterday. Tucker wouldn't be approaching her loony butt any time soon. Her cheeks heated at the memory of the brand of crazy that he'd been a witness to yesterday. He undoubtedly thought she was a first class nutball.

A slight rumbling sound brought her back to the present and she froze. The sound gradually increased until she was able to identify it. It was a truck engine. It gradually got louder, thundering through the tranquility of the morning until it stopped just outside her cabin. Olivia's heart lurched in her chest, her pulse started racing, and her palms grew damp. She sidled over to the front window and peeked through a crack in the old, worn draperies. Who could be coming this far up Longview Drive? And why?

She audibly exhaled when the engine cut and Tucker leapt out. His Timberland boots crunched the ice underfoot. Olivia couldn't help but admire his long, lean legs encased in dark-wash denim jeans. He was wearing a light jacket, nothing more than a Gore-Tex windbreaker that was far too insubstantial for the current weather.

Yesterday, she'd been so shaken up from seeing him again, and the fact that their first face-to-face in however-many years had taken place in her cabin as she struggled into consciousness. She hadn't had the presence of mind to notice much about him except his soulful, large brown eyes. The same eyes that had been locked in her memory for all these years. When he turned to walk up the drive, Olivia ducked from the window, not wanting to be caught spying.

He knocked on the door.

Olivia's tongue was stuck to the roof of her mouth and she found it hard to swallow. She wasn't entirely sure she could handle a one-on-one with Tucker right now. She didn't want him to witness another round of wacko Livvy, and she was feeling so unsteady at the moment that she wasn't at all confident that it wouldn't happen again. On the other hand, Tucker was the only person she knew in Port

Ursa, and their friendship had once meant a lot to both of them. Perhaps it could be rekindled?

Olivia took a few deep breaths and opened the door a crack.

"Hey," she smiled at Tucker somewhat breathlessly. Despite the practiced breathing, she could feel her accelerated heart rate. *Get a grip!*

Tucker beamed back at her.

"How are you feeling?" he asked.

"Fine. Better than yesterday," she answered through the four-inch gap, "I'm sorry about all that."

Olivia hung on to the door, blocking his entrance into the cabin. She knew that manners dictated that she invite him in, but she still felt unsure and slightly wary of his presence.

He nodded. An awkward silence followed. Olivia stared at the floor, noticing the scuff-marks on her battered Converse. She would need a good pair of boots if she was going to trek around out here in the wilderness.

"I brought over the snowmobile you ordered. Thought you might need it sooner rather than later." Tucker gestured over to his truck where she could make out a lump beneath a canvas covering.

"You didn't need to do that!" She exclaimed, "I'm so sorry, I thought that your delivery guys would do it or something."

"It's not a problem," Tucker scratched the back of his head, "I noticed it in the warehouse by chance, and figured I'd bring it up, see how you're doing."

"Thanks very much. I... I really appreciate it."

Damn, he wasn't doing a very good job at this. "Want me to show you how to use it?"

Olivia contemplated the offer. She felt tongue tied in front of him. Their conversation had been stilted and awkward yesterday. He had been so kind to her and she wanted him to stay now, but until she could get more of a handle on her anxiety, she would only embarrass herself in front of him again.

"It's okay. I'm sure I can manage." Olivia replied at last, forcing a smile, so as not to appear unfriendly.

"It's really no trouble," he replied, "We can take it for a ride if you'd like?"

Was that a hint of hope in his voice? No, she must have been imagining it.

"Really - I'll be fine."

"Okay," Tucker started to back away from the door, "I'll just unload it. Anywhere in particular you want it?"

Olivia shrugged, looking wildly around the front yard.

"Anywhere would be fine."

He smiled briefly at her - a very different smile to the one he'd given her when he'd first arrived. Olivia sighed quietly as he walked toward the truck.

The wind caught his jacket as he headed toward the vehicle, blowing it up and backwards awarding Olivia with a glimpse of a perfect ass, firm and muscular. Most of Tucker's appearance looked so unfamiliar to her now - from the back he cut the figure of a hot, well-built stranger. The dark chocolate-brown hair that she remembered from her youth, that was always worn too long and curled in disarray at the ends, was gone. He now sported a short military-style cut. It made him look tougher and more aggressive from the back - but one look at those large brown eyes and you couldn't mistake him for anything other than the decent, kind man he was.

He removed his jacket, shoving it through the window of his truck. Beneath it he wore nothing but a plain black t-shirt, and Olivia's jaw dropped. It was surprising that he was standing in the ice-cold arctic air with nothing more than flimsy cotton separating him and the elements, but what was even more of a shock was the impressive specimen of manhood that Tucker Sterling had grown into.

His biceps were thickly muscled and clearly obtained through outdoor labor, not hours in a gym. She didn't think that would be Tucker's style anyway. They bulged impressively as he single-handedly lifted the snow machine, which was easily the same size as he was, off the back of the truck and gently lowered it onto the ground.

"Hey," Olivia looked skeptically at the Skidoo, "Are you sure that's the right one?"

"Yep." His reply was terse.

"Um, I bought a really old one. Secondhand. That looks brand new."

"It is really old. The owners obviously just took good care of it."

Olivia shrugged. It looked brand new to her, but it wasn't like she was an expert or anything.

"Okay. Great." She tried to smile brightly at him, but on seeing his reaction, she knew the smile must have looked fake. *Jesus*, she was messing this up. She took a deep breath and stepped cautiously out onto the front porch.

Tucker stood still, watching her as she slowly approached. His eyes had a guarded quality, as if he was trying to hold back—the same way one might look when trying to approach a skittish animal that might run off into the wild at any second. *He thinks I'm a freak.*

"Just wanted to get a better look." Olivia murmured, wishing she'd stayed in the doorway.

He nodded, and gestured toward the machine. He cleared his throat before speaking, "It's a really good model, uh... even though it's old. Very safe. Easy to handle."

She inspected it, self-conscious of that fact that while she was, she had the unmistakable feeling that he was inspecting *her*.

Olivia straightened up and turned to Tucker, "It looks fantastic. I can't believe I got it so cheap."

He smiled, somewhat wryly, and she blushed without knowing why.

"Nice to see you, Liv."

He reached out his hand and softly brushed away a tendril of hair that had fallen loose from her barrette. She caught her breath as his fingertips touched her skin. The contact felt so searingly hot that she thought for a moment that he'd branded a mark there. But she didn't flinch. *Progress.*

Olivia could see the relief in his eyes as he lowered his hand. Other than hugging Doctor Young, it was the most intimate moment she'd shared with another human being in years. She'd forgotten what human contact felt like. It was a basic need that she'd denied herself for so long.

She stepped back slowly. She wanted Tucker to know that she wasn't rejecting his touch, but at the same time she felt utterly overwhelmed, not really knowing if she wanted to cry or laugh. Or both. Tucker didn't need to witness her emotional turbulence, and she in turn needed time to process. It was enough for today, but it was progress.

"Tucker," she spoke softly, "I'm going to go inside now. Maybe see you around?"

"Yeah, of course. Whenever you want. You have my number. If you need me. I'm at the store. Okay?"

She nodded her understanding.

Tucker smiled at her wistfully, then turned toward the truck. He took a couple steps, then turned back around.

"*Anything*, Liv. If you need *anything* at all." He stressed. Then kept steady eye contact for a couple more seconds. "Livalot," he mumbled softly. He knew she was terrified, he could smell it. His shifter senses easily picked up her fear, her racing heartbeat, and increased perspiration. What the hell had her so terrified of him?

Once he was in the driver's seat, and the door of the truck slammed shut, Olivia felt her breathing slowly return to semi-normal. She waved at him from the front window, and then headed for the phone to call Doctor Young.

9

Olivia waited impatiently for nightfall. She'd ridden the new Skidoo into town and spent a few hours exploring what Port Ursa had to offer. It had changed a lot since she'd lived here as a child. It was still your average port side town, with fish eateries, tourist junk and small local grocers, but it was evident that the general demographic had changed. The coffee shops now had a cozy boutique feel, and there were quite a few independent retailers that offered pottery and stylish homeware. The ambience was different too, far more touristy, which gave the main town thoroughfare a bustling and lively feel. As she wandered around, stopping once for a coffee and pastry, she found herself growing to like the area a lot more than she had initially envisioned.

The smell of the sea drifting in from the port had also brought back many memories. That, at least, hadn't changed a bit. She remembered her father taking her out for cockles on Saturday mornings when the fish markets opened, then walking home picking them out of Styrofoam cups. They tasted like salt and seawater.

Not all the memories were good ones. Her mother and father arguing in the grocery store, slammed doors when they got back home, her mother crying quietly in her room a few days before they left for good. Olivia escaping the tension and the uncomfortable atmosphere by running into the woods to hers and Tucker's tree house where he would show up a short time later. He hadn't needed to be told that she needed him. He could just sense it, and always came for her carrying a treasure of some sort in the palm of his hand. Unusual rocks, wild flowers, rainbow oyster shells.

She had tried to ignore the unpleasant memories by making herself busy. Cleaning the already spotless kitchen and then checking the fence to take note of where the worst breaks were so she could get supplies next time she was in town.

When the sun showed signs of retiring, she made supper, another stew. It was the only thing she could think to make that would be warming and hearty enough to repel the cold that she was starting to feel in her bones. She recalled Tucker's light touch, and how in that split second, it had warmed every part of her body from the top of her head down to her ice-cube toes.

Doctor Young had been nothing but enthusiastic at hearing about her old childhood friend. She had held back, though, not comfortable revealing her less than platonic feelings, the way Tucker had made her heart rate shoot through the roof, or the way his battered jeans hung from his hips, making her stomach plunge downward.

As far as Doctor Young was concerned, the more people Olivia got to know, the better. She had vowed to heed his advice to mingle more, and as soon as the opportunity arose, she would try her best to push herself out of her comfort zone.

Tonight though, she had a non-human priority. Her guardian bear. She lit the fire and dug out the book she'd bought at the bookstore cafe she'd visited earlier. It was a very thick romance novel - something that would hopefully keep her going for days. She used to be an avid thriller reader, but the last few years had put her off any suspense novels. Her nightmares were bad enough without them.

Olivia settled herself down on the sofa, snuggling with a thick comforter. She would wait until the sun set completely before checking to see if her bear had returned.

The first time she peered out of the kitchen window, she saw no sign of him. The Spruce trees loomed large over the clearing, a sliver of brilliant red sunset still glaring along the surface of the forest floor as it dipped down over the bay. Olivia sighed and retreated to the sofa. Ten minutes later, she was back at the window.

This time, she saw his familiar bulk at the edge of the clearing. He was seated a little further forward than yesterday, and the sunset turned his dark brown fur a deep russet. She leaned closer to the window, watching his still form. He was faced toward the front yard, looking away from the side of the cabin. This way she could admire him freely without worrying that she'd frighten him off. Not that that was particularly likely. He seemed perfectly at ease in 'human' territory.

Leaning closer still to the window, Olivia knocked a serving spoon into the sink. It made an almighty clatter, and she jumped in alarm. When she looked up, the bear was staring directly at her. She was taken aback by how human his expression seemed, inquisitive and questioning, with his head tilted to the side. Olivia smiled at him from the window, and he lowered his stare.

She was going to throw caution to the wind. Turning from the window she pulled on her shoes without bothering to tie the laces and grabbed the thick comforter that was strewn on the couch and wrapped herself. The cold air smacked her in the face as she opened the front door, but she merely pulled the comforter tighter and closed the door softly behind her. She didn't want to startle him.

Her shoes crunched over the icy ground. Olivia found herself praying that the bear wouldn't run off into the woods at the sound of her approach. He would have smelled and heard her by now, no matter how quiet she tried to be. Something inside of her longed for him.

As she turned the corner, the bear sat facing her. It had moved up from its haunches, and was now in an upright position. With his furry underside exposed, Olivia could ascertain that he was male. By his general size and muscle density she had suspected as much. His bold behavior was also a masculine trait; females tended to be far more skittish and wary.

She approached slowly, keeping her palms faced outward and her head low. When she was only a few feet in front of him, she glanced upward. He looked extremely puzzled by her behavior, and as she raised her head to look him directly in the eyes, he lazily scratched at his stomach. Olivia wanted to laugh. It was such a human thing to do, and seemed purposefully obnoxious.

Okay, he's definitely not scared of me, and he doesn't seem to want to eat me either.

She closed the gap between them. In the silence of the forest, she could hear her own blood pumping rapidly around her body, and the shallow breathing of the bear. As human as some of his movements were, Olivia couldn't quite rest easy when faced with the razor-sharp claws at the end of his paws, and the powerful looking frame that could tear her apart in seconds. Yet, she felt more comfortable with this eight-hundred-pound grizzly bear than she did with most humans.

Olivia crouched lower to the ground, to make certain she didn't appear threatening. When the bear didn't move, or seem in any way bothered, Olivia shuffled a little closer. His musky smell of wild animal mixed with the aroma of pine and wood was intoxicating. It smelled so *familiar* to her, almost haunting, as if the bear had climbed out of her old childhood closet.

Slowly, and with a trembling hand, Olivia reached out her fingers. The desire to feel his soft, thick fur had become overpowering.

She met his deep brown eyes, making an unspoken request. His stare managed to speak volumes. She'd never witnessed an animal with such capacity for expression. Feeling that it was safe, she sunk her hand gently into his coat. She felt the grizzly tense beneath her. She held still for a moment, allowing them both to get used to the sensation. When Olivia felt his muscles relax, she continued, stroking down the thick muscle of his deltoid.

He was so warm, the heat passing into her slowly spreading through to her entire torso. Her caress increased in pressure, and she heard a deep resonant rumble that sounded like a juddering motor.

She was stunned for a moment, before laughing softly to herself as she realized he was doing something akin to purring.

"You like that, huh?" she said softly.

The bear nudged his muzzle toward her face, gently grazing her forehead with his nose. She moved her hand upward, threading her fingers in the shorter fur that surrounded the side of his face. It was silkier, and she smiled at the luxurious feel of him beneath her touch.

"You're a beautiful creature, you know that, right?" she cooed at him.

The bear gave a short grunt, as if he was responding to her question.

"Yeah, I know you can understand me, clever bear."

The forest was now drenched in the complete black of night, the only light pooling in splotches across her yard from where she'd left the fire going and her small table lamp on. Olivia thought it looked cozy in her cabin, but she was so irresistibly pulled to the bear, she didn't want to leave him.

She started to feel drowsy, being lulled by the flickering lights and the sounds of her bear's purring. She leaned closer toward him, leaning her body against his torso, intensifying her exposure to his warmth. Hearing no complaint from the bear, she rested her head against his chest.

Soon her eyelids became leaden and she closed her eyes, welcoming a dreamless sleep.

10

He'd left her in the morning. He had held her all night long wrapped against his fur, his intense body heat keeping the worst of the cold at bay, and for once the typically ice-cold air had thawed to a crisp, cool morning. He had transformed back into his human self, and thankfully, got the hell out of there just as her eyelids were fluttering and she began making the soft noises of someone coming out of deep sleep. If she had opened her eyes to see Tucker lying next to her, naked, she would have run for the hills screaming.

Tucker travelled home to change and shower. On his way back to his cabin he'd called his old army buddy, Drake, who was now Alpha of the wolf shifter pack.

Tucker was pulling on an old sweatshirt when the doorbell rang. He went to let Drake in, still drying his hair with a towel.

"Looks like you started this morning late. Not like you," Drake observed as he stepped through the threshold.

"I had good reason. You want a coffee or something?'

Drake nodded, and took a seat at the breakfast bar as he watched Tucker pop a coffee pod into the Keurig. Tucker's cabin was situated at the highest incline on Harpoon Road, a five-minute drive from the port. It was large and spacious but sparsely decorated with very little furniture. It was the only way his "restless bear" as he referred to it, could ever feel at home cooped up indoors.

"So, what's up?" Drake questioned after Tucker placed two steaming mugs down in front of them.

"I have a favor to ask. I know you're still tight with Jackson at Intel. There's someone I need looked into."

Drake's eyes narrowed. He knew Tucker wouldn't ask for a favor like this unless it was extremely important. He nodded for Tucker to continue.

"A female by the name of Olivia Harris."

Drake had been about to take a sip of coffee, but on hearing the familiar name, the cup was left suspended in midair as he tried to place where he'd heard it before.

"Hang on a second," Drake frowned in confusion, "Olivia.... Liv Harris. Isn't that your childhood friend, Old Man Harris's daughter?"

"Yeah," Tucker sighed heavily, "That's the one."

"Hmmph," Drake muttered. "I'd heard she was back in town." *Of course he had*, Tucker thought. Drake pretty much knew everything that went on around here. That's one of the things that made him so good at his role as Alpha.

"Don't you think that if you have questions, you should be asking her?"

Tucker let out a sigh, and rubbed a hand across his closely cropped hair. "I don't think I'm gonna get a straight answer to the kind of questions I need answered."

Drake eyed his friend speculatively.

"When's the last time you saw her?" He asked eventually.

"Last night. She's moved back to Port Ursa."

"Look, there's obviously something else here, something you're not telling me, so let's have it. Spill."

Tucker scratched the back of his head. He didn't know how much to divulge to Drake, but if he was going to ask him to break certain rules to get information, honesty was the best, and probably the only, policy. Besides, he trusted Drake's discretion.

"I'm worried about her. She's a ghost of the girl she once was, jittery, jumpy. Drake, I'd bet my left nut she's suffering from PTSD."

Drake raised an eyebrow, "Tucker, man, I got to ask. Are you sure you're not reading too much into this? People change. It happens. Sometimes they change for the worst."

"Yeah, I know, but this is something else." Tucker paused, wondering how much he needed to say.

"She won't make eye contact, any sudden moves and she jumps three feet in the air." Tucker blew out a long breath, "She's got cigarette burns on the back of her neck, Drake. No one does that to themselves."

Drake sat in stunned silence.

"Okay. I'll look into it."

"Thanks, man. I appreciate it. I just don't know how to make her feel safe."

"Well," Drake shrugged, "Sometimes you can't. She'll just have to get there in her own time. All you can do is be there for her. In a *friendly* capacity."

Tucker smarted at the emphasis, "I'm not trying to hit on her!"

"Dude, it's me you're talking to. I've seen you go through women. *Lots* of them. All I'm saying is that she might need a friend rather than a..." he trailed off, "you know."

"I'm not an idiot. I know she's not open to that. It's not my angle."

Drake nodded, his eyes narrowed as he watched his friend suspiciously. "Sonofabitch. It's not, is it. I've never seen you like this before. You care about this girl, don't you?"

"I think she's... She does something to me, being around her. I mean... it's like she soothes me or something. Soothes my bear."

"You said you think she's... what Tuck? You think she's what?"

"My mate. She's my mate."

Drake nodded, his eyes never leaving his friend's. Drake understood. He could see what this meant to Tucker. He knew a wolf would do anything to protect and care for his mate, he was fairly certain that a bear shifter felt the same.

"It'll take me a few days, but Jackson will come up with the goods. Anything in particular you want me to look out for?"

Tucker hesitated before replying, "Check to see if she's taken any legal action. Claims, lawsuits, whatever. Witness identity protection—maybe look into that."

"Alright. Consider it done."

Tucker nodded, "I owe you."

"Don't worry about it. Sounds like she needs help."

Tucker had known Drake would understand. Drake had been more that an excellent soldier. In Afghanistan, he'd been an endless source of courage and support for the men in their unit. The months after their return to Port Ursa, Drake had been an invaluable friend. They'd provided one another with a shoulder to lean on in those first few months when adapting to civilian life posed challenges. He would trust the man with his life.

"I'm gonna head out. I'll be in contact in a few days' time."

Drake stood to leave, and Tucker walked him to the door. They slapped each other on the back, and Drake made his way down the drive to his truck.

When he was out of sight, Tucker leaned heavily against the doorframe. Liv wouldn't be at all happy if she knew what he was doing, but after the jittery behavior and those bright red marks he'd spied on her skin last night, he was willing to take that chance.

11

It was late afternoon when Olivia noticed the broken latch on the bathroom window. It had been covered by wooden blinds, so she had no idea how long it had been broken. She couldn't help but feel irritated by the contractors she'd hired to rehab the cabin. Surely they should have noticed something like that. Unless, or course, it had happened after she'd moved in, but she couldn't imagine how.

The window was fairly large. Back home she would have assumed the worst, but there was nothing of value to steal in the cabin, and intruders in a place like Port Ursa were almost unheard of.

Well, she told herself, *time to put the 'living alone in the wilderness' skills to the test.*

She trudged out to the small shed in the back, to hunt around for a toolbox. When she eventually located it, she found that her father had kept it well stocked. She felt another twinge of her heart strings as she dug around inside of it looking at the tools. She regretted that she hadn't been able to carry on any type of relationship with him for the last nine years of his life. For some reason, she felt guilty, even though none of it was her fault. It hadn't been his either, yet for all those years, she'd blamed him.

There were so many different tools. There were things she'd never seen before, and had no idea what their purpose was. Grabbing a screwdriver, she trudged back in and went to work trying to loosen the old latch mechanism. The entire thing would have to come out and be replaced. That would mean a trip into town to the hardware store. Again, her mind went to Tucker. He'd said to call him anytime. For anything, and he seemed as though he really meant it. If Olivia was normal, she'd give him a call and ask him to meet her for lunch or something. The thing is, she didn't think she could be normal for the entire hour it would take to have lunch in a public place with people around. She felt disgusted with herself. Sometimes she was sure that she'd never be normal again.

As she looked closer at the window, she could see where the contractors had obviously patched some wood that had been dry rotted. They'd done a good job, so it puzzled her that they hadn't noticed that the window latch was broken.

After sleeping outside last night, she found, unexpectedly, that she had a great deal more energy this morning. Sleeping in the warm embrace of her guardian bear had chased away the fearful nightmares, and for the first time in years, she'd slept soundly till morning. She had awakened to find her bear gone, but the memory of his body heat still cocooning her.

She almost had the latch off. The screws were removed, but the metal was stuck to the wood with old paint. She used the screwdriver as a prybar and pushed against it with her full force. *Almost...* The screwdriver slipped, and slashed against her palm. *Sonofabitch!* Olivia cradled her hand to her chest as the blood pooled quickly to the surface and dripped onto the floor.

Rushing over to the sink she tried to wash away the blood to get a better idea of how deep the wound went, but as she ran water over her palm, the profusely gushing blood wasn't letting up. It was deep, and blood, she was afraid, might trigger flashbacks that she'd be unable to control. She could already feel the panic rising. *Think, think.* The bleeding didn't look like it would be subsiding any time soon. She needed to apply pressure, and a doctor. Tucker had mentioned that there was a doctor in Port Ursa now. She needed to get herself to the doctor.

You can do this, Olivia Harris.

Wrapping her hand in an old t-shirt, Olivia pulled on her coat and grabbed the keys to the snowmobile. She had passed the new clinic on her way into town yesterday; she could make it in under ten minutes.

The motor started right up, sliding off over the iced ground. Olivia's biggest concern was keeping the machine steady with only one hand. She'd avoid the main road for safety, traveling through the forest till she came to the back of the building.

The journey was brief, but by the time she saw the path which led to her destination, her back was dripping with sweat and her t-shirt had been fully saturated in her blood. Feeling light-headed, she wandered up to the back entrance, unsteady on her feet and sending up a swift prayer that she wouldn't collapse on the ground before she could reach the door.

"Oh goodness, you poor thing!"

A nurse, about to take her cigarette break, exclaimed loudly at the state of Olivia.

"Help?"

The nurse rushed down the steps, and helped Olivia into the building.

"I'll fetch Doctor Sterling for you, let's just get you settled in here first."

Olivia was escorted into a white room, and the nurse sat her up on the bed.

"Lie down if you need to, I'll get you some water."

She hurried off, the door whooshing shut behind her.

Olivia took a moment to observe her surroundings. She didn't like hospitals or doctor's offices. They represented nothing but shame and exposure for Olivia. As pleasant as everyone in the medical profession had been to her throughout the years, their penchant for the cold hard truth had sent Olivia into spirals of anxiety before every visit. And there had been many.

This place was the cheeriest she'd been in, though. Everything felt bright and clean, and despite the white room, it somehow failed to feel as clinical and sterile as most. It was probably because it was a local clinic. Olivia had only visited colossally large hospitals before, where everything was impersonal and alien.

"Hello."

An attractive woman with a shower of beautiful red gold hair peered around the door. Olivia smiled weakly at her, surprised to find herself warming to the stranger despite her typical doctor's apparel of a white coat, stethoscope and name badge, normally a flashing warning sign for Olivia.

"I'm Doctor Hannah Sterling, may I take a look?"

She gestured to Olivia's bandaged arm. Olivia nodded, and held it out away from her chest. As Doctor Sterling unwrapped the bloodied fabric, the wound seeped fluid and Olivia winced in pain.

"I'm sorry, this will sting a bit," Doctor Sterling surveyed the wound. "It's a deep cut. I'll need to disinfect it properly. May I ask what happened?"

A bolt of cold fear shot through Olivia, an urgent and guttural reaction to the question. It took a moment for her mind to process the fact that this time she could freely tell the doctor how she'd got her injury. There was no need for the practiced lies or the faux bafflement.

"I cut it...with a screwdriver. I was trying to fix a broken latch on my bathroom window. No idea how it had gotten broken, I paid the contractors a pretty penny to go over everything before I moved in."

"Ah, a DIY," Doctor Sterling smiled at her, "A common reason for a patient visit. Before you moved in? You're new to the area, then?" She asked pleasantly.

"Returning. I've taken over my dad's old cabin at the top of Longview."

"Top of... Oh! *You're* Olivia Harris!" The doctor beamed a full mega-watt smile at her, and practically clapped her hands in excitement, "I've heard lots about you from my husband, Colton."

For some inexplicable reason, Olivia's heart sank.

"I'm Tucker's sister-in-law," she smiled knowingly at Olivia.

Oh. Olivia blushed at how evidently transparent her reaction had been.

"Have you seen the town yet? I imagine much has changed since you were here. Have you seen Wyatt or Colton yet?"

"No. Just Tucker. I haven't really been out much since I arrived. There's been a lot to do to the cabin."

Hannah nodded in understanding.

"It was left for quite a few years, wasn't it?"

"Yeah. I had contractors do a lot to it, and now it's really about making the place feel a bit homier."

"Well, go easy over the next few days," Hannah took Olivia's hand gently in hers, ready with a disinfectant swab, "This might hurt."

She cleaned the wound, and Olivia exhaled a small hiss of pain.

"Most scream the place down," commented Hannah, "Your pain threshold is impressive."

Olivia didn't know what to say to that. She couldn't very well tell Doctor Sterling that she was well versed in extreme levels of pain, and had learned a few years ago how to turn screams into whimpers to avoid the neighbors overhearing.

Hannah deftly wrapped up Olivia's hand, securing the bandage firmly.

"I want you to drink some oral electrolytes, just a precaution due to the amount of blood loss. It will help you feel less woozy."

Hannah fetched a small bottle from the cupboard above the sink in the corner of the room, and a paper cup.

"Here," she handed Olivia the cup, "I'm actually closing the clinic now. I'm going to meet Colton in the tavern right down the street. I'd love it if you came?"

"Oh," Olivia hesitated, "I'm not sure. I should probably get back."

"In that case, I'm requesting your company under doctor's orders. I need to keep an eye on you for a few hours."

Olivia deliberated. The idea of spending some time with Doctor Sterling, *Hannah*, was appealing. It had been a long time since she'd had a friend. On the other hand, spending time in a noisy tavern felt hugely overwhelming, and the Sterling brothers...well. Memories.

Maybe Tucker will be there. The thought came into her mind unbidden. As much as she longed to see him again, she wasn't sure she was prepared to suffer through the awkwardness that was completely her fault. No matter how hard she tried, *normal* escaped her.

She was about to decline the invitation politely when she heard Dr. Young's words in her head. *Be extra careful not to isolate yourself up there in Port Ursa. You need to start making friends, rejoining the human race. You may have to force yourself to take baby steps outside your comfort zone, Olivia.*

Hannah waited patiently for her answer, smiling warmly as Olivia weighed the pros and cons.

"I'd be happy to. Thank you." She replied eventually.

"No, thank you! I'm looking forward to getting to know you better. Colton has mentioned that you and Tucker were attached at the hip when the two of you were kids."

Olivia blushed, looking down at the tiled floor.

"Come on," Hannah held open the door, "First round's on me."

Olivia meekly followed Hannah from the clinic, taken aback by the rapid change of direction her day had taken.

12

The women were met by the blast of warm air as they entered Dante's Tavern. A heady and energetic mix of voices, music and clinking glasses purveyed the air, and Olivia found that rather than fear and anxiety, her spirits lightened a bit.

"Let's find Colton," Hannah shouted above the music, "He'll be somewhere in the back."

They wove their way around the crowded bar, until they reached two large pool tables. Sitting behind them, taking up the length of the back of the room, sat two very large and very well-built men. Colton and Wyatt. Older, certainly, but still recognizable to her. Wyatt had his arm casually slung around a petite woman Olivia didn't recognize.

Colton beamed at Hannah's approach and stood to greet her. Olivia didn't remember Colton too well. What she did remember was a dark-haired little boy with perfect features who always wanted to play with Tucker, and Tucker always wanting to escape somewhere with her.

The man in front of her had the echoes of those beautiful features, but he had grown to become far more masculine. Far more. The Sterling brothers had certainly won the genepool lottery, she thought, each one tall, heavily muscled and handsome in his own way.

"If it isn't Olivia Harris," Colton turned to face Olivia after he'd finished embracing his wife. He still had an arm around Hannah's waist, as if marking his claim on her.

"Long time no see. Tucker told us you were back."

He smiled at her openly and warmly. Olivia took a half-step back, slightly afraid he might embrace her in welcome, but he kept his distance as if sensing, correctly, that she would feel uncomfortable.

Wyatt was up next, moving Colton out of the way and holding his arms open in greeting. When he saw Olivia's eyes fly open wide, he froze and extended his hand slowly instead.

"Hi Olivia. It's lovely to have you back."

Olivia shook his hand limply, glad that neither brother seemed particularly prone to breaching personal boundaries. She was happy to see Wyatt; she remembered him fondly as a level-headed teen who did a great job of looking after Tucker and Colton.

"This is my wife, Haley."

He gestured toward a beautiful, delicate, dark haired woman who smiled at Olivia, also holding out her hand.

"It's lovely to meet you Olivia," she spoke softly, with an almost musical tilt to her voice. As with Hannah, Olivia felt an instant warming to the woman.

"You too," Olivia smiled.

"Olivia let me take your coat," Hannah started to shrug hers off, "and I'm going to get us a bottle of wine - does that work for you?"

"That sounds great." She needed the liquid courage. Olivia knew how easily she could slip into being overwhelmed with so many people here, and how desperately she wanted to keep those feelings at bay.

"Come and sit with me," insisted Haley, "I want to hear all about the work you've had done to the cabin."

Olivia laughed and sat down, gesturing her bandaged hand to Haley.

"DIY has not been my strong suit so far," she rolled her eyes, "Attacked myself with a screwdriver this afternoon."

Haley winced in response. They continued to discuss the merits of different homeware stores, and Haley gave advice on the best hidden gems in Anchorage for decently priced vintage furniture. As the conversation progressed, Olivia felt herself relaxing. She stifled a small giggle. She was doing this. She was really doing this. Dr. Young would be proud, she was actually making friends, and getting out in public.

Haley was an easy conversationalist and more than made up for any awkwardness on Olivia's part.

She glanced over at the bar to see if Hannah needed any help, and found her eyes skirting over Hannah, who was chatting animatedly with the barmaid, and instead drawn to a familiar figure at the opposite end of the room. *Tucker.*

Until that moment she hadn't realized that half of her had been waiting anxiously for him to make an appearance. Their eyes met, and Olivia felt a jolt in the pit of her stomach, queasy and wanting - churning her insides. She looked away.

In the next moment, Olivia took stock of her present situation. She'd woken up this morning in a forest, hadn't been expecting to see anyone today and had worn old work clothes to tackle the chores on the house. Those old work clothes were now blood splattered and caked in dried sweat. She could only imagine what kind of state her appearance must be in.

"Haley, I'm just going to go and freshen up," she said, excusing herself from the table.

She hastily escaped to the ladies room, grateful that she wouldn't have to pass Tucker to reach it. There were three other women crowding around the sink mirrors when she entered. They were all dolled up—a little over the top for a night in a local tavern in Smalltown, Alaska. Tight miniskirts, low cut tops, high heeled boots, the three were collectively wearing so many colors they looked like a pride of peacocks.

Olivia waited patiently at the side for them to finish. They smiled blandly at her before continuing their conversation.

"He's here, and oh my gawd, does he look hot tonight!" One of them shrieked in excitement.

"On come on, he looks hot *every* time I see him," the brunette liberally applied a dark shadow to her upper lids, "I've got a feeling it's *my* lucky night tonight."

The third woman snorted in derision, "Oh come on! Tucker wouldn't look twice at you when he's got *me*."

Olivia flinched, staring over at the women who carried on their bickering without noticing her.

"You've only slept with him once, Emma. You don't own him!" The first girl replied, slamming her eyeliner back into her makeup case and storming out of the room.

Emma laughed at her retreating back, and rolled her eyes at her friend, "She's just jealous."

Olivia felt slightly nauseous. She knew she shouldn't care, she'd been prepared for Tucker having a life here that had nothing to do with her, but hearing it like this felt intolerable.

The two women marched out, leaving a wave of sickly sweet perfume in their wake. Emma was very attractive, tall, with glossy hair and a face that had been plastered with so much make-up she looked like a baby doll. Olivia tried to ignore her less than charitable thoughts toward her, she wasn't naturally a bitchy person but there was something about the woman's overly confident nature that pushed *all* Olivia's buttons. She seemed like a woman who always got what she wanted no matter how much manipulation she had to employ.

When at last Olivia had her turn in the mirror, she wanted to cry.

Her hair was windswept, her clothes felt doubly bland after the peacock girls, and she was unnaturally pale from losing so much blood earlier today. She tried to smooth down her hair, normally her favorite feature, into something that looked less like she'd been dragged through the bushes backwards. The rest, well, there wasn't much she could do about the rest.

Not that it matters anyway. He doesn't see you that way.

Clearly, if he was interested in Emma, or the other peacocks, Olivia didn't have a hope in hell in capturing Tucker's attention. They were cut from a *very* different cloth.

Olivia sighed in frustration and gave up.

13

Where the hell did she go?

Tucker stood by two burly dockworkers playing an intense game of pool. Wyatt and Colt beckoned him over, but he chose to remain where he was and scout for Olivia.

"Hey good looking," Emma brushed passed him and shot a seductive smile, "What you waitin' for?"

Tucker groaned inwardly.

"A friend."

His reply was abrupt, but not enough for Emma to take the hint.

"Anyone I know?" She purred.

"No."

"Well," she looked slightly perturbed that Tuckers gaze remained fixed away from her, "I'll be at the bar when you're in a friendlier mood. About five beers in if I remember correctly." She winked at him, and sauntered off through the crowd.

Tucker sighed and glanced around again, looking for Olivia. Eventually he caught sight of her tumbling brunette hair exiting the ladies room.

He strode over, blocking her path to his brothers' table.

"Olivia," he smiled down at her, before noticing her bandaged hand, "What the hell?"

"Just a DIY accident. Hannah took care of it." She replied.

"You should be more careful. You're pretty isolated up there."

Olivia nodded, and then stepped sideways to return to the table.

"Wait," Tucker hesitated, "Dance with me?"

The jukebox was playing an old country tune and a smattering of couples were dancing further back by the tavern entrance.

Olivia grimaced.

"Not really my thing."

"It used to be."

"What?" she looked momentarily baffled.

"Don't you remember playing old records down in my parent's basement?"

Olivia blushed. Tucker cocked an eyebrow at her, hoping she was recalling correctly the summer they'd taken over the family basement, building a fort from his mother's old scarves and various bedding. They'd tried to learn the foxtrot, for some unaccountable reason, and had spent long evenings laughing themselves sick at Tuckers inability to master a few simple steps.

"Well," she replied, "I hope you've improved your footwork."

Her small smile was coy and teasing, and Tucker laughed.

"I've been practicing." He hadn't. In fact, since that day, he'd had no interest in ever dancing again, until now.

He held out his arms, but Olivia perceptibly shifted backward out of his reach. No touching. Okay, she needed to feel more comfortable first. He could handle that. He put his beer down, and gestured for her to move into the dance 'area'.

Tucker felt his brothers' eyes on him. Without looking over he knew they were watching him and Olivia like hawk, he just hoped she wouldn't sense it too.

Olivia had always been a great dancer, but her movements seemed awkward and uncomfortable. They half-danced for a while, both smiling shyly at one another, until the bumps and collisions with the other, more enthusiastic couples, forced them to move closer.

"I'm not interrupting. I'm just giving Olivia her wine!" Hannah shoved a glass of white in Olivia's hand, and stood grinning a little too broadly at the pair of them before swiftly disappearing back the way she'd come. Olivia looked momentarily stunned before taking a sip from the glass.

"Looks like Hannah's taken a liking to you," he said, in way of explanation, "That means that you've probably made a friend for life there."

"She's great. Your brothers seem very happy."

"Yeah, they are. We've all got a good thing going here."

She nodded, her smile dimming. Tucker couldn't fathom what he'd said to cause the change in her mood. Before he could ask what was wrong, a new song started up. It wasn't anything Tucker recognized, but it was a slow, melodic ballad. Olivia stopped moving.

Tucker decided to take a risk.

Without breaking eye contact he leaned forward, and slowly placed his fingers around the top of the wine glass. His hand brushed hers, and he felt a small tremor travel up his arm.

"May I?"

She didn't say no. She didn't say anything, but it wasn't a no.

He put the glass down on a nearby table, and turned back to her. She was standing still, like a doe caught in headlights. Maybe she could also sense the tension that was building in Tucker, the space between them shifted into something more intentional and needful.

He took a step toward her.

"One more dance." He made his comment a statement, not a question. But still he watched her body language, knowing that he would need to back off the moment he sensed her fight-or-flight response kicking up. As it was, Olivia merely looked hesitant.

He moved closer. He was able to drink in her intoxicating scent, the mix of her conditioner, the Alder pine scent from last night that still clung to her, and the faint tang of blood from her bandage. Within all that was an achingly familiar scent that was pure Liv, the essence of her, an aroma that conjured up his most treasured memories.

"Won't Emma mind?" She asked softly, looking up into his eyes.

"Who?" He had no idea what she was referring to.

"Emma. You know… the… um… she's here. Your… girlfriend?"

Oh great.

"She's not my girlfriend."

He rested his hands lightly on her hips, wanting nothing more than to wrap her in his arms and press her soft body against his. Just being near her had his desire skyrocketing. He longed to pull her into his body and hold her tightly, protecting her from whatever she had become so afraid of, loving her, and touching her the way his body had been yearning to since the moment he'd laid eyes on adult Olivia.

"Oh."

Tucker slowly, so as not to startle, ran his finger along the underside of her jawline, tilting her chin up so that he was looking into her eyes.

"She's not anything," he said quietly, "Just, I got lonely waiting."

She looked puzzled, and opened her mouth to reply. Before she could, Jake Wakefield, a member of Drake's Yupiq pack came and whispered in his ear.

He broke away from Olivia, regretting the timing. But Drake had the information he needed.

"I've got to take care of some things, see you back at the table? I won't be long."

Olivia nodded. He could see the shutters coming back down, but her returning smile was sincere.

"See you in a bit."

Tucker turned regretfully and followed Jake out of the bar.

14

"Ssst," Drake whistled out to him. He was leaning by the side alley of the tavern, completely covert. As the door swung shut behind Tucker, the riotous noise died down to become a background hum, occasionally spiked by loud bursts of laughter.

Tucker leaned his back against the wall next to Drake. After the almost stifling warmth of the bar, the cold air cut like a knife.

"Don't thank me yet."

Tucker recognized his friend's agitation and disquiet. Whatever Drake was going to tell him, it wasn't going to be pleasant.

"Your lady's had it rough."

Tucker sighed, bracing himself for what was coming.

"Eric Sanderson. Mid-thirties. Exec level management job in software development for a major corporation. Met Olivia three years ago when she was working in Public Relations, same company."

Drake delivered the information without looking at Tucker. He had gone into full intel deployment mode, facts and details with no personal elaboration.

"They moved in together six months later. Soon after, Olivia's medical records start popping up. She's been the victim of some nasty 'accidents.' Records continue for a year. I'm not going to go into the details."

Tucker balled his fists and pressed his back into the stone of the tavern wall to try to anchor himself. His bear wanted to seek vengeance for his mate. His blood raced around his body, breath coming out in sharp exhales as he fought to regain control of his temper. If he didn't stay in control, he might easily crush the stone foundation with his fists, breaking everything in sight.

"She leaves him. He finds and kidnaps her. He, uh..." Drake paused, selecting his words, "Repeatedly tortures her for a week's duration before the noises are overheard. Cops intervene and jail him. She was reported to be near death, recovered in City Hospital for over two months. Upon release, she assumes a false identity. Moves to Shreveport, Louisiana and works in a shoe store. Sees a therapist twice a week."

"Repeatedly tortured?" Tuckers voice came out as a low, hoarse growl.

Drake shook his head, "You don't want to go there. To give you an idea, twenty-three fractures, and she was kept in a medically-induced coma for over a week. Look man, if it were me, my mate, and I read these details... I'd never be able to erase them. Just trust me, here."

Tucker felt his bear raging. His bear was pushing a shift, it's insistence becoming urgent and absolute. *Don't do it Tucker.* He needed to keep himself together. Liv was waiting for him inside. He didn't want to disappear on her, or let his fury overwhelm him so he couldn't then go and maintain a normal conversation. Liv deserved fun, freedom and the chance to live a life out of the shadow of her past.

"How long did he get locked up for?" Tucker practically growled in Drake's direction.

"That's the thing," Drake's voice tense, "He got twenty-five years, but was released on a technicality a few days ago. He's a free man."

Tucker felt the ground lurch beneath his feet and his legs almost gave way. *Fuck.*

"Does Liv know?" He spat out.

"I've no idea. If they still think she's living under a false identity they'd be trying to contacting her under that name, not the Olivia Harris that lives here."

He had to go back inside. In bear or human form, Tucker would be guarding Liv twenty-four seven until that monster was dealt with.

"I'm gonna contact you tomorrow, we need to look into this."

Drake nodded, "I thought you might say that, I've got a Yupiq team on standby, ready to travel. We'll find him."

Tucker nodded.

"I can't thank you enough, Drake."

"Don't worry about it. Just make her happy. I saw the file. It's something I never want to see again." Drake shrugged and walked off into the night. Tucker watched him go, amazed at the emotion behind those last few words. Drake was an exemplarily stoic. Whatever had been in that file, Tucker hoped to God he never saw it.

Breathing deeply, he tried to regulate his heartbeat and calm down. He didn't want Liv to notice anything was amiss when he went back inside. He would eventually tell her that Eric had been let off, but now wasn't the time.

Back inside Dante's, Tucker realized he was in no mood for the laughing, chattering bodies enjoying their Friday nights.

"Hey stranger, what you been up to?" Emma purred at his shoulder as he tried to break through the crowd on the dance floor.

"None of your goddamn business, Emma."

She looked stunned and upset, and Tucker regretted the words as soon as they left his mouth. He wanted to apologize, but Liv was his priority right now. Now and always. He pushed past her, ignoring her forlorn face and made his way over to the table.

Olivia was nowhere to be seen.

"Where did Liv go?"

He turned to Haley and Hannah, who were finishing off the bottle of wine.

"She took off," Hannah replied, "Said she was tired and wanted to turn in early. No worries, I had Cletus give her a ride home. She can pick up her snow machine tomorrow." Cletus owned the one and only taxicab on the island, a Jeep 4x4, and was often hanging around Dante's as a designated driver, sipping soda waiting for his next fare.

Shit.

"Tucker, will you go and look at her window tomorrow?" Haley asked.

"What do you mean?"

"Her window. The latch was broken on her bathroom window and she tried to fix it, that's how she cut her hand. I think you should take a look, because she's not going to be able to do anything with bandages."

Hannah nodded, looking expectantly up at Tucker.

"When did the latch break?"

Hannah and Haley both appeared confused by the question.

"She said something about the contractors having overlooked it when they gave the place an overhaul. She only noticed it was broken early this afternoon." Hannah replied.

Tucker had thoroughly checked every single window and every possible point of entry to the cabin the first night she was there. Every one. All the window latches had been secure.

He felt the blood drain from his face.

"I've got to go." He whispered the words hoarsely, before turning and fleeing the bar.

His mate wasn't safe.

15

"Thanks a lot." Liv called to the cab driver as the car pulled up at her cabin. She handed him her cab fare plus a few dollars tip, surprised at how cheap it was.

"Have a good night, and be careful."

The driver surveyed the forest behind her house anxiously, thinking how strange it was that a lovely young lady like that lived up in old Harris' place seemingly all by herself.

He did a U-turn and backed down Longview Drive. Olivia watched the Jeep go, cursing that the front path to her cabin didn't have solar lights.

The cabin was in darkness, and for the first time since she'd arrived it seemed genuinely ominous. It was probably just the stark contrast between her empty home and the laughing, warm bar where she'd been surrounded by people wanting to talk to her, that threw her home in such an unappealing light.

I don't want to go in there. The thought came loudly, unbidden. She shoved it aside and thought of what Doctor Young would say, *you can't let fear rule you, Olivia.*

She was being silly. Squaring her shoulders, and reaching inside her pocket for the keys, she strode across the front yard. She had nothing to worry about anyway, her guardian bear would be here tonight. If her cabin suddenly felt unappealing, then she could sleep outside again, wrapped in his warmth.

She felt ashamed for leaving the way she did. For leaving Tucker. What she'd done had been rude. She should have waited to say goodbye to him, but the walls had started closing in and she was terrified of having a crazy attack in front of her new friends.

She had watched him walk away, his every step purposeful and confident, his body perfect, toned, muscular, a match to his striking features. He was easily the most handsome man in the room. She wasn't his type; she was about as far from one of the peacock girls as you could get, but Tucker had seemed interested in her. Not just as a friend. Which meant a load of scary things she didn't know if she was ready for. Telling him about her past was one thing, but being intimate was another.

She'd thought about making love with him. What if she did something awkward, what if she had one of her anxiety attacks at completely the wrong moment? Oh my God, what if she was naked when it happened? She might never be ready for that kind of relationship. Her own thoughts had made her nervous and extremely anxious and she'd suddenly felt the room getting smaller. She'd had no choice but to get out before she had a complete meltdown in front of everyone.

The night was still and quiet, an occasional hoot from an awakening owl broke through the silence, and if she listened hard enough she could hear the ferocity of the sea breaking against the jagged rocks that surrounded Port Ursa and the rest of Kodiak Island.

The moon just peeked over the tall Aspen trees, nothing to help her guide her way to the front door, but it turned the tips of the trees a dark silver and Olivia took a moment to marvel at their beauty. It might take her a while to get used to the nights up here, but it certainly was a tranquil and awe-inspiring place to live.

Olivia let out a slow breath. Once again, she felt disgusted with herself. She knew she was getting better, getting stronger and coming out of her shell more and more every day, but she was still a freak. All because she couldn't get a grip on her irrational fear.

She fumbled with her key, taking a couple of tries before she heard the tumblers of the lock click. She swung the door open and stepped into the darkness, her hand reaching out to search for the light switch on the wall next to her.

"Hello Olivia."

She dropped the keys in horror. *That voice.* Her legs almost gave way beneath her.

He stepped in front of her, a large, hulking figure with his features blacked out in shadow. The smell of Jim Beam and Marlboro purveying the smell of her home.

Bam.

Without warning, he punched her hard in the face. Her head jolted backward, hitting the frame of the door and she slid slowly down to the floor. Olivia could feel warm blood trickling down to her lips. He'd busted her nose. *Again.*

He leaned over her, his smell overpowering. Olivia knew better than to move, but she doubted that she could if she tried; her body had turned to jello, almost as if, instinctually, it knew better than her the inevitability of the scene that would be played out.

She felt his hands at her scalp, gathering up her hair. He stepped over her, and yanked at the makeshift ponytail, pulling her out of the doorway. She felt the bottom frame scrape at her neck, grazing her skin.

"Did you know they let me out Olivia?"

His question floated over to her, the pain at her scalp and face caused her grip on consciousness to become hazy. The cruelty in his voice, the grating knife-edge malice that dripped from every word, *that* couldn't be ignored.

I'm going to die.

She felt the paving stones of her front yard give way to grass as he dragged her in the direction of the forest. She wanted to cry out, convinced that her entire scalp would be ripped off her skull before they reached his destination. Both of her hands clutched beneath his grip trying to keep him from pulling her hair out of her scalp, other than that, paralyzing fear made her powerless to fight back.

"I'm guessing you didn't. It was hard to find you though. Alaska of all places," he laughed heartily before continuing, "All alone in a cabin. Olivia, who knew you had it in you?"

She heard the clink of glass as he paused to take a gulp of whisky. He drained the bottle and flung it over on the grass.

"But it's convenient for me, in the end," he added in an off-hand manner, "There are countless wild creatures here. Every hunting season something goes amiss. If I'm lucky, your body won't be found till next year, when the snow melts, if at all."

He was slowing down now, dragging Olivia's body across the ground was taking its toll. He was also drunk, and the more tired he got, the sloppier his footsteps became, no longer in a straight determined line, but weaving left and right as he tried to stay on course.

Maybe my bear will get you first.

She wanted to laugh out loud at the possibility. Eric mauled by her guardian bear, meeting the awful end that he had wanted to stage for her in the first place. That would be true justice.

"Your pathetic crying to the cops has caused me to lose everything."

He gave her hair an especially ferocious tug, and she felt strands ripping away in his hand.

"My job, friends, family. I have nothing. And here you were in your father's cabin. This is pay-back, you cunt, fair and square."

She could feel the grass start to get longer, and the ground beneath her become more uneven. They were nearing the edge of the clearing. If her bear were anywhere near, he would have seen them by now, smelled the blood on her face. The absence of him caused tears to spring across her vision. She was in a hopeless situation. No guardian bear was going to save her. She had been suffering from deluded fantasies.

"Shit!"

She heard Eric's loud expletive. Wondering what had happened, she tried to tune into her surroundings. She could hear the distinct sound of a truck rumbling up Longview road, it's lights on full beam, darting in and out of the darkness as it navigated the road.

Please, please, stop!

Olivia wondered if she should risk calling out loud, but the chances of the driver hearing her all the way over here were practically nil. It would also mean a swift kick in the head or punch to the mouth if she tried.

You're going to die anyway, call out for Christ sake!

She took a lungful of breath, and opened her mouth to scream. All that came out was a strangulated high-pitched moan, followed by a gurgle as the blood from her nose flowed backwards down her nasal cavity.

"Stupid bitch, shut the fuck up!"

The kick was aimed at her stomach, and the toe of his boot hit the underside of her rib cage. She saw stars, and whimpered in pain.

She closed her eyes, unwilling to have false hope. The truck would either drive past or stop at one of the houses lower down the road. She should admit defeat. Perhaps that way, there might be some dignity to her end.

With renewed vigor and panic, Eric continued to pull at her hair, stomping through the undergrowth, desperately wanting to meet the canopy of trees before the truck drove any closer. Sharp stones and twigs cut into her back, but Olivia barely felt them.

"Jesus, is there no privacy these days!"

Eric's voice was bordering on the hysterical. The truck's headlights were fixed on Olivia's cabin. She and Eric were still in darkness, but it had stopped. The truck had stopped. Whoever was in that truck, they were here for her.

Tucker, God, please let it be Tucker.

"Well, it looks like there will be two bodies found next summer."

Olivia heard Eric fumbling around by his belt, followed by the sounds of a safety catch being released. He had a gun. Tucker, or whoever was in that truck, wouldn't save her, they'd die alongside her.

16

He could spot them easily in the woods. He smelled Liv's blood and fear a mile off, the night was saturated with her pain. As his eyes met hers, his bear became enraged with fury, unable to be contained in human skin.

It was almost a sweet relief to let his human body be cast aside. He welcomed the rage, anger and hate, letting it flow freely through his veins, consuming him and transforming him into his bear. He bellowed loudly into the night sky, shaking his truck and the ground beneath him. There was no need for a surprise element. He was going to tear Eric limb from limb.

He thundered through Liv's front yard and out into the open. He could hear the gun being cocked, ready to fire at him. Tucker wasn't afraid. His rage was so great, he felt as if the bullets could pass through him without slowing his bulk down. Nothing would stop him.

The bullets did fly. Shooting off into the sky, as if wielded by a drunken man. He heard them splice through the air and hit the ground, missing Tucker with every shot. He felt one skid past his face, grazing his shoulder blade, but it was nothing, he hardly felt it. He was gaining on his victim.

He could see the horror on the man's face. The grotesque realization that a man had just transformed into a bear, and that the beast, with jaws gaping and salivating, was heading straight toward him. Olivia was silent, but he knew she was still alive. Hurt, but alive.

The gun went off again, and even at this distance his aim was off. Tucker could smell whiskey on him, and his fear mixing with Liv's.

At only a pace away, Tucker launched himself at Eric. The man screamed, once, in shrill desperation.

Tucker's jaws closed around his face. Locking into his flesh, he pulled his head backward, mauling the man that had threatened his mate. Another shot went off as Eric's body jerked in pain. Tucker ripped a claw down Eric's torso, slashing his flesh to ribbons.

"Tucker."

Her faint voice called him back from his blood lust.

"Tucker, help."

He turned, wiping his muzzle on the forest floor to remove the blood. Another tang took over, far more potent than what he'd just tasted. Liv had been shot.

Tucker padded over, horrified at Liv's pale face, almost ghostly in the moonlight. It was covered in bruises from Eric's handiwork. Her nose and cheeks were already starting to swell.

He wanted to transform back into a human, provide some comfort to her, but his bear wasn't ready yet. His mate was injured, and he couldn't give up on her.

Tucker nuzzled her neck, whimpering at her pain.

"I should have known it was you," she smiled softly and reached out a hand, burying it in his fur, "You're so beautiful Tucker."

He could smell death on her.

He couldn't locate the entrance of the bullet with so much blood, but he could sense her life slipping away from her. All of Liv's vitality, long repressed by Eric, looked like it would be lost once and for all. Tucker knew, staring into her eyes as they shone softly with a strange sense of peace and ease, that part of him would die along with her.

There was one hope, a scant one, but it was a chance he had to take. All shifters had regenerative powers and could heal incredibly quickly. If he bit her now, there was slim chance that she could transform into a shifter fast enough that the wound would heal. But if the wound was too grave, his bite might only accelerate her death. Shifters weren't immortal. If the wound was severe enough, even as a shifter, she wouldn't heal sufficiently for her life to be spared.

You're running out of time, Tucker!

Her body could also reject the transformation. It wasn't unheard of for humans to be bitten and just bleed out, without any of the shifter abilities taking hold.

He pawed at the ground in agitation. Liv's hand was still at his neck, softly moving up and down against his fur. But her eyelids had fluttered closed, and he could feel her heart rate dropping with every passing second.

It's now or never!

He wished he could warn her as to what he was about to do. *I'm so sorry, Liv. I can't live without you.* He nuzzled her neck one last time, watching her as she smiled softly at his loving gesture.

Before he could change his mind, Tucker opened his jaws and bit down in the same place he'd just touched her so tenderly. The bite was savage and deep. She cried out, an ungodly sound that pierced like a dagger through his heart as he tore the flesh at Liv's neck.

17

Olivia woke with a start. Something was different. She looked around wildly. Tucker was sitting on the arm chair opposite her, looking like he'd just witnessed a car wreck. A fire crackled in the grate, warming her little cabin.

Tucker had looked up, hopefully, as she'd sat upright. Now he seemed guarded, waiting for...something.

Her body. She scanned down, checking for bruises, cuts and bandaged wounds. She should be *dead*. She should at least be battered bruised and achingly sore. Instead, she felt powerful and strong, her body humming with bright sparks of electricity and full to bursting veins of healthy, robust blood thudding through her.

The memories started to creep into her consciousness. Eric wanted to kill her. Tucker was there. So was her bear. No, wait, that's right, Tucker was her bear. Did that happen? Was that the truth, or was her mind just confusing things. An effect of horror and trauma, perhaps? But the bear's eyes, she was sure they were Tucker's, and then.... the bear bit her.

"You bit me," her voice was dry and gravelly.

"I'm so sorry Liv. It's the only way I could save you."

"Am I...?"

Her voice trailed off into a question. *What* was she? She looked the same, but something within her had altered dramatically.

"Yes," Tucker's voice was hoarse, "You have a bear inside you now."

Olivia was stunned into silence. She could almost feel it. Some potent thing inside her made her feel as if she was inextricably linked with everything around her, that nature was calling out to her most primal instincts, welcoming her home.

Tucker interrupted her thoughts, still looking unsure as to how she was digesting the news. She wanted to laugh, to jump up from the sofa and throw her arms around him.

"You don't need to be sorry, Tucker," then, "I can't believe you gave me a grizzly."

Her voice held only a molecule of the astonishment and excitement that she felt. He smiled a ghost of a smile at her.

"No one will ever be able to hurt you again."

There was pain at the back of his voice. She realized then that he must have somehow found out about Eric. He wasn't asking any questions, and she could see in his eyes that he'd been scarred by what he'd heard.

"Thank you." *For so many things.*

She owed Tucker her life. Not just for killing Eric and transforming her into a bear, but for the days before when he'd made her feel alive and hopeful. For knowing her secret and not judging her to be weak and feeble, deserving of what she got if she couldn't stand up to a man.

"Tucker. I want to... I mean... how do I?" She smiled shyly at him, eager to meet her own bear.

"You want me to tell you how to shift? How to change into your bear?" He looked surprised by her request, but quickly covered up his expression with a beaming smile. "Of course. Just close your eyes and allow it to take over your body. Give it permission. That's all there is to it." He rose from his chair, "We should go outside, though."

"No," Olivia held her palm out to him to stop him. "I mean..." He nodded. She wanted to do this herself without his interference.

"Okay, just stand in the yard," Tucker announced, "Are you a fan of those clothes?"

She looked down at her blood-soaked t-shirt and ripped jeans, smeared with mud and debris from the forest. She raised an eyebrow at him in response.

Tucker laughed and then cleared his throat, "Okay, sorry."

She stood still, glancing over at him to see if she needed to do anything else, say a magic word or speak her intention to the universe or whatever.

"It will come. It's a completely natural process." Tucker reassured her, watching her walk over to the doorway to the cabin.

She considered grabbing her coat, but thought better of it. She wasn't even remotely cold, as if her temperature was running at about twenty degrees higher than normal.

Olivia stepped out into the grass, and closed her eyes, focusing on her body and her breathing. She could feel *it* inside her. Heating her stomach from the inside, fizzing away and crackling like fireworks. She let it build up, filling her senses, tingling its way up her spine.

Olivia let out an almighty roar. The change was upon her. She dropped forward onto all fours, her arms thickening to hold her, her legs retracting to bring her closer to the earth. She felt her jaw elongate; her teeth grow sharper inside her mouth. The sensation was strange, but not unpleasant. Tucker was right, it did feel natural. Her body felt more comfortable in this state than she ever had in her human skin.

Tucker watched through a crack in the draperies. He didn't want to spoil the moment for her, but he wanted to be there for her if she needed him. Shifting for the first time was not just about the body mutating and changing, but a being's entire perspective on the world, and their place within it.

Her bear was beautiful, majestic and sleek with a glossy coat of thick mahogany fur, so like the color of her hair when she was young. Olivia turned toward the cabin, pawing at the ground, unable to keep still. She grunted, surprised when words didn't come out.

His own bear tugged within him, called by her new form. He felt his need for her consume his body, tightening the jeans at the crotch.

He watched, wanting her, keeping his distance. Olivia turned suddenly and ran off toward the forest. He let her go. Her bear would want to roam, to feel at one with nature's surroundings.

He decided to wait for her in the cabin. She might have questions on her return, and would need someone to talk to. He left the door slightly ajar, and went to sit down and wait.

18

Tucker paced the cabin feeling like an absolute idiot. Olivia had been gone for hours, and he was starting to seriously worry. He should have gone with her. He should have at least followed at a distance to make sure she was okay. She was new to being a bear. God only knows what could happen to her in those woods. He suspected a few rogue shifter wolves from the vanquished Altik pack still meandered in the depths of Kodiak Island.

Calm the hell down.

Tucker's pacing increased. Maybe he should try to track her. Better to be safe than sorry. Yes, he may be the last person in the world she wanted to see right now, but he needed to find her, just to make sure she was safe. He would keep a distance, and let her have her space.

He strode out onto the porch and froze still in the doorway. Light flooded from behind him, casting a glow across the dusting of freshly fallen snow in the front clearing. She was approaching. Emerging from the tree line, striding toward him, naked and unashamed, moonlight gleaming and catching the waves of her glossy hair. Olivia. Only, this wasn't the Liv that he'd been witnessing the past couple of days. No, this woman was very different.

This Olivia strode as if she owned the very ground she walked upon. Her back was straight, her chin tilted upward, challenging the world and everything in it. He had never seen Liv like this. Tucker recognized the signs. The unspoken challenge in her movement, the sheer power and grace of her walk. He had never felt such power, in fact he had to fight the instinct to expose his neck to her in submission.

"Well I'll be dammed," he whispered softly as Olivia approached. She's dominant.

She said nothing. Striding toward Tucker she took his face in her hands and kissed him. It was deep and sound, forceful and sweet at the same time. It sent Tucker's head spinning.

"Get inside," Olivia murmured against his neck, "I need you in my bed."

She smelled like the forest, of fallen birch and willow, fresh moss and ice-cold water. Tucker felt his heart rate spike. He'd never been so eager to follow an order.

"Yes ma'am." A huge grin spread across his face.

As he strode toward the bedroom, Olivia watched his backside and broad shoulders drown her narrow cabin hallway. She felt her insides churn as they'd done only hours earlier at the tavern. That felt like a millennia away.

Once in her room, she walked toward Tucker. Looking into his eyes, where his longing mirrored hers, she slowly undid the buckle of his belt never breaking eye contact. She could hear his light panting, see the strain against his jeans - causing his top button to pop open with minimal effort from her.

She greedily reached inside his boxers, her hands enveloping his hot erection and springing it free from the elastic. He was sinfully large, stunning Olivia for a moment. She parted her lips unconsciously, wetting them with her tongue in anticipation.

"T-shirt." She managed to rasp out.

Tucker didn't need to be asked twice. He pulled it off in one swift movement, his muscles bulging and flexing in all the right places as he moved. Olivia observed his tight six-pack, riddled with faint scars from his own battles.

She pulled his jeans down the rest of the way, pooling them at his ankles. He stepped out of them, standing naked before her. He raised an eyebrow as if to challenge her, *where do you want me next, Liv?*

She chuckled at him - she knew exactly where she wanted him next.

"Get on the bed."

He sauntered toward it, his erection thick and throbbing, waiting for Olivia's touch. She knew she had him at her mercy, and the power he gave her was intoxicating.

Tucker lay across the bedding, resting up on his elbows. He couldn't take his eyes off Olivia. A bead of precum emerged from the tip of his cock as he observed her large, full breasts with their tight and erect nipples. He was aching to take them in his mouth and make her moan in surrender.

She padded softly toward him, every inch as confident as she'd been outside. She moved up onto the bed, parting her thighs so she straddled him either side. When her hands reached out to clasp his cock, he inhaled sharply which turned to a shudder of ecstasy as she slowly moved them up and down stroking his length.

His hips rose to meet her rhythm, and she moved closer to him, running the tip of his erection alongside the silky layers at the apex of her thighs. Tucker groaned.

Her wetness soaked Tucker's shaft, and as the sensation grew inside Olivia she couldn't wait another moment, he pushed the tip inside her. Tucker moved his torso upward, grasping Olivia's backside, digging his fingers into her ample cheeks as he guided her over him and thrust himself deeper.

She ran her hands through his hair, clasping his head and bringing her mouth over his. He kissed her passionately, protectively, fiercely, their lips melded together so that their entire bodies were touching, joined in every conceivable place as if neither of them could bear to separate.

As Tucker sped his rhythm, Olivia pushed down on him, finding the friction that her body had been aching for. Tucker broke from the kiss, burying his face in Olivia's breasts as his breath hitched.

"Oh, fuck, Liv."

His plea was wrestled from the back of his throat. Olivia clenched her thighs tighter at the sound of his voice, driven crazy by its evident want and desire.

She felt Tucker's lips clasp around her nipple, followed by a gentle biting sensation that set her skin shivering with an ice-cold fire. He sucked harder, grunting against her, his muscles slippery with their sweat.

Olivia felt a heady sensation growing within her. At first she thought she was going to shift, but it was so different from the feelings she'd experienced earlier. This sensation began deep within her abdomen, a heavy, full tug that increased her wetness, widening her core to welcome more of Tucker's girth inside her.

"I want you behind me," she whispered into Tucker's ear, "Now."

He lifted her up swiftly, twisting her onto her front so her face fell into the pillows. He grabbed her backside and pushed it up in the air and toward him running his hand across her cheeks, admiring the soft, silken skin and the glimpse of her widening, wet core beneath.

He released a growl from deep in his chest. Liv was driving him crazy. He'd never desired a woman more in his life. He had known, at the back of his mind for years, that Liv was his mate. Her scent, even as a distant memory that hung around the Harris property, had always called to his bear.

He slammed into her, unable to hold back another second.

"Harder, please!" Liv cried out to him.

He grasped her backside again, thrusting inside her and she gripped the pillow beneath her, crying out in pleasure, feeling free to call out and release the emotions within her.

He leaned forward, clasping her breasts in his hands, luxuriating in their firmness and teasing her nipples with his fingers. She gasped.

"Tucker, I'm close..."

She screamed, arching her back upward. Tucker buried his face in her hair, panting against her as he felt her orgasm overtake her.

Seconds later, he followed, calling her name in a whispered moan as he released himself inside her.

They both collapsed on the bed, each of them fighting for breath, their racing heartbeats slowly regulating. Tucker pulled Olivia against his firm body and cradled her in his arms.

She buried her head into his chest listening to his heartbeat which perfectly matched her own. She didn't understand what was passing between them. It was something so *other*, so strange and magical, as if she could feel their souls entwining as they lay together, her inner bear purring at his closeness.

"Liv, are you okay?"

She rolled her head to look up at him, smiling into Tucker's kind brown eyes.

"Better than okay, that was amazing."

Tucker nodded, softly kissing the top of her head.

"I'm glad you liked it, but that's not what I meant."

She turned to face him. "Tucker, I haven't felt like this in years. I'm back to normal. No, better than normal. I feel… I feel… like inside I'm a badass five hundred pound apex predator with six inch claws and four inch incisors, and no one in their right minds would *dare* fuck with me!" There was complete silence for a moment before she giggled hysterically at her own words.

Tucker let out a low whistle and chuckled.

"There's something else about bear shifters you should know," he hesitated before continuing, "When we mate, truly mate with someone, it's different."

He couldn't say more than that. He didn't want to scare her off. Someday he would explain that that when shifters found their mate, the bond was for life, and that Liv was and always has been the one for him. Always. She would be part of him till his dying breath.

"I know. I can feel it, too." Liv whispered.

Tucker wrapped his hands into her hair, drawing her lips forward to meet his. He drowned once again in her kiss, only in that moment taking the time to notice that he too felt different. His restless bear was no longer restless. For the first time in years, Tucker felt utterly content.

He felt his groin tighten in response to Liv's soft lips touching his own, and dragged her back into his arms. She clutched at his broad frame, pulling him further toward her. He buried himself within her again, determined to pull more cries of pleasure from her lips.

Later, as she slept in his arms, he watched her face, still and content in sleep, her thick eyelashes casting soft shadows across her cheekbones.

Being careful not to wake her, he lifted her hair off the nape of her neck. He lightly brushed away the small tendrils stuck to her skin with perspiration. He smiled. The cigarette scars that had been ugly red puckered gashes on her beautiful skin had been transformed into small white dots.

They would never disappear completely, neither would Liv's memories of all that she'd endured. But her scars made her stronger, a fierce and magnificent bear that he loved, as he always had, and always would.

19

"Happy birthday dear Leila, happy birthday to you!" Applause rang out across the table, as a delighted dark-haired child giggled with excitement as two waiters carried over a ginormous cake.

"Blow out the candles little bird," Haley kissed her daughter on the cheek, "and make a wish!"

Wyatt stroked back Leila's hair as she leaned over the candles, ever the watchful father. Tucker smiled at his brother, and then observed the rest of the family gathered around the table. Uncle Joe had even taken the afternoon off from chain smoking and watching sports.

Hannah and Colton were wrapped in one another's arms, watching as Leila puffed furiously at the candles. He felt Liv's hand close around his, and she glanced at him out of the corner of her eye.

He pulled her head toward him, kissing the softness of her hair and inhaling her scent. He wanted to take her back home already, have her dominate him utterly in bed. She winked at him, guessing where his train of thought was jetting off to.

"Let's all raise a glass to family," announced Wyatt from the head of the table, "Long may we have our health and our immense happiness."

Everyone raised a glass of champagne, reaching to clink glasses across the table, as the liquid sloshed on the snow-white tablecloth.

"Liv?" Hannah questioned.

In Liv's hand was a glass of water, the champagne glass sitting discarded on the table.

"You're not drinking," she observed, "Any particular reason?" Her eyes danced with merriment.

The entire table turned to face Tucker and Liv. She blushed and then broke into laughter.

"I'm pregnant," she turned to Tucker, "We're going to have a baby."

"It's a girl." Tucker announced.

Tucker smiled at the whoops and cheers of his family. Haley and Hannah ran over to Liv immediately, hugging her tightly and expressing their congratulations through shrieks and kisses. Wyatt raised a glass to Tucker.

"Nothing beats it brother."

Colton laughed, doubting the truth behind Wyatt's words. No doubt Hannah would want one next, and there was nothing on this earth that Colton wouldn't give her.

Liv bent down and kissed Tucker. As they broke apart, a look passed between them. It was a new beginning for them; a girl that would be as fierce and confident as her mother, a girl that would banish the last of the shadows from her mother's past in the light that she would bring to their lives.

"I love you Livalot." He whispered into her ear, "Always."

For more books, please visit:

https://books2read.com/candaceayers

https://lovestruckromance.com

Candace Ayers ♡